The Devil's Wingman

by

J. M. Davis

The Devil's Wingman

COPYRIGHT © 2015 by Jillian Davis

Cover Art by *Angela Anderson*

The Wild Rose Press, Inc.
PO Box 708
Adams Basin, NY 14410-0708
Visit us at www.thewildrosepress.com

Publishing History
First Black Rose Edition, 2015
Print ISBN 978-1-62830-866-2
Digital ISBN 978-1-62830-867-9

Published in the United States of America

Acting on a whim, I brought my hands up and pressed my palms against his cheeks. They burned like a fever. I wasn't sure if I'd ever get used to that.

His black eyes latched onto mine. I waited as he struggled with something internally, pain and confliction clearly written across his face. Eventually, his expression shifted, the hard planes of his features softened into a sweet smile. As our faces drew closer, my breathing became ragged with anticipation. When he wet his lips, it was nearly my undoing. My chest heaved with expectation, trembling each time his breath crept across my skin. I looked into his eyes; the crimson specks were recessing, like a fading tide within a murky sea of black ink. They were hypnotizing.

"If I am under a trance, don't ever rouse me," I murmured.

His eyes glimmered just before he pressed his warm lips to mine. Our mouths moved together in perfect unison, as if they were molded to fit one another. The kiss deepened, and together we were swept away by our unraveling emotions, pawing at one another as though each other's breath was the only oxygen we had.

When we finally parted for air, we both stood staring at the other, panting. Dominic took my hands, his touch warming me like a soothing balm. He cast his eyes down to our intertwined fingers, his long lashes fanning out over his high cheekbones, and he said, "My fraying willpower makes it hard to walk away from you."

"Then don't," I whispered.

Dedication

To my kids:
Dream big, and then chase that sucker relentlessly.

Acknowledgments

Special thanks to:

My husband, Alex, for your unwavering love and patience through my erratic, late-night writing schedule.

Gail Abrams and Shannon Ford, who read this in its earliest and roughest draft. I am forever grateful for your encouraging words.

My critique partners, Bethany Shaw and Cecilia Robert, for the invaluable feedback and advice.

The Wild Rose Press, Inc., and my editor, Lill Farrell, for never growing tired of me, or my persistence.

And finally, to my parents, for stoking my creativity at a young age and insisting that I never let it idle into embers.

Prologue

Love is a selfish beast. It doesn't care if you're carefully treading depression, or recovering from tragedy. It doesn't care what demons you're battling, whether your heart is healed or if it bears fresh scars. Love strikes suddenly, and fiercely. Seizing your heart without mercy, until you finally realize it is no longer your own to possess. I gave my heart away voluntarily, but the battle for my life and soul was a harder fought victory.

J. M. Davis

Chapter 1

"He who does not see the angels and devils in the beauty and malice of life will be far removed from knowledge, and his spirit will be empty of affection."
~ *Khalil Gibran*

My eyelids felt heavy, but I forced them open anyway, only to have to blink against the blaring fluorescent light overhead. *Clicks* and *beeps* of machinery hummed nearby and the sterile smell of iodine and bleach filled my nose.

"She's coming home with me." The familiar voice of my mother drifted through the curtain. I turned my head, listening as she continued. "She will just have to transfer schools. There is no way in hell I'm allowing her to stay. It's obvious she's not coping well." She choked back something, her tone quieter as she said, "Neither of us are."

Why am I here?

I lifted my eyes, finding an IV stand, with two bags of clear liquid hanging from it. There was one window. The blinds were open, but not a speck of light shone through it except for the glow of a distant lamppost. I attempted to push myself upright. Pain exploded in my wrist, causing me to fall back against the pillows, gritting my teeth in agony. I clutched my bandaged hand, remembering, but also trying to forget. I recalled the steps that led me there. The depression, the emptiness, the will to die greater than the will to live. My vision grew spotty around the edges, as hot tears ran down my cheeks.

The curtain drew back. The harsh hospital lighting outlined the silhouette of my mother. My roommate Jen peeked around the corner of the opened door. She flashed me a strained smile.

"Kara?" My mother hurried to my side, peering into my face. Her eyes were red from crying, her features tight with worry. She punched the call button frantically, her breath hiccupping in her throat the way it did when she was nervous. A strange voice crackled from the speaker beside my head.

"Nurses' station."

"Something's wrong with my daughter, please hurry."

"Someone will be there soon." Static, then silence.

"Kara, honey." Her fingers grazed my forehead, before she raked them through my hair. Her touch was comforting, but the pain remained, spreading up my arm and neck. My fingers felt odd. I tried to wiggle them, but they prickled, like dozens of needles sticking me all at once.

A doctor charged through the door, a nurse on his heels. He did a quick assessment, noting my groans and tear streaked face, before touching my elbow gently.

"Did you bend your wrist?" the doctor asked, leaning over me. He smelled like aftershave. The mix of pine and musk was overwhelming.

I nodded, wincing when he touched me.

"I'm going to remove the bandages. I'm afraid you've popped the stitches." His tone was pleasant enough, but the cut and dryness of it wasn't reassuring. The nurse hung close to the wall, scribbling notes in a chart.

My mother's lips quivered. She pressed her hands together as if she were praying, and brought them to her mouth, her eyes tight as she watched me. My heart tugged, knowing I was the cause of her sadness.

Slowly the doctor unwrapped the bandages, the pressure releasing as each layer loosened. I tried my best not to look, but like a crash scene on the highway; my eyes remained glued to the chaos. The gash was recently sutured, but now it was a gaping wound. Bright red blood oozed from the pink, almost frayed flesh of my wrist.

The scent of copper and salt wafted through the air, mixing with the doctor's obnoxious piney aftershave, making my stomach turn. I heaved, gagging on the smell. The nurse flew into action, shoving something under my chin. I didn't bother to open my eyes, when she began murmuring words of comfort as I retched into what I assumed was a wastebasket.

When I was through, I lifted my gaze, ignoring the smell of vomit as my mother wiped my mouth and face.

The nurse disappeared with the puke bucket, then returned a moment later with a syringe. She inserted the needle into my IV tube, and pressed the plunger. The sting of the drug burned as it worked its way through my veins.

"We're giving you something the dull the pain," the doctor said. "I'll need to restitch this." The doctor smiled as he patted my shoulder. "You need to be more careful." His words seemed silly, considering what brought me there in the first place. My heart clenched at the memory. I didn't fight it, I couldn't. It was still fresh, raw, like the wound on my wrist. Ignoring either is impossible, and it is foolish to even try. I recalled the desperation.

The compulsion to fill the empty hole in my heart the only way I knew how. By stopping it. If it ceased beating, then the pain would finally end. A stilled heart meant release. My eyelids grew heavy, and my thoughts became erratic and slurred. Unable to control either, I let my mother's voice become distant, whispering to me as I drifted into the dark world of the unconscious.

****

Three months later

I stepped over boxes and book bags, scanning the numbers on every other door I passed. Some were still the simple typeface numbers you could buy at a home improvement store for your mailbox. Others were replaced with hand-made signs of construction paper and glitter. Silently, I prayed my door was simple, devoid of colorful sparkles and stupid drawings. Plain suited me just fine.

A blonde in a lime green t-shirt blew past me. The neon straps of her panties peeped out the top of her pants. She carried an oversized zebra print bag and a huge stuffed monkey.

I shifted the cardboard box I was holding and looked down at myself. My eyes skimmed across my gray t-shirt, and down my faded jeans. They were snug, and virtually impossible to wrinkle. My best friend Becca gave them to me during my senior year at Old Fort High. They were too long for her and since nobody, aside from old men, ever hemmed a pair of jeans, she bestowed them on me.

I took a quick peek at my worn sneakers before glancing back at the monkey-toting bombshell. *I wish Becca were here.* She'd have some sort of wisecrack, and we'd notch the air with our fingers, keeping an invisible tab of all the thong and bra straps we've seen.

I started walking again, and bumped into a bony shoulder.

"O'myfuckin'gawd!" a voice snapped. "Watch the shoes!"

"Sorry," I muttered, blinking at the brunette girl. Her eyebrows had been plucked, shaped, and waxed into thin wisps. Her bra strap dangled over her shoulder, and again I thought about Becca. I attempted to smother a smile, but failed.

"What the hell is so funny?" she shot, her voice loud and drawing unwanted attention to me. "You think ruining my stilettos is funny?"

My cheeks warmed as I slid my gaze around the crowded hall. Everyone was craning their necks to watch us. She glanced around; the corner of her mouth flicked upward, giving me a smug smile.

Damn drama queen.

"You won't be laughing after I snatch your hair out your head," she snapped. Her heels clicked against the floor, as she took a step back, her dark eyes surveying me up and down.

I grew self-conscious, shifting from one foot to the other. I wanted to melt into the floor. *My first day is a disaster*, I thought. The girl watched me expectedly, as if waiting for an apology, and I almost gave her one until she laughed in a condescending manner, shaking her head as though I was some sort of joke. Irritation flared within me. I gripped my box tighter, trying to steady my shaking hands.

"Since nothing happened to your precious *hooker stilts*, the world can continue to spin," I said. "And the bonus for you is, you won't get knocked on your pretty little ass today," I added with a smile.

Her jaw dropped as her miniscule eyebrows nearly reached her hairline.

Ha! That shut her up. I continued to smirk at her as I stalked past her and resumed my quest for Room 178.

As I ventured down the hallway, I noticed a tall redhead stationed beside a small table. She grinned at me. Feeling like a trapped animal, my eyes darted around, searching for an escape route. There was none. *Damn.* I regarded her with apprehension as I drew closer. Free pencils and pennant flags littered the table. She held an armful of fluorescent orange papers. An intricately woven braid cascaded over one shoulder and her ears were punctuated with sapphires the size of blueberries.

"Rush week is two weeks away. Hope to see you there," she said enthusiastically, handing me a flyer that read, *Π M Σ! Join the sisterhood!*

I groaned. Sorority recruitment. "No offense, but sororities aren't my thing." I shoved the orange proclamation back at her.

"A united sisterhood full of learning, loyalty, and lifelong friendships aren't your *thing?"* she asked in a sickening sweet voice. She had a smile plastered so tight on her face; I thought her skin would crack.

"Organized friendships that require you to pledge loyalty is lame. It's for those who have an inept longing for acceptance." I met her icy stare, just before my eyes drifted down the length of her. She wore a tangerine colored t-shirt, knotted above her annoyingly flat stomach, and a pleated purple skirt. "Besides, any group that forces you to wear orange and purple— *together*—should disband. Can you say, *fashion fatality*?" I wrinkled my nose in distaste.

Her mouth twisted into a snarl. "Screw you. Phi Mu Sigma wouldn't have you anyway."

I snorted. "Phi Mu Sigma? You're kidding, right?"

She looked thoroughly confused and equally pissed.

"PMS? Your initials are PMS! Oh, that's rich!" I laughed. "It's fitting though," I added.

Her ears and cheeks flushed crimson. "Bitch." She snatched the flyer from me, turning away in such a tizzy, her braid nearly slapped me across the face. Fixing a grin back in place, she straightened her shoulders, and regained her composure. "Rush week is two weeks away," she began. "Phi Mu Sigma wants you."

I shook my head as I walked away. *Sororities are so stupid.*

A mop of curls waltzed past me. Golden tendrils bobbed and jiggled as she moved, reminding me of the curling ribbon my mom used on my birthday gifts. The girl suddenly stopped and spun on her heel.

Tucking a curly lock behind her ear, she asked, "First day here?" Her big blue eyes held mine as she waited for me to answer.

I nodded.

She smiled, revealing two deep dimples in her cheeks. She wore khaki Capris, a bright yellow shirt, and strappy leather sandals. She was cute, in a pixie sort of way. "Well, welcome to Belman! Need help finding your room?"

"No, thanks." I forced a smile to show that I wasn't a complete social misfit.

"Okiedokie. See ya around." She gave a little wave and bounced away.

I watched her, pursing my lips as she veered to the right and practically skipped into the room on the corner. My eyes flicked sideways and caught the number 175. *Oh no.* I groaned as I trudged toward the inevitable. *She's going to bake cookies and force me to participate in sing-a-longs.* As I grew closer, I wearily scanned the pink stationary that hung from the door. I wanted to bang my head against the wall. There it was, in bubbly handwriting: Room 178.

I shifted my cardboard box; my wrist was starting to ache from the weight of it. Focusing on the pain, I mentally prepared myself. *If you can get through eleven stitches in your wrist, you can get through this.* I rounded the threshold and sure enough, there she was, standing on one of the twin beds, plastering posters of Taylor Lautner and Johnny Depp on the wall. She looked over her shoulder and grinned. "Team Jacob or Team Edward?"

"Uh." Caught off guard, I forced myself to zero in on her button of a mouth.

She frowned slightly. "Oh, come on. You have to have a favorite." She turned and crossed her arms over her chest. I mentally wished I could fasten that button mouth closed.

"Actually, Jasper is more my style," I answered.

Her shoulders sagged with relief. "Thank heavens. For a moment, I thought you were going to tell me you never saw the movie or read the books."

"Actually, I've never seen the movies," I said. "But I have read the series." I flashed a hesitant smile.

Her mouth dropped open. In fact, I thought her jaw might unhinge and crash into the floor.

"Books are better than movies," I said with a slight shrug.

She continued to gape at me.

I felt my eyebrows lift. "Oh-kay. Well. I guess you've already picked your bed?"

"The early bird gets the worm," she sang as she plopped down on the bed. "But I'm flexible. You can have this one, if you want." She smiled at me, her curly hair framing her petite face. She seemed sincere, which made it harder to dislike her.

I placed my box on the floor, relieved to finally put it down. I rubbed my sore wrist and said, "No. You keep it. Wouldn't want you to tear those posters."

Her smile broadened before she turned, and smoothed the corners of the posters with her fingers.

I scanned the room. It smelled of fresh paint and didn't look much different from my old dorm. There were two twin beds, each lined with built-in shelves, two standard desks and a dinky bathroom. I glimpsed inside the minuscule closet. A couple of empty wire hangers hung lifelessly from the middle of the rack. The bathroom was exactly as I thought it would be, except for the shower curtain. It was clear plastic with blue bubbles and yellow rubber ducks splashed across it. *I'm guessing curly-locks brought that.* Bottles of shampoo, conditioner, body wash, and face scrub filled the sides of the tub. A pink loofah sponge hung from the faucet handle.

"You can use my shampoo and stuff," she said as

she walked up behind me.

"I've got my own, but thanks," I muttered as I sidestepped around her. "So what's your name?"

"Cassie. What's yours?"

"Kara." I made my way back to my box, and knelt beside it, setting to work on the packing tape.

"Senior?" she asked.

"Yup," I answered as I unpacked.

"Me too. Did you just transfer in?"

"Yes." I quelled the urge to roll my eyes.

"Cool, from where?"

"DGU." *Aren't my short answers an indication that I'm busy?*

"What's your major?"

Obviously not. "Well, here it's art. But it *was* photography. Unfortunately, Belman doesn't offer photography as a major," I said, my tone a little darker than I expected. I missed Del Grace University. Their photography courses were stellar, and I aced most of them. I bit my cheek, reminding myself that I was in that "glass half empty" mind frame again. "Luckily most of my credits transferred," I added.

She nodded knowingly. "So, what kind of photographer do you want to be? Something legit right? Not like, paparazzi?"

My eyebrows shot up as I gave her my famous *you've got to be kidding* look.

She only continued to stare at me, her face serious. My lip twitched, threatening either a smile or a wisecrack. "I don't think there's a major for that," I said finally. "Although, I'm sure a Stalking Stars 101 course would be popular."

Cassie chuckled, which sent her pale locks jostling

wildly about her face. Her eyes suddenly darted behind me. I followed her gaze, glancing over my shoulder, expecting the resident advisor to be standing there. RA's always poke their chipper little heads into each dorm, ensuring everyone is happily content. My jaw went slack.

"Kara! There you are! I can't believe I found you amidst all this chaos."

"Mom!" I couldn't hide my surprise. "What are you doing here?" I stood, rushing to hug her neck. I was thrilled to see her. Since moving back home, I noticed the little things she hid from me while I was in Florida. Like the sadness that lurked behind her smile, and the way she'd retreat to her bedroom as soon as dinner was over. Since Dad died last year, she had been secretly lingering in a deep depression, hiding it behind a fake smile. I knew better though. I saw myself in her. The emptiness. The broken heart.

That night at the hospital, through the haze of painkillers and blurred tears I saw it. There wasn't a fire in her eyes anymore. It was as if someone blew out the flame, smothering her passion for life. She merely existed now. Drawing myself out of the memory, I frowned, glancing down at the jagged scar across my wrist. *Who am I to judge*? I thought bitterly, quickly tearing my eyes from the ugly mark, and adjusting my bracelets to conceal it.

"I have something for you," she said.

In her hands were two boxes, each wrapped in blue and yellow plaid paper. Both were bursting with bundles of tightly coiled yellow curls. I briefly thought of Cassie and her head full of ringlets.

"I wanted to make your room more…homey." She

lifted the boxes and smiled warmly.

"Aw, Mom. You didn't have to do that," I said as she shoved the presents at me.

"Hush. Just open them." She watched expectedly, gnawing her bottom lip. Something was bothering her. She only chewed her lip when she was worried. I ignored it for the moment, noting that I should ask her about it before she left. I tore into the first box. I was eager to please her, and buying me presents pleased her. I ripped apart the plaid paper and lifted the lid of the box. I ran my fingers across soft fabric, pulling it from the white tissue that surrounded it. I held it in the air. It was a pale pink fleece bathrobe. It looked like it belonged in a spa. I draped it over my arm and rubbed the fluffy material.

"Thanks, Mom. Looks comfy."

"I know! Doesn't it?" She patted the robe, and then her caramel eyes shifted to mine. "It will keep you warm too." She seemed happy. For the moment anyway. I wanted to keep her that way, so I hurried to open the other present. I peeked through my lashes at her, as the wooden picture frame emerged from the shredded gift-wrap. My breath caught in my throat. There was my father, smiling back at me from behind a thin layer of glass. Tears pricked at my eyes and my nose felt that familiar tingle when I was on the verge of a breakdown.

"Oh Mom," I whispered. I traced his face with my finger. *So that's why she's worried. She's not sure how I'll react.*

I glanced at my mom. She was watching me quietly, her lips pressed together until they were nearly nonexistent as she waited for my response. I gave her small smile before looking down at him again. *God I miss him.*

A teardrop slipped down my cheek and landed on the glass. Mascara mingled with sorrow splattered across his handsome features. I wiped it away, leaving a smudge across the glass. I pulled up the hem of my shirt and feverishly scrubbed at it until it was spotless again.

Our last family portrait. Dad always picked on my mom about our famed photo shoots. Each December, my mother would pick out coordinating clothes for the three of us and make our yearly appointment with the photo studio. We would stand in a cluster, grinning like idiots for the camera. The poses were lame, but my father and I had fun giving the poor photographer a hard time.

Place your hand on Mom's shoulder. Look at her admiringly. Cue the doe eyes and dramatic gaze. We would roar with laughter. *Lie down on the floor and prop yourself up on your elbows.* Fluttering eyelashes and cheesy smiles. Once, we were supposed to pretend we were decorating a Christmas tree. The mock living room had a fake fir tree, chock-full of garish ornaments and tinsel.

Dad hung two large plastic ornaments from his ears and wrapped silver garland around his neck like an extravagant boa. That picture made it onto our Christmas cards that year.

Mom longed for serious, sentimental pictures, but that was against our grain of nature. You could count on Dad and I to turn a photo shoot upside down. That was part of *our* charm. Two goofy peas in a pod. The hazel eyes that peered up at me from the frame tugged at my heart. I clutched the frame to my chest, searching my mother's face.

"I wasn't sure if you'd be ready to put it out, but I wanted him to be here with you." She pursed her lips together again, trying to suppress her emotions, but her brown eyes sparkled with tears.

"I'm glad he's here," I murmured. "And I'm glad you are too." I hugged her with my free arm, glimpsing Cassie as she pretended to busy herself by unpacking her suitcase. I inhaled my mother's sweet scent and closed my eyes. I remembered how she would put a bandage over my scrapes with a touch that was light as a feather. Then she would hug me and gently kiss my hair.

As a young girl, I would get lost in her flowery aroma of tea olive and jasmine. That was my mother's healing power. A heavenly scent and an angel's touch. As if on cue, my mom brushed her lips across my forehead. It was as if a butterfly fluttered against my skin. Instantly, my aching heart hurt a little less. *A mother's mojo. It's some powerful stuff.*

Chapter 2

"What classes do you have today?" Cassie asked as she wriggled her toes into a pair of white flip-flops.

"Intro to Art History II and Drawing. You?"

"Foundations of Education, Intro to Urban Education, and Human Evolution."

"Wow," I mouthed.

"Yeah, I know."

I parted my hair and clipped it with a barrette. "Well, I better get going. Got to get to the Archer Building by nine," I said, slipping my arms into the straps of my gray book bag. "See ya later."

I turned and headed to the door, catching my reflection in the mirror. My button-up ivory shirt was snug in all the right places. I matched it with a long necklace that held multiple charms. The tiny trinkets tinkled prettily as I walked. I also wore my beloved "feminine fatigues," a pair of fitted sage green pants that held multiple pockets at the thighs and calves, and of course, my trusty black sneakers.

"Hey," Cassie called. I looked over my shoulder as she was snatching up her bag and purse. "Need help finding the Archer Building?"

"Nah. I'll be fine."

"Okay. Later, tater," she said as she scooted past me and out the door. She weaved in and out of the crowded hall and disappeared.

I melted into the rush of bodies, following the flow through the hall and out the double doors of the building. Belman's finest were strutting across the courtyard, shielding their faces from the relentless sun. Their micro-mini pleated uniforms looked fresh from the dry cleaners.

I tried not to hate them just because of their role here, but cheerleaders always annoyed the hell out of me. I mean, what is up with "spirit fingers"? And the way they clap—was it required that they cup their hands like they're cradling a butterfly? I marched past them, scolding myself for being so negative.

In the distance, I saw a sprawling two-story building, with a bold sign that read The Archer Building. I squinted against the glare of the sun. There were three sets of double glass doors under expansive archways. The red brick was inviting and actually attractive against the white pillars that stood stately around each entrance. The green lawn of Belman ushered me directly underneath the shade of the massive building. The rugged outer façade was beautiful against the brilliant blue sky and climbing ferns. I slid off my book bag, and retrieved my camera. I powered it on and focused, taking in the image before me. In the tiny frame, I found the perfect angle and the right lighting. Clicking it several times, I captured the Archer Building forever on my SD card.

My eyes drifted along the brickwork until they landed on a dark haired boy, leaning against the wall. His cool posture commanded attention, but the sharpness in his features demanded respect. I found myself oddly curious, yet deeply drawn to him. As if sensing me, he lifted his head. I stood rooted, my feet refusing to move as his eyes slowly swept across the space between us. The intensity within them seemed to close the distance between us, fading the world around us until all that was left was this beautiful stranger and me. He stared at me as though my eyes were a lifeline, holding on until I became overwhelmed by our intimate exchange. Heat rushed to my cheeks as I tucked my hair behind my ear, and looked down at my shoes. *He's looking at me as though I'm the only person on earth.* Compelled to look once more, I lifted my eyes, startled to find an empty wall. I searched the area for him. *Where did he go?* Turning around myself, I struggled to make sense of it all. *Did that really happen?*

Confused and still a bit unnerved, I headed to class, taking in the collection of students at Belman University along the way. It was a typical assortment of specimens. A group of muscular boys tossed a football back and forth on one side of me, while across the lawn sat a gaggle of spaced-out looking individuals. I shook my head at them, noticing a cluster of people wearing outdated hoodies and sandals over my left shoulder. I pressed on, skirting around the preppy kids, whose parents probably pushed them to attend college and gladly footed the entire bill. Those kids could choke on their silver spoons for all I cared.

I walked up to the double doors, just as a blond guy reached for the metal handle. He opened it and stepped back, allowing me to enter first.

"Um, thanks," I muttered.

"You're welcome. Where you headed?" he asked in a deep voice.

"Drawing," I answered.

"Me too. May I walk with you?" he asked.

I looked up at him. All I could muster was a pathetic nod. His height was perfect for basketball, but his size was ideal for football. I wondered if he played either. His eyes were clear blue, mimicking the oceans of Barbados, complete with the glistening sun reflecting off the surface. My eyes drifted to the cleft in his strong chin. His skin was golden-brown. He obviously loved the sun and the feeling was mutual. His body wasn't just sun-kissed; it had been lapped like a melting Popsicle.

We walked in silence up the stairs and down the foyer of the first hallway. I let him lead the way, since he seemed to know where he was going.

"I'm Cayden, by the way."

"Kara," I replied.

"Nice to meet you." He beamed down at me.

"Same here," I murmured.

He slowed his pace, his eyes darting to the open door to our left.

"Here we are," he said, halting suddenly. "Ladies first." With a fluid wave of his hand, he gestured toward the door.

I smirked in amusement, figuring he was raised in the south, where manners are instilled deep into one's very marrow. Being raised in Garet, I knew some women who were more proud of their sons' impulse to pull out a girl's chair, than their grade point average in school.

When I stepped inside, I took a quick assessment of the room. There were four large windows along the far wall. Slatted blinds allowed the sun to filter through the panes. Empty easels filled the right corner. A long wooden table stationed at the head of the classroom held stacks of canvases and a mason jar full of pencils. Nearly every inch of the wall was covered with posters of famous artwork, mixed with the creativity of past students. I scanned the names as I strolled by. Van Gogh. Penny DeLuth; Class of 2008. Pierre Renoir. Sheryl Davis; Class of 2010.

I scooted down the center aisle and sank into a chair. My gaze lifted to Cayden as he strolled down the rows of desks to my right and plunked down into one. I glanced over my shoulder. He raked his fingers through his blond hair, his bangs falling back over his forehead as his eyes shifted to mine, catching me peeking. He smiled. Heat rushed to my cheeks; I turned back around, hoping he hadn't noticed.

There was commotion in the hall. The room fell silent as everyone turned their attention to the woman shambling through the door. Her purple muumuu nearly tripped her as she tussled with a laptop, a shiny garbage bag, and an Army-issued thermos. With a grunt, she tossed her wares onto the table, then adjusted the collar of her dress.

"Good afternoon, class. I'm Professor Dixon." With a stubby index finger, she shoved her specs against the bridge of her wide nose. The frames were solid black and the lenses were square. For a moment, I thought she was wearing a pair of those silly Halloween glasses with the bulbous nose attached. All that was missing was the bushy moustache.

"Welcome to Drawing," she began. "I presume each of you have met the prerequisites for this class." She looked at us expectedly. Someone coughed from several rows behind me.

"I'll take that as a yes."

She unzipped the laptop case and withdrew a stack of papers. She rounded the table, bumping the edge with a chunky hip and handed the mound of papers to a boy in the front row.

"This is your syllabus," she said. "You will need the listed literature and supplies."

The syllabus slowly made its way around the room. "I expect everyone to be prepared by the next class." A moment later, there was a light tap on my shoulder. I shifted in my seat, meeting Cayden's broad grin as I took the stapled papers.

"Thanks," I muttered. *Boy wonder is a bit too cheery for me.* I thought of Cassie, with her blond locks and perpetual smile. *She'd be perfect for him.*

"If you have any questions, my office location and phone number is on the syllabus," she continued, tucking her hair behind her ears, revealing tiny pewter cats dangling from her earlobes. *Oh God, she's a cat person.* I pictured Mrs. Dixon as a crazy cat lady. Cooing at them as she tried to scoot through her kitchen with dozens of felines meowing around her feet, all clambering for attention. *Cat people are a breed of their own.*

"I find it to be a complete waste of time to go over the syllabus. Since you've made it this far with your education, I assume you all can read. So without further ado, I'd like to see first-hand your drawing abilities. I need to know if I'm teaching the next Picasso, or merely the next champion doodle artist." She chuckled to herself as she turned around. Her plump rear end caused her dress to hike up in the back. Stout legs funneled into padded leather sandals. Her hand reached around and raked at her left cheek. I shook my head, sighing inwardly. *Oh, Mrs. Dixon. You are no doubt a calamity in sensible shoes.*

She whirled around, clasping the garbage bag in her left hand. Again, she approached the boy at the head of the class. She reached in the bag and withdrew a plastic banana. He took it, confusion spread across his face, as he watched her saunter off without an explanation. She made her way around the room, presenting each student with faux fruit. As she handed someone a green pear, she said, "I want you to sketch this fruit. Sounds simple enough right? I don't care how you draw it. Just do what speaks to you. Make it a cartoon, make it realistic, make it abstract. Make it *yours*."

Then it was my turn. Mrs. Dixon stood next me, the smell of cheap perfume and joint cream filled my nostrils. I discreetly covered my nose as she reached deep into the bag, then withdrew a bundle of purple grapes. She smiled, smearing bright pink lipstick across her teeth. I reached for the grapes, being extra careful to not stare at her mouth. She brushed past me and made her way to Cayden. When the bag rustled behind me, I couldn't contain my curiosity any longer, so I turned to watch.

"Let's see, what will be your inspiration?" She made a production of searching the depths of the bag, before she dramatically revealed a polished red apple. It could have come straight from a farmer's market. It made my mouth water.

"Ah, an apple," she gushed. "This has the potential for many avenues of self-expression. I can't wait to see what you do with it." Cinching the bag shut, she bustled back up the aisle, and said, "I have sketch pads here, if you don't already have one. You may begin."

I rummaged through the contents of my book bag, my fingers searching for my sketchpad. When I felt the spiral spine, I pulled it out and laid it on the desk, smoothing the worn pages with my fingers. My sketchpad was more like a journal to me. It chronicled my past two years. It was full of silly doodles, clipped poetry, and general musings. I flipped to a blank page, and then stared at my bundle of plastic grapes. I worked the tip of my pencil back and forth across the woven fibers of the page until the grapes took shape. I delicately shaded in the leaves, my brows furrowing as I concentrated. Finally satisfied with it, I sat back, my eyes flickering to the clock. *Fifteen minutes? It took me only fifteen to draw that?* I glanced around the room and noticed everyone else was still working diligently. I looked down at my creation. It was pretty good, but perhaps it was a little boring. I tapped my eraser against my chin as I studied it some more. I began seeing drops of dew, exaggerated stems, and even a vineyard in the horizon. With a few strokes of my pencil, I added the lush details before leaning back, cocking my head at the drawing. A smile pulled at my lips. *Much better.*

Feeling the weight of someone's stare, I lifted my face, scanning the room before spotting a figure in the hallway. The wall obscured half of his body, but the heat from his eyes melted me into place. *It's him.* I tried to swallow, but my tongue was too dry, sticking uncomfortably to the roof of my mouth.

"Time's up. Pencils down." Mrs. Dixon's voice interrupted the drone of scratching pencils around me, and I whirled to look at her, a little flustered by the boy's presence. "Please hold up your artwork so I can see them."

I looked back at the doorway. He was gone. *Where did he go?* I stared down at my paper. My heart was beating so hard I was afraid the entire class could hear it. Was he looking for me? And why was he looking at me *like that*? Like he was trying see through my skin, and into my very soul. I had to know the answer, so I stood on unsteady knees and crossed the classroom, distantly aware of Professor Dixon's look of question. Taking a deep breath, I stepped out into the hallway, searching the length of it for the mysterious boy. It was empty.

I made my way down the hall until it opened up into the lobby. It was relatively isolated, except for a few students lingering near the vending machines. Outside the double doors of the building, the boy stood with his back to me. I took in his slight, but muscular shoulders. The way his dark jeans hung provocatively low on his waist. His slick black hair, tousled precariously around his head.

He turned just slightly, looking at me over his shoulder. His eyes swept from my feet to my face, then clung to my gaze, refusing to let me go. And I didn't want him to. I could have stared at him forever.

The sound of wheels on tile roused me, causing me to break our exchange. A girl with a walker was slowly inching her way across the floor to the front door. She smiled at me, just before a lanky redhead stepped in front of her, dropping a notebook by the wheel of her walker. Before I could warn her, the wheel caught the edge of the notebook, jarring the walker and thrusting her forward. I rushed to her, even though I knew I wouldn't make it in time to catch her. I had to at least *try.*

A blur of movement swirled past me. My eyes widened when I noticed the mystery boy clutching the girl's hand, steadying her as he righted her walker.

Jesus! How did he move so fast?

He placed the walker in front of her, holding her firmly until she gripped the bars solidly with both hands.

If it wasn't for him, she would have landed on her face, I thought. *But how in the hell did he do that?*

Her round eyes looked up at him. She seemed just as startled by his quickness as I did. She gave him a small, grateful smile as he murmured something quietly to her. Initially, I tried to listen, but then felt guilty for intruding so I averted my eyes. *How did he make it from there...?* I shifted my gaze to where he stood now. *To here so fast?*

My eyes drifted up his lean body, admiring his strong profile. His raven hair flopped over his forehead as he spoke to the girl. I watched as he brought his hand up and sank his fingers into his deliciously disheveled locks, combing it back with one smooth motion. Then, he coolly strolled to the door and held it open, as the girl pushed her walker through the threshold, and out into the sunny lawn of the courtyard. As the door closed behind her, the boy turned. His face now pinched, and hostile. The temperature seemed to drop, and the tension in the air was almost palpable.

Oh, shit. I looked to the redhead. His mouth hung open, appearing unsure about what he should do as he watched the boy lift his notebook from the floor. My gaze followed him as he stalked toward the redhead with the notebook fisted tightly in his hand.

This is going to be bad. I held my breath as he slammed the notebook into the guy's chest, causing him to wince slightly.

"You ought to be more careful," the boy hissed. "And you're damn lucky that was an accident." His dark eyes narrowed at him, his voice lower when he added, "This time."

What did he mean by, this time? I wondered.

The redhead nodded woodenly, and swallowed hard. His trembling hand took the notebook, then he darted away.

The boy's gaze fell on me, and again I felt the strong attraction igniting the space between us. I was compelled to get closer, wanting to ask him his name. "You better get back to class, *anima bella*," he said before he turned his back to me, and strolled out the door.

Anima bella? What did that even mean? I stood there for long bewildered moment, replaying the last few minutes. His presence was intimidating, there was no doubt about that, but seeing him rush to help the girl revealed a hint of what he held inside, and I was intrigued. *Who is this boy?*

I traveled down the hallway, running my hand along the wall as I thought about his eyes, as dark as midnight and entrapping, like quicksand, and I was pretty confident I would rather sink deeper than to be rescued. I rounded the threshold of the classroom, and blindly made my way down the aisle of desks, lost amidst a cloud of *him.* His ebony eyes clashing against his pallid skin. His husky voice, and the way his lips caressed the words *anima bella,* as though he were seducing me right there in the lobby.

"Uh huh. Very nice," said Mrs. Dixon. She was still examining the sea of papers before her, waddling through the rows, occasionally leaning closer to the sketches to inspect them further.

She stopped at my desk, just as I sank back into it, thankful to be off my shaky legs. Lifting the thick frames from her eyes, she peered into my sketchbook. I noticed her eyes were brown, nothing noteworthy. No flecks. Not a hint of another hue. Just dull old brown. She squinted at the fading landscape of vineyards. "Not only do we know that this is a drawing of delicious grapes, but we know their origins. Fantastic!" she said as she scuttled past me. "Love the dramatic shadowing!" she squealed to the Goth chick in the back row.

I was vaguely aware of everything around me, my mind still entrapped by the dark-haired mystery boy. His captivating eyes entranced me, and what's more, I couldn't help but think he was entranced by *me*.

"Oh my!" Mrs. Dixon said. "What an artistic voice you have, my boy. A creative spin on such an ordinary object! I'm eager to see what else you have up that sleeve of yours."

Trying my best to be nonchalant, I slowly shifted in my seat. Mrs. Dixon patted Cayden's shoulder and walked away. My eyes fell on the image, and I felt my chin sag as I gaped at it. Feathery lines and swirls filled the page. The apple practically lifted off the page. The flowing contours and sweeping scrollwork was almost lost on the simple pencil lead. It belonged on a ceiling in Italy somewhere. It was beyond college art level, beyond the scope of a fifty-minute class. It was beyond beautiful. Then I noticed it. Delicate fingers curled around the edges of the apple. A blurred image of a woman was shadowed in the foreground. Her hair was long and figure was slight, and her face showed no detail. The gray and black shadows of his strokes made her features obscure, but for some reason she looked familiar. My breathed hitched when I noticed it. Even cloaked in dark charcoal smudges, there was no denying what was on her feet. There, in the splotch of dark pencil lead was a pair of beat-up black sneakers.

Chapter 3

"That's it for today," Mrs. Dixon announced. "Remember to be prepared for the next class. See you Wednesday."

Still in shock, I shoved my sketchpad in my book bag and rose from my seat. Mrs. Dixon tidied up the table as the class filtered through the aisles and out the door.

As I moved through the hall, I tried to convince myself that either I was seeing things, or it was a complete coincidence. I quickly ruled out the first explanation. I knew what I saw. It was a pair of black sneakers. The girl in the picture was *me*. I shook my head roughly. *Don't be so full of yourself. Why would he draw you? A lot of girls wear black sneakers, so it has to be a coincidence. Right?*

I had a few minutes before my next class, so I found a bench in the courtyard and sank into it. My book bag jabbed uncomfortably into my spine, so I shimmed out of the straps and pulled it into my lap. I picked at the zipper vacantly, barely registering the sound of approaching footsteps.

"May I sit with you?"

Startled, I inclined my head, meeting Cayden's sparkling blue eyes.

"Sure," I mumbled, sliding over to make room.

"Where ya headed next?" he asked brightly.

"Art History II. What about you?"

"Biostatistics." He gave a thumbs down and blew a raspberry. "Boo."

I laughed. "Better you than me. I hate math. I suck at it."

Cayden chuckled. It rang off my ears like a soothing hymn from a church choir. "It's not so bad. I actually enjoy it."

"Well, then you're just weird," I shot playfully.

"I like figuring things out. Solving problems." He eyed me briefly, catching me off guard.

I began toying with the charms on my necklace. He regarded at me as though he was trying to place my face. The way you study a stranger who you know you've seen somewhere, but unable to remember where. It was unsettling, and a bit annoying. I cleared my throat, trying to shake free of his stare.

He blinked, then said, "I'm actually quite good at solving problems."

I rolled my eyes. "What *aren't* you good at? Math whiz *and* amazing artist." I snapped my mouth shut, pursing my lips tight. *Why did I say that?* My muscles tensed as I tried to read his expression.

The corners of his lips suddenly quirked up as he studied me for a long moment.

"Singing," he answered finally. "Can't carry a tune. Oh, and cooking. Although I can make a mean pot of mac n' cheese."

I giggled. The aura around us instantly relaxed. I wanted to ask him about the picture, but when I opened my mouth, the words fell silent. Sinking back into the bench, I glanced sideways. He leaned back and crossed his ankles. He appeared completely at ease, as if I wasn't a stranger, but a long lost friend.

I decided to ask him something simple. "Are you from North Carolina?"

He shook his head.

"I thought gentlemen were raised in the south?" I smirked at him.

"Not true," he said pointedly.

"So, not a southern boy?" I cocked a brow at him, not sure if I believed him.

"No." He seemed to be pondering something. "I'm a Yankee to the highest degree."

That's odd. He doesn't have an accent, I thought. "With a tan like that?" I stated, taking in his golden skin.

"I said I was *from* the north." He bumped my shoulder with his. "But I spend a lot of my time here."

"Oh," I whispered. "Of course."

"And you?"

"I've lived in North Carolina my whole life. I applied to DGU just to get out of here."

"What brought you back?"

My body shut down. The doors leading to the painful, buried memories of my father slamming shut, and refusing to open. I knotted my fingers nervously. I felt his eyes burn into me, waiting for my answer. I swallowed the lump of resistance that filled my throat, and without looking at him, I said, "My father." I closed my eyes as though the darkness would help me finish the words. "He died last year. Cancer. I came back to be closer to my mom." I pried my lids open, but stared straight ahead, sitting with my back and shoulders rigid. I fought to appear unnerved, but internally, I was a wreck. I felt the bite of impending tears nip at the corners of my eyes, so I clamped them shut, trying to will them away, but it was too late. I felt a warm tear slide down my cheek, and with it, a flood of memories washed over me.

I remembered sitting between my mother and my Uncle Cliff during my father's funeral. My eyes raw from hot tears and countless tissues. My heart felt as though it had shattered into pieces, and the frayed shards now flowed through my blood stream, cutting me, reminding me what I had lost. I shuddered as I relived the memory, recalling the endless, one-armed hugs I received from strangers and family that practically fell into the same category. I cringed at their words. *Sorry for your loss. My thoughts are with your family. I'm praying for you.*

By the end of the service, my nerves had hardened into steel. I clung to my chair, staring at nothing as I dug my nails into the seat cushion. My brain slowly registered that the pastor finally shut his yapping mouth. Guests mingled around the room, waiting like vultures to swoop in with their limp hugs and lousy words of encouragement. I struggled to avert my eyes from their sympathetic gazes, but they burned into my skull. The soles of my feet remembered the pounding they took as I bounded across the parking lot to escape. All of these sensations were so vivid; it was as though I endured them just yesterday. I shook my head, trying to break free from it.

Cayden touched my shoulder. "I'm sorry," he said quietly.

I usually balked at any words of condolence, but somehow those two little words filled me with an unexplainable peace. My eyelids fluttered open and I slowly turned to face him. Genuine concern etched his face.

"I don't know why I told you that."

"I'm glad you did," he said softly.

"I normally don't spill my guts to strangers," I replied, suddenly aware of his hand still lingering on my shoulder. He must have felt my muscles tense beneath his fingers, because he quickly withdrew his hand, allowing it to fall into his lap.

"It's good to share your thoughts, especially your burdens with others. No one should have to endure hardships alone."

What college boy talked like that? Burdens? Endure? Hardships? I would bet the entire east wing of the boy's campus never used those words in an English paper, much less a conversation.

"Well, I better let you get to Art History, you have less than ten minutes to get there," he said as he rose from the bench.

"Where do you have to go?" I questioned.

"Furman Building."

"That's clear across campus. Unless you can fly, you're going to be late."

His body blocked the sun, the rays filtered around his frame and reflected off the golden highlights of his hair.

"I'll be there on time, with plenty of time to spare." He winked. "See you around." He strode around the bench and proceeded to jog across the field. I noticed the crowds of students began to disperse around me, so I stood and gathered my book bag. I turned to take one last look at Cayden, but he was already gone.

Chapter 4

I made my way across the courtyard toward Ansley Hall. The massive structure was identical to the Archer Building. I guess you could call them "sister buildings" since they mirrored one another, with only a strip of manicured lawn separating them.

I entered the double doors and surprisingly found the classroom easily. I realized that most of the seats were already full, so rather than drawing attention to myself by fumbling down a row full of book bags, purses and sports bags, I slipped into the nearest empty desk. I scanned the room. A few students waited anxiously for the professor, sitting upright in their chairs, their notebooks opened to a blank page. Others were chatting with friends, or attempting to make new ones. A few were lost in the tiny screens of their cell phones. Their fingers moving like mad across the buttons.

A lanky man with thinning gray hair entered the room. He carried a leather brief case in one hand and a Styrofoam cup in the other. "Good day everyone," he greeted as he slapped his briefcase on the podium and briefly survived the faces before him.

"This course defines the history of art from the ancient worlds to the twenty-first century," he began, his upper lip hidden by an untrimmed moustache. "We'll start with primitive man, and the crude art they scrawled on cave walls." He stepped around the podium with one hand in his pocket, the other still grasping the cheap white cup. "And by the end of the semester, we'll be discussing modern art and its current artists." He paused to take a long sip, which enhanced his jagged cheekbones. He swallowed hard and his face drew into a hard grimace.

"There are historical periods I am enthusiastic about." His gaze focused on each pair of eyes that met his. "And then there are others I'd gladly omit from our discussions. However, that would be doing a serious injustice to you, as art is ever-evolving and each style influences the other."

The next forty-five minutes went by in a blur. My mind kept meandering back to the brick wall and the boy who adorned it like a piece of art. His pale skin contrasting against his dark hair, his coolness, and the heated exchange we shared. I wondered who he was, what he studied, and if I'd see him again. I even created entire scenes and conversations that we'd share if we ever crossed paths again. I was so absorbed in my daydreams that I hardly noticed that Professor "what's his name" had stopped droning on about some cave in France.

I snapped into awareness at the sound of shuffling around me as everyone gathered their belongings. The professor, (whose name was Professor Ray Milton, I learned after I referred to my class syllabus), briskly pitched his empty cup into the trash and hastily shoved his notes into his briefcase. He, along with the rest of the class exited the room as I sat alone, scolding myself for possibly missing a vital piece of information, which may bite me in the butt later. I sighed inwardly and collected my sketchbook and pen, dropping them into my book bag. *Get a grip, Kara. What are you? Sixteen?* I hadn't day dreamed about a boy since the eleventh grade. *What is it about that boy that affects me so?*

I trudged across campus and by the time I made it back to my dorm room, the mystery boy wasn't at the forefront of my mind, and I was glad about that. I could focus on other things, like checking my email, and downloading the newest paranormal romance novel to my tablet. I had close to two hours of alone time, when the bouncing ball of sunshine burst through the door.

"Hey! How was your first day?" Cassie asked as she flopped belly first onto her bed.

"Good." I hesitated, unsure if I really wanted to ask about hers.

"My professors seem nice," she declared, tucking a loose curl behind her ear. "I start student teaching this semester, which I'm totally excited about."

"The experience will be good for you," I said when I noticed she was expecting a conversation. "I was in the work-study program at DGU," I continued. "For one semester I worked as a lab assistant. I learned quickly that biology wasn't my thing. I cleaned slides and changed light bulbs in microscopes all day long. On top of that, I prepared trays of dead frogs, crayfish, and fetal pigs." My nose wrinkled involuntarily at the memory.

"Ew," she mewled, "I would have totally quit." She examined her fingernails thoughtfully, then a slow smirk broke across her face. "Got any cuties in your classes?" she asked, wiggling her blond eyebrows.

I couldn't help but laugh, allowing it trail off awkwardly.

"Ah ha! So you found yourself a hottie already?"

"I never said that!" I squealed.

"What's his name? I might know him."

"There is no hottie," I pleaded. The images of the dark haired boy lit up my memory like fireworks. I felt the heat flush my cheeks, but I refused to acknowledge it.

"My BS detector is beeping like crazy," she chided. "But since you're being all secretive and stuff, I'll just drop it…"

"Thank you."

"For now anyway," she added, as she picked at her hot pink nail polish. Her gaze slid to mine and the corners of her mouth quirked up slyly. "Want to hear about the eye candy in my Evolution class?"

I rolled my eyes. "Cassie, is that all you think about?"

"Of course not," she pouted, appearing hurt. "I just can't help myself. It's in my DNA to appreciate the male species."

"Appreciate?" I snorted. "More like ogle and drool after."

"Well, that too." She grinned. "Hey, I'm starving. Want to head to the Galley, pick up some lunch?"

"Sure." My stomach chimed in just then, causing Cassie to giggle. I rifled through my book bag and pocketed my student ID. Cassie snatched her purse from her bed and looped it over her head. The red strap of her giraffe print purse ran across her chest like a seat belt. She played with it as she chatted about her classes, the cost of her books, and the impending papers she would be writing.

We walked across the courtyard and past the

Belman Book Store, where you could purchase anything from books and school supplies, to snacks and CDs. We eyed the display window, and I made a mental note to come back and pick up the navy blue aluminum water bottle.

"So what grade do you want to teach?" I asked, once there was a lull in our conversation.

"Third grade, or maybe fourth. I haven't decided, but I know it's definitely going to be elementary kids. I'd rather be the meat between a Gary Wattle and a Philip Lander sandwich than work with middle school kids." She visibly shuddered at the thought.

I felt my eyebrows shoot up. "Who?"

"*Hello*? Don't you watch *Drop A Beat*?"

I gave her a blank stare.

She rolled her eyes. "Reality show?" She paused, waiting for me to make sense of her words."

I didn't, so I continued to gape at her.

"Kara! It's only the best show out there about up and coming disc jockeys."

I laughed. "You really will watch anything, won't you?"

She scowled. "It's good."

"That stuff will rot your brain."

"*Drop A Beat* has taught me something."

I give her an incredulous look. "What could reality television possibly teach you?"

"It taught me that just because a guy has a sexy voice doesn't mean the rest of him will be."

"Wow." I hid my amusement and just shook my head at my roommate. She smiled sheepishly before her gaze skipped over my shoulder. I automatically turned to see what caught her eye.

"Cayden," I whispered.

"So there *is* a hottie!" she screamed, smacking me lightly on my upper arm. "No wonder you were holding out on me. He is more than a hottie…he's smoking hot! Introduce me!"

"If I get the chance, I will," I said as I tore my eyes from him, urging her to continue walking.

"I think your chance is coming," she muttered as she ran her fingers through her mop of curls, jostling them into a frenzied mess of perfection. I turned my gaze back to Cayden, realizing he was closing the space between us quickly.

His eyes were set on mine and a smile tugged at his lips. When he reached us, he said, "Hey, Kara."

"Um, hi."

"How was your second class?"

I hesitated. *What was my second class again? Cave Man Art 101? No. Art History? Yes, that was it.* "It was all right. Typical first class, you know…" I hoped my face didn't reveal more. *Like how I have no idea, what we went over. Like how I'm not even sure I remember what the professor looked like because all I did, was think about some boy I don't even know.* Cassie nudged me in my ribs, jarring me back to life.

"Oh, um, Cayden…this is my roommate, Cassie."

Like a curtain at a theater, Cassie's lips drew back and her pearly whites glimmered at Cayden. "Hi." She lifted her hand and wriggled her fingers in a petite wave. *Geez Louise. You might as well dig your toe into the dirt and tweak his nose.*

Cayden's eyes washed over my sex kitten of a roommate, as she soaked in the attention, practically purring as she coyly twirled a loose curl.

"Nice to meet ya," he said.

"Likewise."

"We are on our way to the Galley," I said. "So I'll guess I'll see you Wednesday in class?" I took Cassie by the hand, and pulled her away.

"Is it all right if I tag along?" he called.

"Of course!" Cassie replied. "Come on, the more the merrier."

I shot her a long look, which I was sure she didn't understand. Becca would have known that look. All best friends share *a look*. It wasn't as if I didn't like Cayden, he seemed like an all right guy, but I had a feeling that he was interested in me, and I wasn't ready to address that yet. I glanced at the flirty and ever grinning Cassie and knew I wouldn't be able to pry her away from Cayden, so I steeled myself for the inevitable and forced a smile. "Sure."

Cayden smiled brightly and in two long strides, he was again within my personal space. I swallowed, noting the sweet scent that surrounded him. We walked in a small cluster for several moments before I finally dropped Cassie's hand. Like a puppy being let off her leash, she quickly darted away from me. She skipped ahead and turned around. "Cayden, you look familiar. Do you play any sports?" She was walking backwards with expert ease, flowing with the pavement, never stumbling or colliding with a fellow student.

"Baseball," he answered. Do you watch the games?"

Baseball? I figured he played some sort of sport, but I pegged him for a quarterback or center for the basketball team.

"I've seen a few," she said. "But I may just attend

41

more, now that I know one of the players." She grinned and turned on her heel, bounding through the double doors of the cafeteria, with Cayden and me following behind her. As they collected their trays, I examined my surroundings. It was pretty packed. Tables lined end to end stretched across the expansive room. Blue plastic chairs edged each table. Shiny sign holders were sporadically scattered amongst the tables. They reminded students of Galley hours and specials.

Glass freezers lined the right wall. They held bottled water, various sodas, fruit juices, and milk. Another held cold sandwiches, salads, and fruit cups. The buffet style kiosks were full of warm comfort foods. Fried chicken, macaroni casserole, mashed potatoes, brown rice, and pork n' beans. *Wow. You could tell we were in the south. The only thing missing was hash and pulled pork.*

I took a glimpse of the dessert cart and found small bowls of banana pudding and Mississippi mud pie. *Double wow. Where are the moon pies and colas?* I eyed Cayden, who seemed to be sampling everything on the menu. He plucked two bowls of banana pudding from the cart and piled them on top of his heap of steaming southern food.

Cassie's tray was more reserved. It consisted of a salad, a small bowl of casserole, and bottled water.

I trudged along, still silently fuming at Cassie. I snagged a turkey and swiss sandwich from the shelf, along with a packet of mustard and made my way to the drink freezer. *Lord help me get through this lunch with the tanned sex God and the mop of curls who worships him.* I grabbed a bottle of soda and headed to the register. Cassie was already in front of me. She handed her student ID to the clerk, who was perched on a barstool. The cafeteria worker's attitude radiated bitter annoyance. She was probably in her mid-forties, but it was hard to tell. Her mousy brown hair was pulled into lopsided bun on top of her head. She wore a hair net and a starched white apron over her pale green uniform, which looked a lot like medical scrubs. Her nametag read Colleen. She barely acknowledged me as she swiped my ID card through the reader. She handed it back with disinterest, and I nearly flinched at her dingy yellow fingernails. I wrinkled my nose at the stale stench of smoke that wafted from her. Did she recently quit, or was she craving a cigarette? She reached past me to retrieve Cayden's card.

"Hello," he said in a soothing tone.

Her head snapped up and her slack features quirked into a tight smile. She swiped his ID, never taking her eyes off him. He reached for the card, brushing his fingers across hers fleetingly.

"You have a good day, Ms. Colleen," he said smiling. "Take care of yourself."

She nodded vigorously and watched us walk away.

I peered at Cayden.

"What was that all about?" Cassie asked my unspoken question.

"What do you mean?" Cayden walked briskly to an empty table and sank into a plastic chair.

"Uh, hello? She wouldn't give us the time of day, but she goes all goo-goo eyed with you," she continued as she took the empty seat across from him. "Not that I blame her." She grinned at him.

"Goo-goo eyed?" He laughed and dug a spoon into his mashed potatoes. I perched myself next to Cayden, careful to keep my knees from touching his, since he seemed to take up most of my personal space.

"Maybe she's a cougar," she said, her eyes flickering with mirth. I sniggered as I unwrapped my sandwich. Cayden stiffened, but his laughter erased any tension that went with it.

"She's an acquaintance of my family. She's struggling with some…issues."

"Issues? Like what?" Cassie's eyes darted back to the lackluster woman on the stool.

"Addiction," he said simply.

"Addiction? Should she even be here, if she's an addict of some sort?" Cassie asked, obviously appalled.

"She's a recovering addict. She's been clean for years, but sometimes the demons of her addictions come back to haunt her." His voice was calm, as though he dealt with these kinds of issues all the time. I sat in silence for a while, absorbing his words and the peculiar aura that surrounded him. Cassie was also visibly affected. She quietly consumed her casserole, mindlessly scraping the bowl when she was through.

"Are you going to eat?" Cayden asked, jerking his chin toward my untouched sandwich.

I shook myself from my stupor. "Oh yeah." I tore the mustard packet with my teeth and squirted it along the length of my hoagie. I took a bite and got a mouthful of dry bread. I forced it down and reached for my soda.

"So…Cassie. What's your major? Cayden asked, trying to perk up our lifeless conversation.

"Education. What's yours?"

"Psychology."

"Whoa. You're gonna be a shrink?"

I snorted, remembering the way she pieced together my desire to be a photographer with a future career in paparazzi.

"A psychologist actually," he snickered. "After I get my PhD of course," he added.

"Wow. Impressive." She nodded her head in approval.

"I forgot to get a drink," Cayden said. "Be right back." He rose and strolled confidently through the crowded lunchroom.

"I'd lie down on a couch and identify ink splotches with him any day," Cassie purred when he was out of earshot. I nearly choked on my turkey and swiss. Sputtering, I snatched my soda and downed half of it. Cassie giggled like a teenager as I wiped my mouth and attempted to recover my composure. *The girl is ridiculously boy-crazy.*

Cayden breezed by, his sugary smell following him, as he settled back into his seat, tucking his knees beneath the table.

We chatted for a while about nothing, and it was actually pleasant. Cassie was growing on me like a fuzzy mold on aging cheese. Her booming laugh was infectious. *Maybe I was wrong about her,* I thought. I found myself enjoying her company, as I watched her talk animatedly about *Drop A Beat*. She was like your best friend back in middle school. Pinky swears and all.

Chapter 5

"Oh man! I better get going," Cayden said, just before he planted the last dollop of banana pudding into his mouth. "I've got practice," he said from behind his spoon. He quickly gathered his empty plates and trash. Plucking the spoon from his mouth, he said, "Kara, I'll see ya in class?"

"Yep," I said. "See you later." I gave him a small wave.

He stood and collected his tray. "Later," he called over his shoulder. Cassie and I watched him toss his trash and deposit the tray on the counter. He disappeared through the doors and soon passed the cafeteria window.

"Wow, Kara," Cassie said through a deep sigh. "He's amazing. You should totally go for it."

"What?" I gaped at her. "I'm not interested in Cayden."

"Are you kidding me?" She stared at me, practically frying my skull with the intensity that was coming from her eye sockets. "How could you not be attracted to him? He's gorgeous."

"He's not my type," I insisted, recalling the mystery boy, who was Cayden's complete opposite in every way. Cayden was a sunny beach in California, with his warm smile and golden skin, while the boy was a deserted alley in New York, shadowed and a little frightening. I frowned at myself for a moment. *Why am I attracted to someone I'd compare to a dingy back alley?* Then I remembered. Those damn eyes. No one could look at me the way he had.

Cassie slapped a hand across her forehead and huffed. "Not your type? Kara, you are crazy. That guy is *every* woman's type. I know he definitely is mine," she said. "I picked up some mad vibes from that delectable bod of his."

I arched an eyebrow at her. "Oh really? And what was his delectable bod saying?"

"That he needs a good girl to do some bad things to him." She bit her lip, her eyes becoming distant, as she no doubt pictured herself in the role of the "good girl."

I pursed my lips to keep from laughing. Taking one last sip of soda, I said, "Come on, let's go."

After we tossed our things in the trash, Cassie and I started our walk back to our dorm room. I pelted her with questions, attempting to keep the discussion from circling back to Cayden. I learned that she was the middle child, in a family of seven. She was born and mostly raised in Polk, Wisconsin, before her family migrated to Georgia to escape the bitter winters. Aside from shamelessly boy-crazy, she was equally enthralled with coffee, reality TV, and anything produced in the 1980s. I never realized how much you could learn about someone in the matter of a ten-minute walk.

Cassie unlocked our door and pushed it open. I was relieved to be back in our room and headed straight for the shower. As I turned the dials on the tub, I heard the muffled voices from television commercials as Cassie flipped through the channels.

I quickly stripped out of my clothes and stepped

into the hot stream of water. I washed slowly, savoring my quiet alone time. The water eventually cooled, sending a shiver along the length of my spine. *Shit. Cassie's going to kill me.* Feeling guilty for hogging all the hot water, I hurried to rinse off and dried off equally as fast. I wrapped my towel around my wet hair and nestled into the fuzzy bathrobe my mom gave me. It smelled new, the crisp cotton still carried a hint of tissue paper scent. I cinched the belt tightly around my waist and reluctantly emerged from my oasis.

"Finally," Cassie complained, as she threw the remote control onto the bed. She darted inside the bathroom and shut the door as I nosed through my dresser. I shifted through the clothes until I found an old pair of gray yoga pants and a black tank top. I cocked my head toward the shower and heard Cassie belting out the chorus of some eighties pop song, so I figured it would be safe to change where I stood. Then, I meandered to my stash of evening supplies. I'd always had a bit of bedtime ritual. Brush, braid, moisturize, and lotion. In that order.

I retrieved the remote control from Cassie's bed and flipped the television on. I sat cross-legged on my bed and set to work on my knotted hair. The water shut off and a few minutes later, Cassie emerged, scowling, wearing a knee-length nightgown with clouds and sheep on them. Her hair was pulled on top of her head, in a messy attempt at a bun.

"Thanks for saving me some hot water. Lucky for you, in a family of seven, I'm used to cold showers." Her eyes flickered to the television. "What are ya watching?"

"Nothing really." I tossed her the remote. "You can

change it."

I worked at my hair, until it was smooth, then carefully braided it.

"You want to go to Movie Night? I hear they're playing a really gooey romance," Cassie asked as she plundered down onto her bed.

I pressed my lips together to keep from laughing, sweeping my eyes across her unassuming face. She was regarding me with hopeful eyes. *Oh my God, she's serious.* I sighed and unscrewed the lid from my moisturizer bottle. "I think I'll take a rain check."

"There's a 'Build-A-Buddy' workshop. I've done that one before. Look." She reached around behind her back and revealed a plush purple bunny, wearing a tie-dyed t-shirt. "Super cute, right?"

"Yeah," I said with false enthusiasm, dabbing on some moisturizer. I smeared it across my forehead, chin, and cheeks. It reminded me of butter and felt just as silky. As I rubbed it in, I thought of my father. He called it my war paint. I smiled to myself briefly before Cassie interrupted my pleasant memory.

"What about 'Bling my Flops'?"

Irritated at her intrusion, I rolled my eyes. "What?" I asked curtly.

"'Bling my Flops.' For one buck you buy a pair of flip flops and then you can bedazzle them with sparkly crystals and beads."

"Are you serious?"

She nodded with nauseating gusto.

"Cassie, look. I don't really...*do* things like that. I just, go to class. I might catch a couple football games here and there, but I don't do...*activities.*"

"Why?"

49

"I...I just don't." My lips pulled into a frown.

"Are you a loner?" she asked bluntly.

"No," I shot.

"You sure?" She arched a blond eyebrow at me.

"Yes. I just don't do anything that involves a lot of people."

"So, you're a loner."

"I am not." I poked my chin out stubbornly.

"You don't participate in college activities, so why bother living on campus? Your mom lives like twenty minutes from here."

I looked down at my hands. They were gripping the brush so tightly my knuckles were white. Somehow I was able to say, "My dad died about a year ago," without my voice cracking. "That's why I transferred to Belman, to be closer to my mom. But I can't stand the thought of being in my house. Not yet anyway. There are just too many memories there." I took a deep breath, forcing myself to stop there. I couldn't tell her the rest. The true reason I was back in North Carolina. How my mom forced me to come home. And how she insisted that I attend suicide support meetings. Or how the damn doctors agreed with her, and even went as far as threatening to put me in a secured mental ward if I refused. Needless to say, I didn't.

"Oh," she breathed, her blue eyes round and full of sympathy. "I'm sorry, Kara."

"It's all right." I tried to look at her, to show I was all right, but I just couldn't bring myself to do it. I picked nonexistent fuzz off my pants instead. "You didn't know."

Cassie fell back against her pillows. I chanced a quick peek, her small features were laden with guilt.

She watched me carefully from a distance, and surprisingly, she left me alone. Tears began to fill behind my eyelids. I lay down and flung my arm across my face. My chest felt hollow, and the memories of my father hacked away at my brain. *Oh Daddy. Will this ever get easier?* I never finished my bedtime ritual that night. My bottle of apple-scented lotion stood untouched on my nightstand. Instead, I crawled under my comforter and cried myself to sleep.

Chapter 6

The next day was uneventful. I attended two classes. Philosophy of Art and Beauty followed by Ancient Architecture. Both were held in the Archer Building, so I quickly grew comfortable maneuvering my way through its hallways. Ancient Architecture was full of unfamiliar faces and brain-numbing information. I was in heaven. I enjoyed the monotonous voices of professors as they drilled facts into our heads. I scribbled notes and underlined sentences with bright neon highlighters. Yep, it was my kind of paradise. Academically I had always soared above my friends. Becca was bright, but she was far too engrossed with all things frilly to care about her grades. I'd pore over my books, studying for tests, while she combed and braided my hair. She loved to give me makeovers while I did *our* homework. I swear, if wasn't for me, Becca never would have graduated.

There is always one professor who loads you down with tons of homework on the first day of class, and this semester, it was Professor Hollings. He was a relic of a man who had seen the school progress from the years he attended Belman as a student through the forty plus years he had spent teaching there. He had seen eight deans and the expansion of four buildings.

He wore an outdated gray suit and thick-soled shoes with Velcro straps. He barely acknowledged the class as he reviewed the syllabus.

We watched a brief video about Italian architecture and then he proceeded to ramble on about famous buildings and the inspiration behind them. Without hesitation, he assigned a massive amount of reading and chapter summary essays (no less than two hundred words a piece) and a short report about our favorite architecture style. Before releasing us from his merciless grip, he topped it all off with a not-so-subtle hint that there would be a pop quiz next week.

God bless Professor Hollings. He was definitely the old school type. There would be no emailing him questions about homework. No fancy PowerPoint presentations or excuses that you lost access to Wi-Fi. He was straightforward and traditional to the nth degree. He was all number-two pencils, chalkboards, and wide-ruled paper.

Drawing myself from my desk, I realized my day was over. As far as classes go anyway, so I decided to head to the Belman Book Store and finish buying all of my necessary textbooks. I stood awkwardly in the center of the aisle, scanning the shelves of endless books. I bit my lip and searched for the titles I needed. A boy, who barely looked old enough to attend college, sidled up to me. His face was full of acne and he reeked of musky cologne. It was overwhelming, as if it had sat in his father's cabinet for years before he pilfered it from his stash.

"Need help finding anything?" he asked.

His tag read "Lenny." My first instinct was to say no, just to get rid of him, but I really was lost in the midst of the stacks of books. I fought the urge to plug my nose as I spoke to him. "Um, yes actually." I shoved my list of books into his hands and strained to stretch my neck away from his radiating stench.

"I got you covered." He buzzed around the aisles like an amped up worker bee. I watched him work at a dizzying pace as he collected an armload of material. "I'll leave this at the counter for you," he said as he zipped past me.

"Thanks," I said, stepping aside, allowing him to hustle my stash to the register. I breathed deeply and strolled to the back of the room where the school pride products were kept. I fingered through the rack of shirts and hoodies before I moseyed over to the display of water bottles. Once I made it to the register, I decided that I also needed a pack of bubble gum, a bottle of lemonade, and a packet of sunflower seeds. As the clerk rang up my goods, I looked down at my bounty. Aside from my tower of textbooks and last minute items, I also purchased a water bottle, a new notebook, and a t-shirt. It was made of soft cotton and had the Belman Bobcat clawing its way out of the navy blue fabric. I loaded as much as I could into my book bag and still had to carry two plastic bags back to my dorm. My arms ached by the time I got to my room. I was thankful Cassie was there to open the door for me. It saved me the hassle of searching for my key. I dropped the bags at my feet and tossed my backpack on to my bed. It was nearly bursting at the seams. I quickly relieved its stress by unzipping it and emptying its contents across my crumbled comforter.

"Bought all your books today?"

"And a few other things," I added, a bit winded.

"I see that."

I divided the books, shoving the books I needed for

tomorrow's classes back in my book bag and left the others stacked on the desk.

"How were your classes?" Cassie asked as she plopped onto her bed, scooting backwards until her back was against the wall. She opened her laptop and laid it across her thighs.

"Blissfully mundane," I sighed, shoving everything aside so I could sit down.

The gentle hum of Cassie's computer whirled to life as I unscrewed the cap from my lemonade bottle. Downing a quick swig, I glimpsed Cassie's face as it lit up from the illuminating screen in front of her. The rhythmic melody of tapping keys filled the air. At the rate her fingers were flying, if she were an accomplished pianist, Cassie would be pounding out a powerful symphony right about now. I wiped my lips with the back of my hand and felt a sudden longing for my friend Becca. I fished my cell phone out of my pants pocket and scrolled through my recent calls, pressing SEND on Becca's contact screen. It rang once. I gnawed at an annoying hangnail as I waited. It rang twice. Then I heard her familiar voice on the other end.

"Hey!"

"Hi," I said as I stretched out across my bed.

"What's up? How's school?"

"It's good. I miss DGU though," I answered, as I plucked stray hairs from the pillow.

"Aw, I'm sure. You had your heart set on graduating from there. But Belman is a great college, Kara. Give it some time."

"I know. I just hate being back."

"Kara, you can't run from your dad's death, you know."

I groaned and buried my face into the pillow.

"Oh, poo on you, Kara Maven. I'm right and you know it. You always do this. You don't like something, you run. You get hurt by someone, you run."

I closed my eyes and pinched the bridge of my nose.

"It's called fight or flight, Becca. It's a survival instinct. All animals do it."

"You're not an animal, Kara." I could practically feel her annoyance through the phone. "Come on, you need to face some things head on."

"I didn't call for a lecture, you know." I scowled at the phone.

"I know. But someone's got to put a boot up your ass every now and then."

"I don't need a boot up my ass, thank you."

"Well, then get your head out of it."

"Whatever." I pouted, rolling over and reaching for the small bag of sunflower seeds. "How's school going for you?" I asked as I tore at the packet with my teeth.

Becca howled into the phone. "Sounds like I'm attending an Ivy League college or something," she said. "Just call it what it is, Kara."

"Ok, how's *beauty* school going?" I asked, slurping a handful of seeds into my mouth. I winced slightly as the salt bit at my tongue.

"*Cosmetology* school," she corrected, "and it's going great. They say I'm a natural. I'm really enjoying the courses about skin care; more than I thought I would."

"So, now you're going to be an esthetician?" I spit the seeds out into my hand and slung them into the trashcan.

"I don't know yet," she said thoughtfully. "We'll see. I'm thinking about going into massage therapy next."

Good ole Becca. If she has the slightest interest in something, she pursues it, no holds barred.

"There's a few schools right in Lexington that offer certification, so I'm going to look into it."

"Tell me again *why* you chose to move to Kentucky?" I asked dryly.

"'Cause it has the best fried chicken," she quipped playfully. "And I wasn't sophisticated enough to keep up with the bright lights and big city of Garet, North Carolina," she drawled dramatically. "It was too much for this country girl."

I chuckled, but in fact, she was right. Garet was far from highfalutin. It was cozy and steeped in decades of old southern traditions. However, even carefully tucked into dogwood trees and magnolias, the small town was slowly progressing.

"Besides," she continued. "I already told you. In order to learn *real* cosmetology, I had to leave. If I stayed in Garet, all I'd be doing is teasing beehives, and giving crew cuts to all the men in town. Kentucky's not exactly New York, but at least here, I'm learning more than just how much hair spray is needed to withstand a twenty mile per hour windstorm."

I listened patiently as she told me about perms, facials, and how to thread someone's hairline. The conversation eventually lulled, and Becca had to go practice her techniques of exfoliating a client's cuticles.

"Bye, Becca. I'll talk to you soon, okay?"

"You got it. Oh, and Kara?"

"Yeah?"

"I miss your face," she said gaily before hanging up the phone. I shook my head and smiled. When I looked up, Cassie had shut down her laptop and was stowing it away in a bright purple case.

"Did you eat yet?" she asked.

"Do sunflower seeds and lemonade count?" I replied.

"If this was midterm week, yes," she said as she sprung from the bed. "But since it's not, let's go get some real food."

"You consider the slop at the Galley, real food?"

"Of course not, silly." Cassie clutched her purse and motioned for me to move along. "We're going to Lexi's Mexi Joint!"

****

"Are you sure you don't want me to drive?" I asked as we made our way through the parking lot. "My car is parked just over there." I indicated to my car several rows down, secretly hoping she'd take my offer. After watching Cassie maneuver her way through countless lunch lines, I had little faith she was a competent driver.

"No, I'm good," she said, as she unlocked a green two-door car and tossed her purse inside. As I rounded the trunk to the passenger side, I heard a low rumble of an engine, vibrating the air around me. I jerked my head toward the grumbling sound. A shiny black muscle car stalked past me, like a leopard on the prowl. Its low-scooped hood poured into two small round headlights, reminding me of beady bat eyes. The windows were tinted, but I could make out a masculine shape behind the wheel. I watched the impressive vehicle as it parked smoothly a few spaces away. Curiosity pulled at me like a magnet. I was compelled to see the driver. With my hand still clutching the door handle, I stood motionless, like time had literally stopped as I waited for him to emerge.

"Come on, get in. I'm starving!" Cassie pleaded from behind the wheel.

"Just a sec," I murmured as I opened the car door. The smell of vanilla washed over me as Cassie's car clicked to life. The buzzing from the engine sounded like an annoying fly compared to the monster a few spaces away.

Finally, the car door swung open. A messy mop of black hair lifted into the air. What was attached to it, made my mouth drop. An incredibly handsome boy with pale skin emerged from the classic car. His eyes calmly took in his surroundings as he slammed the door shut behind him. *It's him,* I thought. *The boy from the other day.* I watched him as he strolled through the maze of parked cars, right past the front of Cassie's car. His hands were jammed into the pockets of his gray vest. The black t-shirt beneath it was snug. He looked like a modern day James Dean.

Bad boys are so fucking hot, I thought. *They ooze confidence and the sinful way they strut their sexiness around is hypnotic.* His dark eyes swung in my direction. His expression was deadpan, but edged with a hard exterior. He looked through me as if I were just a piece of trash littered on the pavement and glided toward the building behind me.

"Earth to Kara," Cassie chanted. "Hello? Earth to Kara."

Shaken from my stupor, I sank into the seat. *He barely looked at me.* I set my eyes on the little yellow tree dangling from the mirror. *That was far from the special moment I thought we had shared the other day.*

"Put your seatbelt on," Cassie instructed as she slowly backed out of the parking space.

I fumbled with the strap, relieved when I was finally able to sink it into the lock.

"Kara, what is up with you? You act like you've seen ghost or something."

"That guy." I stared at her, quelling the urge to shake her. "Didn't you see him?"

"Of course I did. Is that what's got you acting all weird?"

"You didn't think he was cute?" I asked astoundingly.

"Yeah, he's cute…in a dark sort of way. That's just not my type."

"I thought male was your type."

"Just about," she chuckled, turning onto the main road. "He's just too intense for me."

"Too intense for Cassie Harris?" I mocked playfully. "How so?"

"I don't do dark and mysterious. I prefer hot and dumb."

I laughed, allowing myself to forget about the disinterest in his eyes and the disappointment I felt when they didn't reflect the intensity of our first exchange.

Chapter 7

I slid into my desk and pulled out my sketchpad. The tattered cover shifted and disconnected further from its spiral spine as I opened it. I was just about to doodle when a hand brushed across my shoulder, causing me to jump.

Cayden stood over me, smiling. "Hey," he said simply.

"Hey, Cayden. How did practice go the other day?" Not being good at small talk, I bit my lip anxiously, waiting for his answer.

"Tiring, as always," he said. "Coach is pretty demanding. But that's the way of the game. Practice hard, play harder. You should come to one of the games. We play Swanson tonight."

"Oh, I don't know." I lifted a shoulder.

"It's a home game."

His blue eyes held firm to mine, waiting for an answer.

I didn't have the heart to tell him no. I forced a smile and said, "Sure."

"Great." He smiled. "I'll have my very own cheerleader." He gave me a wink before continuing to his seat. Again, he sat to my right, just behind me so I'd have to turn my head to see him. My eyes swept across the empty chair beside me and wondered why he didn't sit there. I heard a raucous stirring at the head of the class and knew Mrs. Dixon had arrived. Papers spilled from her arms, her army thermos dangled from her fingers and a giant tote bag hung from her shoulder. With a low grunt, she unlocked her arms, spreading her loot onto the table with a clatter.

"Good morning, sweet peas." She straightened and shoved her glasses back against the bridge of her nose. "Did anyone watch the special about Paul Cezanne last night?"

The room remained quiet as most of the class shook their head in response, while others looked around the room to see who may have answered yes. No one did. She sighed in exasperation as she fished out a folder from her stack of paperwork.

"It's too bad no one watched it. It highlighted a famous artist of post-impressionism, which is what we're studying today. Can anyone tell me about that artistic style?"

"It's based on light," Cayden answered soundly. Mrs. Dixon's gaze fixated on him.

"Very good, Mr. Adams." She swept her frayed bangs from her glasses and grinned. Her white blouse was oversized, even for her robust frame. Large red and white buttons, which resembled peppermints, were stuck along the front of her shirt.

I leaned forward and started sketching a butterfly in the corner of my blank paper. Movement at the door caught my eye. When I looked up, I saw him. It was the boy in the muscle car. The mystery boy whose been haunting my thoughts and dreams. My pencil suddenly felt like an iron pipe between my fingertips. I dropped it, along with my jaw. *What is he doing here?* It was though destiny insisted that our paths crossed, and my heart pounded joyfully with gratitude. The boy casually drifted through the aisle to my left. If life had a soundtrack, a badass theme song would accompany this beautiful stranger everywhere he went. Mrs. Dixon's beady eyes darted to the clock above the door.

"You're late, Mr..." Her eyebrows lifted as she waited for his answer.

"Benenati," he replied coolly. He sat down beside me, glancing at me momentarily. "Dominic Benenati."

Dominic Benenati. Finally he had a name.

Mrs. Dixon conferred with her notes. "Ah, yes. You were absent last class. What an impressive start to our time together, Mr. Benenati." She peered at him over her glasses.

"I apologize, Mrs. Dixon. I swear, I won't be any more trouble," he said, giving her a smug smile.

"I should hope so," she huffed as she reached for her thermos.

I stole a glance at him. He sat hunched, with his lean arms slung across the desk as he scanned the room. When his head turned in my direction, I quickly looked away. I could feel his eyes on me. I shifted uncomfortably in my seat, my cheeks flushing with heat. I slid my gaze to him, catching his stare. His face was slender, and angular, casting shadows under his eyes and cheekbones. His skin, the color of oyster shells, was as smooth as polished granite, and his raven hair was a disarray of perfection. A red t-shirt clung to his lean muscles, and he wore black jeans that were folded into oversized cuffs. He lithely reached into his bag and removed a worn sketchpad. *Worn like mine.* I wondered what was in there. Drawings? Poems?

Mrs. Dixon's voice faded as I dissected every

detail about him. A sharply curved chin, that sloped into a creamy throat that begged to be nipped. Slender nose and unsettling dark eyes. I devoured his movements, from the tantalizing way he mussed his hair in concentration to how his deft fingers moved as he sketched.

Somehow, class ended without me even noticing. The uproar around me as everyone gathered their belongings jolted me from my daze, sending me into a flurry of motion as I hastily collected my books and shoved them into my book bag. When I looked up from my desk, he was gone. Flustered, I threw my bag over my shoulder and stomped out of the room. *He barely noticed me.* I thought about the first time I'd laid eyes on him. The intensity of his stare, the way it clung to me like a memory, refusing to fade.

I heard a voice behind me, but I didn't acknowledge it. Dominic's face consumed my thoughts, making it hard to focus on anything else. My frown deepened as I considered the fact that I may have misread our exchange. *Was this so-called deep connection all in my head?*

"Kara."

I felt a hand on my shoulder. I stopped and whirled around. "Cayden."

"I'm sorry," he said. "I called your name. I thought you heard me." His brows furrowed with worry.

"Sorry," I said with a sigh. "I guess I didn't."

His eyes softened but were rimmed with apprehension. His mouth was set tight as he regarded me carefully.

"Um, so…what's up?" I asked distractedly as I shifted from one foot to the other.

"I just wanted to remind you about the game tonight," he said, finally releasing my shoulder. "You are still coming, right?" He shoved his hand into his jeans pocket.

"Oh, right, the game. I wouldn't miss it." I said that with honesty. Cayden was a decent guy, and I actually liked him. Besides, it would be a welcome distraction from Dominic and my obsessive need to rehash the first day I saw him.

"Great. I'll see you tonight," he said as he took a few steps back. "Later." And with that, he turned around and strode away, the sweet smell of wisteria trailing behind him.

"Bye," I replied softly. My eyes landed on the pair of worn baseball gloves that spewed from his back pocket. *Why do good things come in twos?* I wondered about that, as I compared the gracefulness of Cayden to the devilish allure of Dominic. *But then again, I also heard misery comes in threes...*

****

I clambered through the door and dumped my book bag on my bed. Flopping down beside it, I took out my Art History textbook and settled into some studying. I flipped on the radio and turned the dial to a low murmur. I needed sound; the emptiness of the room was unsettling. Several hours passed before Cassie finally fluttered through the door.

"Hey, Kara! How was class?" She lightened her load quickly, dispensing her bag and purse onto her desk.

"Remember that guy we saw in the parking lot?" I ventured. I was pretty sure I'd regret bringing it up, but I was dying to tell her. "He drove that old car?"

"Yeah." Her voice indicated she was interested, even though she had her back to me. She was rifling through her collection of nail polish. The tinkling of tiny glass bottles filled the air.

"He's in my Drawing class," I explained.

Cassie twirled around, her eyes set on mine. Her lips were quirked up in a goofy smile.

"What?" I asked as I shoved myself upright, standing with my hands on my hips, irritation filling my veins. "Stop gawking at me like that," I snapped.

"You've got a thing for him!" She bounded toward me and peered into my face. "Yep, you're hooked. You've got it bad for him." I slapped at her. She leaned back, giggling, crossing her slim arms in front of her.

"Shut up. I don't have a *thing* for him," I said. *Yes, I do,* I thought. *How could I not? He's so damn sexy.* "He's just…interesting." I recalled his confident stride and the cool aura that surrounded him. My heart hiccupped at the memory, and my lips threatened to pull into a grin. I fought against it, and won.

"Interesting, huh? Okay, if that's what we're calling it…" She sniggered.

I sighed heavily and plopped back on the bed. It creaked slightly under my weight. My eyes washed over the alarm clock across the room. The illuminated red numbers beamed five o'clock.

"Oh crap!" I jumped up and darted to the mirror.

"What's wrong?" Cassie's brows shot upward as she stumbled out of my way.

"I almost forgot! I told Cayden I'd go to his game." I ran a brush through my hair, and pulled it into a ponytail. I looked down at my clothes. I was wearing cropped white skinny jeans and gray t-shirt. *This will work.*

"Can I come?" Cassie asked. She came up beside me, her hands behind her back innocently. "Please?" she begged, her hands suddenly clasped in front of her as if pleaded with me. "Pretty please?" She smiled broadly.

I rolled my eyes as I squeezed toothpaste on the bristles of my toothbrush. I slid my gaze sideways, she was still staring at me, her eyes hopeful.

"Fine," I muttered around my mouthful of paste.

"Yay!" she squealed, and then ran off to her closet. She emerged wearing a khaki Belman ball cap, her curls dripping past her slight chin. She was wearing denim shorts and a soft pink tank top. "I'll skip the flip flops until I can tend to my toes." She smiled at me as she stepped into her sneakers. "Do you want to grab something to eat before we go?" she asked, fishing her student ID out of her bag.

"Sure," I replied, just as my stomach rumbled in agreement. We hurried to the Galley, eager to scarf something edible down before we went to the game. The cafeteria was relatively desolate. Several students nibbled quietly by themselves as they pored over thick textbooks. Cassie plucked a bowl full of French fries from the warmer. She slathered it with cheese and bacon bits. I snagged a bowl of fruit and cottage cheese from the cooler, along with a bottle of soda.

Stationed at the register in her usual green scrubs, was Ms. Colleen. She appeared haggard, though she didn't look that old. Her hair was woven into a messy French braid. Flyaway strands sprigging out over her ears made her look disheveled and frazzled. She took our ID's with indifference and didn't say a word as we left with our purchases.

The chair legs scraped loudly across the floor as we settled into our seats. Between chewing, Cassie and I talked about utter nonsense. I learned that not only did she star in her high school's production of *Oklahoma*, but she also had an unnatural penchant for panda bears and disco music.

As she yakked, a flash of pale skin caught my eye. My breath hitched. *Dominic*. He moved like a shadow across the floor. My thumping heartbeat suddenly drowned out Cassie's voice. I watched his full lips move as he spoke to Ms. Colleen. Her head nodded in slow agreement, before she nearly jittered off the stool. Walking stiffly, she followed Dominic through the swinging doors of the kitchen. Curiosity ate away at my gut. My gaze sprang to Cassie; she was smearing her finger in the remaining clumps of cheese.

"I'll be right back. I need to use the bathroom," I said as I stood, my knees feeling like they had been replaced with beanbags. I forced them to function, as I scurried to the kitchen doors, quickly peeking through the small hatch windows. I noticed Ms. Colleen exit through the back door. I spotted another set of doors, and figuring they led to the back of the cafeteria, I hurried toward them. My chest tightened with morbid fear. *What is going on?* As noiselessly as I could, I pushed the doors open and slipped outside.

I crept along the building until I heard muffled voices. Pressing myself against the stone wall, I strained to listen. I couldn't make out anything, so I peered around the corner, gasping at the sight. Ms. Colleen digging deep into her purse. An air of desperation surrounded her as she sought the depths of her bag.

A man with a shaved head watched her, then finally she lifted her hand, and thrust a wad of money at him. After examining the lump of green bills, he shoved them into his back pocket and took a fleeting look around the otherwise deserted back lot before he handed her a small bag of white powder. Her eyes widened with eagerness.

I shifted my gaze to Dominic, swallowing hard as I watched him turn away. His face looked drained of any emotion, but his eyes looked resigned, almost guilty. He moved quickly, not looking back as he crossed the parking lot. My stomach wretched. *Why did I have to be so damn nosey?* Cramming my fist to my mouth, I fought back the waves of queasiness that rippled through my abdomen.

Chancing one more glance, I see Ms. Colleen, alone, crouching against the rusty trash dumpsters. She tossed a lighter and spoon to the ground; her purse lay open and emptied at her feet. With shaky hands, she jabbed a syringe into her arm, and winced. Her head fell limp as she sagged into the smelly dumpsters behind her. The sound of her body rang off the metal. I cringed and slid down the wall until I was sitting on my heels. Like a car wreck, I continued to stare at her, engrossed by the ugliness of the scene. Her head drooped forward, her skin quickly taking on an ashen sheen as she plucked the needle from her vein. Shocked to the pavement, I watched, sickened, as she shambled back inside the cafeteria. *Damn it! Why did I follow them?* My stomach churned with disgust and regret. I sat for a few moments, waiting for the nausea to pass before I climbed to my feet. Taking a deep breath, I walked back into the cafeteria and took a seat next to Cassie.

"There you are," she said. "I'm ready to feast my eyes on cute boys with long bats and hard balls." She wiggled her brows at me.

I forced a taut smile.

She studied me for a moment. "Are you okay?"

"Yeah. I think the cottage cheese was expired or something. My stomach isn't acting right." I had to lie. There was no way I could tell her I had just watched a woman succumb to her inner demons.

****

As we made our way across campus to the baseball field, I promised myself that I would wait until after the game to think about Ms. Colleen. I needed time to sort out what just happened, and try to make sense of it all. There had to be an explanation, but I wasn't sure I wanted to find out what it was.

The stands were full of spectators. Most wore Belman's blue and gold, but some sported the opposing team's colors of green and yellow. We found an empty spot close to the dugout and settled ourselves into the seats. Cassie fidgeted to my right, obviously excited to be there. I smiled and shook my head as I surveyed the players before us. A few were stretching, while others swung invisible bats.

I finally spotted Cayden. He was in deep discussion with a teammate, slipping on white leather gloves as he spoke. He looked impressive in his uniform. The snug material accentuated the muscles in his long legs. From the back, to the front, he filled his pants out perfectly. His eyes shifted momentarily, landing on mine. He smiled suddenly, and gave a small wave. His companion, a stout boy with deep-set eyes, glanced at me and dipped his head in acknowledgment.

"Heavenly beef cake," Cassie purred. "Cayden is smoking hot."

I gave her a sideways glance and giggled. The bodies on the field collected into two huddles. The Belman Bobcats talked animatedly, their blue and gold caps bobbing up and down energetically. The rival team examined their opponents, before dispersing like a frazzled ants, scattering to their designated posts.

Cayden's companion emerged from the dug-out wearing a catcher's mitt. He sauntered just beyond the home plate and squatted down. He punched at his glove idly as he adjusted his footing in the dirt.

Belman's pitcher was a lithe brunette with ears like grapefruit wedges. He whirled his arms around like a windmill before spitting crudely on the ground. He nodded once, signaling the first batter up.

The Swanson team member was African-American, with a strong jaw line. His muscular arms flexed as he swung the bat twice before staring intensely at the pitcher. The thin boy curved his back like a cat, scrunching his lean legs into his chest. His frail body leaned with the throw, his mouth twisted with determination as he flung his arm outward, hurtling the ball toward his opponent.

The crack across the wooden bat was the only indication that the ball connected. The boy was off like a rocket around the bases as others rushed to retrieve the soaring ball, but he made it third base with ease.

"I'm going to get us a drink," Cassie announced. "What do you want?"

"Anything that's not diet."

She shimmed past me and disappeared around the

stands. Another player approached the plate and the entire scenario repeated itself. By the time Cassie made it back, the teams had switched places.

"Where've you been?" I asked as I shifted in my seat, allowing her to push past me.

She handed me a red paper cup and sat down. "Sorry, I saw some friends. Did I miss anything?" She sucked on the straw, her eyes sweeping across the field. "Where's Cayden?"

"I'm guessing he'll be up soon. It's our turn to bat."

"Good. That's what I came to see," she said, leering at me. "Cayden bending over in those tight pants." Her pale eyebrows wagged suggestively. "Oh, there he is!" she said as she slapped my knee.

"Ouch! What is it with you and hitting?" I scowled as I rubbed my smarting kneecap. My eyes lifted to the field as Cayden jogged to home plate. His golden hair shined in the sunlight. His back muscles rippled as he gripped the bat and held it high over his broad shoulder. His fingers unfurled and tightened repeatedly before he seemed content with his position. The Swanson pitcher scrutinized Cayden from behind his prescription sports glasses, before slouching his shoulders and whirling the ball toward Cayden. It arced slightly and flew past him.

"Strike one!" someone called. A few players rumbled quietly, but Cayden didn't even flinch. Again, the pitcher launched the ball, and again, Cayden didn't budge. "Strike two!" The pitcher flashed a smug smile, then let the ball fly. This time, Cayden's body burst into a flurry of motion. His arms flexed as he brought the bat across his body. It connected with the speeding ball in a deafening clash. He flung the bat aside and took off for first base. His body seemed to blur as he ran. My eyes tried to follow his movement as he rounded second and third base.

"Geez, he's fast!" Cassie hollered, jumping to her feet.

"Yeah," I said, gaping at him as he elegantly fluttered across the home plate. His eyes searched the crowded stadium until they found mine. I smiled at him, and he grinned back as he trotted off the field.

Chapter 8

The following Monday, in Drawing class, I found sheets of pastel paper laid out across each desk. Mrs. Dixon was busy filling a tray with colored chalk. Cayden was already seated, thumbing through a sports magazine. As I made my way to my desk, he looked up and waved.

"Hi," I said as I settled into my chair. "How was your weekend?"

"It was all right. Caught a flick with the fellas. What about you?

"Nothing really. Cassie was gone most of the time, so I took advantage of the peace and quiet by reading." That was partially a lie. What I should have said was: *I tried to take advantage of the peace and quiet by reading.* Instead, I constantly found myself reliving the horrific image of Ms. Colleen stabbing herself with the syringe, and pushing the plunger with those eager, quaking fingers. Just the thought made my stomach churn.

I glanced at the clock. Class was about to begin. "So, looks like we're drawing with chalk today." I gestured to the paper in front of me. "Kind of reminds me of drawing hopscotch on my parent's driveway."

"I never did that." He smiled, and I returned it.

"Good morning, class," Mrs. Dixon said. "As you can see, you'll be expressing your creativity through chalk today. I have provided the pastel paper and will be passing around chalk in just a moment."

Dominic strolled through the door. Mrs. Dixon's eyes narrowed as she watched him move through the rows of desks.

"You seem to have a trend going," she said. "But let me say, tardiness does not become you, Mr. Benenati.

"I apologize, Mrs. Dixon. I was helping an old lady cross the street, and let me just say, that dress certainly *becomes* you."

The class giggled. I scanned her lime green kimono and looked back at Dominic. He was smiling, which made him look boyish, and absolutely charming. I couldn't help but smile myself.

"Flattery will get you nowhere, and neither will fabricated stories." She removed her glasses and cleaned them with the sleeve of her dress.

"You don't believe my old lady story?" His lower lip puckered, and his eyes sparkled mischievously.

She slipped her spectacles back in place and scowled at Dominic. "Even if I did, it doesn't excuse you being late. A good deed does not cancel out a negative action. Now, if you please, I'd like to commence with class." She collected the tray of chalk and handed it to the red head in the front row.

My gaze swept across Dominic. He looked distant. His smile had faded, and I wondered what she had said that affected him. His eyes suddenly shifted to mine, startling me. My cheeks warmed, and I quickly looked away.

The tray slowly made its way down the aisles and soon it reached Dominic. He selected a piece of chalk and turned to pass the tray to me. My palms felt sweaty as I reached for it. It was like a scene in one of those teen movies, and I was cast as the awkward nerd girl. I tried to focus on what I was doing, but I could feel his eyes burning into me.

I lifted my gaze, meeting his intense stare. The room around me seemed to disappear. It was just him and me, and the tangible electricity between us. My fingers brushed clumsily across the tray, knocking it from his hand. It fell with a loud clang, and chalk scattered everywhere.

Oh, my fucking God! I'm such a klutz! I sank to my knees and started picking up the pieces. My hands trembled as I worked, feeling the entire room's eyes on me.

"Let me help you with that." Dominic crouched beside me. He smelled like strong spice, but it was nothing like cologne. It was natural, and absolutely wonderful. I watched as his long fingers plucked the chalk from the floor, quickly filling the tray. When he was through, he handed it to me, his eyes set on mine. I noticed he had thick eyelashes. Normally I would be jealous, but honestly, they looked better on him than they ever could on me.

"You got it this time, *anima bella*?" he whispered.

There's that word again. Anima bella. What did it mean?

He smiled, one eyebrow lifted in a sexy, but challenging gesture. His grip did not loosen from the tray until I gave him a feeble nod.

I climbed back into my chair, and surveyed the room around me. Everyone was staring, so I hurried to select a piece of chalk and pass the tray behind me.

Mrs. Dixon started explaining our assignment, but I barely heard her. I was walking on air, and wondering how in the hell I got there in the first place.

****

The days that didn't involve Dominic came and went, with no significance or meaning. I attended classes and floated through lectures. Dominic Benenati upset my entire core. His brooding good looks and cool aura consumed my thoughts and devoured my sanity. I never believed in love in first sight before, but I found myself wondering if it were possible. Could that mystical stuff of fairy tales and romance novels really happen for me?

Dominic and I shared the same class for over three weeks, but we hardly spoke. I'd watch him through stolen glances, memorizing his moves and the curve of his full lips.

One Friday morning, I awoke an hour early. I was eager to get to class and see him again. Although I was in a hurry, I carefully chose my clothes and methodically brushed my hair. I even lined my lips with gloss and pumped up my lashes with several coats of mascara. I checked my reflection in the mirror. I was happy with what I saw.

I dressed in a pair of dark denim skinny jeans and a vintage plaid shirt. I wore my silver cross pendant and my trusty sneakers. I hurried across campus, my stomach roiling with the anticipation of seeing him. I felt silly, but there was something overwhelmingly compelling about him that I couldn't ignore. When I got to class, of course no one was there. I was fifteen minutes early. I settled into my seat and smoothed my hair back into place. After a few minutes, I grew bored, so I wrestled my sketchpad out of my book bag and opened it to a blank page.

Slowly, everyone started to trickle in. As the seats filled up, my eyes kept flickering to the door. Finally, Dominic strode through the threshold. One hand held his tattered sketchbook; the other was wedged into his jeans pocket. A pencil was lodged behind one ear. He wore a denim shirt, the color of pewter. The sleeves were rolled up over his sleek biceps.

I half-expected to see a box of cigarettes jutting out of the fabric. His black jeans fit perfectly and hung tantalizingly low on his narrow hips. Today, he oozed confidence and the strong smell of sex, which irked me. Jealousy flared within me, though I'm not sure why. He didn't belong to me. We barely even spoke.

He slid into the desk beside me. My blood warmed and my heart quickened, but inwardly, I cringed. I found my ability to gloss over the horrible incident with Ms. Colleen, disturbing. I knew in my gut that Dominic somehow played an evil part in it, but I simply didn't care. He was mysterious. Dangerous. Oddly fascinating and completely unattainable, but I was undeniably attracted to him.

"Good day, my lovelies," Mrs. Dixon announced cheerfully. My head snapped up. I was shocked that I didn't hear her crash through the door.

"Today we are going to do some simple sketching. I have charcoal pencils for anyone that doesn't already have one." She collected a fistful of pencils and began passing them down the aisles. "I don't care what you sketch, just be sure to *use* the texture of the charcoal pencil to guide you." She ran her fingers through her dark hair before setting them on her hips. "May the artistic force be with you."

My eyes jumped to Dominic. He sat hunched over his notebook, making long strokes with his pencil. I glanced back at my own paper. I bit at my lip, wracking my brain for some inspiration. I twirled my pencil as I stared at the blank page before me. Finally, I swiped the charcoal point across it. Feverishly, I sketched the profile of man. His features were severe, and heavily shadowed. He had a billowing pompadour hairstyle and hooded eyes. The image reminded me of a very gloomy Elvis Presley.

"I'll show you mine, if you show me yours," whispered a husky voice. My heart nearly did a pirouette. I had been admiring Dominic from a distance for so long; I had almost convinced myself that I was invisible. My skin prickled with excitement as I turned to face him. He leered at me, his dark eyes dancing with ferocious intensity. I shifted nervously in my seat. "Come on," he urged gently. "I won't bite."

I smiled sheepishly and slid my sketchbook toward him, gnawing on my bottom lip as he evaluated my work.

"You're quite the little artist," he admired. With a quick flick of his wrist, he flipped his notebook toward me. Reluctantly pulling my eyes from his face, I scanned the page. It was full of disturbing depth and jarring angles. The abstract image was scrawled crudely, but beautifully, deep into the fibers of the paper. Thick vines twirled across the page. Almost lost within the snarled mess, was partially bloomed rose. Thorns, like shark's teeth cut into the delicate petals. Coiled like barbwire, the vines seemed to be choking the delicate bud. My eyes lifted, meeting his intense glare. His mouth curved slightly into a mischievous grin. I bit my lip, secretly wishing I were biting his. He remained quiet, his sharp eyes focused on mine.

"It's really good," I started. "A little depressing, but good."

Amusement colored his stern features. "Depressing?" he said mockingly. "And your sulking Elvis isn't?"

"He's not sulking," I said, practically pouting. "He's thinking. And it's not Elvis."

"Sure looks like him." He drew his sketchpad back toward him and regarded his artwork thoughtfully.

"What do you know about Elvis anyway?" I grumbled, irritation edging my voice. Dominic was like dark chocolate. From the desirable tasty exterior, right down to the bitter sting on your palate.

He snickered. "More than you'd think." He struck the tip of his pencil across the paper harshly, adding more menacing thorns. Prying my eyes from him, I swung them to Mrs. Dixon. She was standing over someone, discreetly critiquing their work. Her straight hair hung like the bristles of an old broom. I watched her vacantly, silently analyzing my two-minute discussion with Dominic. Before I could come to any conclusions, Mrs. Dixon's round bottom brushed my elbow.

"Miss Maven," she trilled. "Let's have a look at your work." She bent forward, lifting her black frames and squinting into my sketchpad. "Wonderful use of shadowing, it makes the portrait ominous, but yet you still capture his appeal." She replaced her glasses squarely on her face. "He's a hunk of a man, that Elvis."

My mouth gaped open as I heard sniggering beside me.

"That velvety voice still gives this old gal goose bumps," she gushed as she swatted my back playfully, jolting me forward. "Well, it looks like I've kept everyone over. Apologize to your professors for me. Those of you whose work I didn't see please bring it next class, and I will look over them first thing. Have an inspiring day."

Everyone around me whipped into motion, packing their belongings and filing out of the door. I glimpsed Dominic strolling under the threshold and out into the mass of moving bodies. Even Cayden had left the room in a hurry. *Cayden.* I tried to remember if I had even said hello him today. *What is it about Dominic that makes me forget about everything else?* I collected my books, and my thoughts, before slowly proceeding through the rest of my day. Time spent away from Dominic seemed dull. I sank back into my lackluster life, pining for the boy who shined so brilliantly, I was nearly blinded.

Chapter 9

I used to think nothing interesting happened on Tuesdays, but I was wrong. *Dead wrong.* I was reading in the courtyard when a crowd of boys wearing nothing but cutoff shorts, and knee-high tube socks ran by. Their bare chests were covered in silver paint, and they were chanting, "Kappa knights ho! Kappa knights ha! Kappa knights rule this town!"

They stopped and lined up in a military like formation, then proceeded to do squats while several guys with wooden paddles observed. A dark haired boy in black denim caught my eye. *Dominic.* My heart beat a little faster. He gripped a long handled paddle over his shoulder as he strolled in front of the line of boys.

"That's enough," yelled a blond standing at the edge of the formation. "Run your pathetic asses back to the ritual site for the final initiation and pinning ceremony." He smacked his palm across the paddle with a loud *thwack*. "I said move it!"

The group of boys staggered to their feet and hustled away. *They have to run in just socks?* I watched as Dominic and the others disappeared across the lawn. *Why would anyone degrade themselves just to be in a fraternity?* I tried to picture Dominic during his initiation, but I just couldn't. He didn't seem like the type of guy who would allow others to humiliate him. He seemed better than that. Like he didn't give a damn who liked him and who didn't.

"Fraternities can be rewarding, if they are held to certain standards," a voice beside me said.

Startled, I dropped my textbook and clutched at my chest. Cayden reached down and retrieved my book, handing it back to me with a smile.

"I didn't mean to scare you."

"How can you be so quiet? You're like six foot two. Do you have wings on your feet or something?"

Cayden chuckled and shook his head. His blond hair caught the sunlight.

"I'm just light on my feet," he replied.

"Apparently," I said. "You about gave me a heart attack."

"Sorry, but you looked upset. Is everything all right?"

I waved him off. "I'm fine. I guess it was watching those poor guys embarrass themselves for some silly fraternity." I slipped my textbook into my bag, leaving it on my lap so I could toy with the zipper.

Cayden shoved his hands in his pockets and nodded. "Some chapters disgrace tradition by bullying their pledges. But fraternities were established to enhance member's characters."

"Well, I think the Kappa knights missed that memo. They have those poor shmucks jogging in daisy dukes and socks."

"I believe that's all in good fun. It's what they will endure tonight that worries me." He frowned.

"What will happen tonight?" I asked, crooking my neck to look at him.

"I'm not sure, but a freshman from the team is pledging tonight. I'm going just to watch his initiation."

Suddenly curious about Dominic's role in all of this, I found myself blurting out, "Can I come?" I pursed my lips after I heard the words. *What the hell am I thinking?*

Cayden lifted a brow at me, his face unreadable for a few long seconds.

"I suppose so. We won't be able to watch the pinning ceremony. That's sacred and only members are permitted to attend."

I rolled my eyes.

"When does it start?" I asked, standing and slipping into the straps of my book bag.

Cayden checked his watch. "Anytime now. They start early so they have plenty of time to celebrate afterward."

He started walking, so I followed.

"Where is it? At the Kappa house?"

"The pinning ceremony will be held there," he said. "And the after party."

"So where's the initiation held? And how do you know so much about it? Are you in a fraternity?" I watched his face, but his expression didn't change.

"No. I've just been to a few initiations." He stared straight ahead. I noticed his jaw flex before he spoke again. "They're usually held in the football field."

We walked the rest of the way in silence, until I saw the lights of the football stadium ahead.

"The dean allows them to use the field for this?" I asked, scanning the scoreboard in the distance.

"As far as he knows, it's all innocent fun. You know, 'boys will be boys' type of thing."

As we drew closer, I could hear chatter coming from the stands. The excitement in the air practically crackled like electricity. I was instantly overwhelmed by the smell of freshly cut grass. I followed Cayden through the rows of chairs until he finally sank into one. He ran his fingers through his hair, and I noticed his features appeared tight.

Cayden looks as nervous as I feel, I thought. As I settled into my seat, I searched the field for Dominic. It was empty except for a couple of boys with bullhorns meandering around. I tapped my foot impatiently, my stomach churning with anticipation. I was about to ask Cayden something, when the high-pitched feedback from the bullhorns interrupted me.

"Attention Belman Bobcats," the voice announced.

I searched for the speaker, finding a broad shouldered boy, with russet-colored skin. His ebony hair was spiky, and his voice held a trace of an accent I couldn't place.

"The Kappa knights' final initiation will now begin," he continued. "What you are about to witness is a privilege. It's a tradition of the knights and this tradition will continue long after we leave this field tonight. What you see here, *stays* here."

I bit my lip. *Here we go.*

"Bring in the pledges!" he called.

There was sudden rush of commotion as the clumsy group of Kappa knight wannabes entered the field. They were now dressed in matching gray sweat suits. I glimpsed at their feet. They wore shoes this time.

The same guys from earlier trailed behind them. Each still carrying a wooden paddle. My eyes darted from one body to another until I found Dominic. He was still wearing the same black jeans and dark denim shirt. He looked amazing. Like he just stepped out the page of a sexy cologne ad.

"There's Ben," Cayden said, pointing to a slight redhead keeping pace with his fellow pledges.

They formed a line, with Ben on the far end, and stood at attention. Dominic strolled in front of them, watching the ground as he walked.

"Think of today as a birthday. The day you were born a Kappa."

I pulled my gaze from Dominic and found the blond bully from earlier, speaking into a bullhorn.

"It's an honor to be a knight. So happy birthday, brothers. For your final initiation, we're going to commemorate your big day by giving you your birthday whacks." His face broke out into a devilish grin, sending a shiver down my spine.

"Commence receiving positions," he ordered, as he dropped the bullhorn and slung his wooden paddle over his shoulder. He strutted like a proud peacock across the field to the start of the line. As he rounded the first pledge, he spat at the poor sap's feet.

The line of boys bent over, some gripping their knees, while others held their ankles.

I wanted to cover my eyes, but couldn't.

The first pledge closed his eyes, and I held my breath.

Whack! The sound rang out throughout the stadium. The boy buckled and fell to his knees. The beating did not stop. My stomach sank as I watched his face tighten. It was obvious; he was trying not to cry out. There were some whoops from the stands.

"Who is that asshole?" I asked Cayden.

"I think his name is Troy," he answered.

"Well, Troy is a royal dick," I muttered. I looked over at Cayden and noticed his fists were clenched tightly in his lap.

One by one, each boy received a beating of ten or more strikes. Most absorbed the pain, but others were visibly affected. Their faces were red, or even lined with tears.

Troy was finally at the end of the line. It was Ben's turn. Cayden sat forward in his seat, his face serious as he watched Troy saunter around the slim freshman. He didn't just hold the paddle; he wielded it like a weapon.

The young boy steeled himself for the beating. As the paddle connected with a loud crack, Ben's face twisted in agony. He flew forward, sprawling out in the grass.

"Get up!" screamed Troy, as he adjusted the paddle in his hands.

Ben lifted himself on shaky arms. As soon as he was back in position Troy slapped the wood across his backside with all of his might. Over and over, he brought the paddle down hard. Ben could barely stand. Tears streamed down his face.

"Are you crying? That will get you ten more licks."

Troy beat him relentlessly. I felt as though I was about to vomit. *How can everyone just sit here and watch this?* My stomach fisted violently. *Why am I?*

Ben finally fell to the ground. Troy stood over him, his face full of arrogance.

I ran my clammy palms over my jeans. *Thank God it's over.*

But it wasn't. Troy suddenly kicked Ben in the ribs, sending the boy into a fetal position. My stomach wretched, and my breath caught all at once.

My hands covered my mouth, as I searched for Dominic. *How can he belong to this barbaric fraternity?* He was slowly approaching Troy, his face relaxed, almost bored. The paddle hung from his fingers, and I was thankful he hadn't used it on anyone. He inspected Ben briefly before speaking. His words fell silent, but it was clear that Troy heard them. He smiled, but it was a creepy, horror film smile. The kind that sends goose bumps across your skin.

I couldn't believe my eyes when I saw Troy lift his leg and bring it down hard on Ben's side. Adrenaline and anger pumped through me. I couldn't take it anymore. I stood up, wishing I could beat the living crap out of Troy. I turned to leave and was surprised to find Cayden's seat empty.

Chapter 10

Confused, I searched the stands for Cayden. I didn't see him anywhere but noticed the stadium was nearly empty. I ran down the steps and flung myself through the gate of the field. *What am I about to do?* I had no clue, but I knew I was going to do *something*.

I darted across the grass, and before I knew it, I was standing in front of Troy.

"That's enough," I said. "This isn't an initiation. This is hazing. And hazing is a crime. You willing to get your ass thrown in jail for some dumb ass fraternity?"

Troy stared at me, his nostrils flaring. Beads of sweat ran down his temples, darkening his blond sideburns. "Fuck off, bitch."

"No, *you* fuck off, *Troy*. I'm not leaving without him." I gestured to Ben, who was hunched over, sputtering and moaning. Spittle dripped from his lower lip and grass stained his sweat suit. He looked awful.

I knelt beside him, not sure what to do. He groaned, and tried to climb to his feet. I steadied him by slipping under one of his arms. Although he was small, he felt heavy on my shoulders. Perspiration and the scent of wet grass wafted off him.

"I haven't dismissed you yet," Troy hissed, stepping in front of us.

"Oh, get over yourself," I shot. "Someday, college

will be over. And *this*…" I looked around the field at the collection of newly initiated frat boys. "*This* won't matter. *You* won't matter." I glared at him, challenging him to do something, to say something.

Troy raised his fist. I told myself not to flinch, but I did anyway, steeling myself for the impact. It didn't come.

Then, I saw Dominic.

And Cayden.

Dominic was gripping Troy's clenched hand, and his teeth were bared. He was practically snarling, like a rabid dog as he snatched Troy by his shirt and yanked him close. "Initiation is over, Troy," he said with authority, then released him with a shove.

Troy stumbled back and glared at him. It was a tense exchange that seemed to stretch on for hours. Troy's neck and ears were flushed. He was breathing hard through his nose, his chest heaving. Dominic remained calm, his face even softened a bit as he said, "The kid is in, if he still wants to be a knight."

Cayden tucked himself beneath Ben's other arm, taking the brunt of Ben's weight off me.

Troy looked at Ben, his jaw flexed once before he spoke. "Knights fight their own battles." Then, his eyes fixated on me, burning with hatred for a few long seconds before he turned to leave. He spit on the ground as he strolled off the field. "Pledges! Back to the Kappa compound for the pinning ceremony," he shouted.

There was a flurry of activity as the pledges broke out in cheers. They gave each other high-fives and pumped their fists.

Dominic turned to face us, his gaze falling on me. I

swallowed hard as his dark eyes seemed to reach through me, right there on that field and touch my soul. "Are you all right?"

I nodded, holding onto his stare as long as possible. His mouth curled into a slight smile, before his eyes shifted to Cayden, then to Ben. The softness in his face disappeared, morphing back into the stone-like features he often wore.

"You still wanna be a knight?" he asked.

"Hell, yeah," Ben said, straightening himself.

Is he really going to go through with this?

I felt my mouth hang open as I watched him beam at his fellow pledges, holding his ribs, as he laughed lightly.

"You can't be serious? You still want to be a Kappa?" I asked.

"Troy's a prick, but the rest of the guys are like my brothers."

I snorted, shaking my head in bewilderment. "I can't believe this," I said, throwing my hands in the air. *I didn't like fraternities before, but now I officially despise them.*

"I can take him from here," Dominic said to Cayden. His tone held a bit of iciness to it, though I'm not sure why.

"Ben, are you certain?" Cayden questioned, regarding him carefully.

"Cayden, it's cool," he answered as he took his arm from Cayden's shoulder. "I'm fine. It's over. Nothing's broken or cracked." He felt at his chest, wincing once before saying, "Maybe bruised. No big deal."

No big deal? I thought. *Sure, I always stay friends with people who beat me to a pulp. Not.*

Cayden's face was tense, as he narrowed his eyes at Dominic. "I'll be checking up on him throughout the evening."

"I'm sure you will." Dominic's lips twitched just slightly, as he spoke to Ben. "Your *friend* here tends to crash parties." His eyes flickered to Cayden. "You're more than welcome to drop in on the *festivities*." He made the word "festivities" sound forbidden, and somehow erotic. I pressed my lips together to keep from asking if I could join. There was an edge of danger to everything about Dominic. The way he spoke, the way he walked, the way he looked. Even the tantalizing way he licked his lips held a hint of risk. Somehow, I just knew that one taste would captivate me to the point of obsession. I stared at his lips, losing myself in thought as the corners of his mouth curled into a seductive smile.

Ben's features were washed with confusion. "Well, I guess I'll see you later, Cayden." His eyes moved to each of us, but when they landed on me, he quickly looked at the ground. He acted like a shy child, apologizing to his mother for breaking a dish. "Thank you. For sticking up for me. You don't even know me."

I didn't know what to say. I forced a smile and a nod, but inside I was pissed. *I was about to punch or take a punch for this kid and for what? Not a damn thing.*

Cayden and I watched Ben and Dominic as they melted into the crowd of pledges. The hoots and hollers followed them as they made their way across the field and out into the night.

I let out a loud breath, still unable to wrap my head around what just happened.

"You're pretty brave," Cayden said, stepping up beside me.

"I just reacted." I shrugged. "I didn't even think about what could happen to him, or to me."

"That's bravery."

"That's stupidity," I muttered, wrapping my arms around myself. I just wanted to get out of there, go back to my room, and forget all about it. I didn't want to think about the beatings each pledge took or the pain on their faces. Or, how someone could overlook all of it, just to be accepted. And for some stupid reason, I hated that Dominic was a part of all that superficial garbage.

"I just don't understand, *why*," I said. "*Why* put yourself though the hurt just to be liked? You might as well let someone rip out your heart, then allow them to kiss the wound."

"I wonder the same thing about you."

I jerked my head to gape at Cayden. "What do you mean?"

"Explain to me what it is about Dominic. What do you see in him?" Cayden asked.

My breath caught and I stood still.

"How can you be attracted to him?" he continued. His brows were rumpled over his strikingly blue eyes.

"Is it that obvious?" I whispered.

"I've seen the way you look at him." He hesitated, licking his lips before saying, "I wish you could look at me that way."

I inhaled sharply, my head suddenly felt light. He had never said anything like that before. Weeks ago, that declaration would have sent me swooning, but now that I'd met Dominic, it just complicated things. My initial attraction to Cayden was innocent, but something about Dominic superseded him and every other boy walking the earth for that matter.

"What does he have, that I don't?" he questioned.

"Cayden, I don't know. You're both so different. It would be pointless to compare you." *That would be like comparing cheesecake to Red Hots,* I thought.

"The only thing Dominic can offer you is a broken heart."

I started walking again, my head spinning. This was all too much. We finally made it out to the edge of the campus courtyard. Curious, I asked, "What do you know about Dominic?"

"I know all about *his* kind," he shot.

My gaze slid sideways to him. His normally kind face was twisted into a sneer.

"What does that mean?" I felt a shiver work its way down my spine.

His eyes met mine. "Just be careful, Kara. A guy like that will leave you broken. And I'd like to say that I won't be around to help you pick up the pieces of your heart." He shoved his hands into his pockets, and looked wistfully out into the empty courtyard before us. He sighed deeply. "But the truth is…I'll be there, bleeding right along beside you."

Turning on his heel, he headed straight for the boys' campus. I watched him for a while. His blond hair bouncing as he moved. *Loving Cayden would be safe.* I shook the thought away as I made my way back to my dorm. *But I don't want to play it safe.* I lived my entire life, safe. Too afraid to take risks for fear that I'd get hurt. But not this time.

I looked up at the moon before going inside the building. It was glowing softly behind a dusting of gray clouds. *Man took a risk by landing on the moon,* I thought. *It may be a long shot, but I'm going to shoot for the moon too.*

Chapter 11

"I'm heading down to the Post after class today," Cassie said as she popped the lid off a tube of lip balm and dabbed it over her bottom lip. "Want me to check your box?" she said before crushing her lips together.

"Sure," I answered as I turned back to my opened textbook.

"You're welcome," she huffed as she yanked the door open.

"Thanks," I called over my shoulder.

I heard the door click shut, and I resumed my studying. I didn't notice the hours slip away until the doorknob jingled. Noise from the hall interrupted my train of thought as Cassie blundered in, falling back against the door, slamming it behind her. In her arms, she carried an oversized box and various envelopes. "When I offered to get your mail, I didn't think you'd be getting a monster package!"

I pushed away from the desk as Cassie handed me the box. It was light, but it must have been awkward to carry. Scooping it into my arms, I inspected it thoroughly. My mother's handwriting was penned neatly across it. I opened it, but Cassie peered inside before I had to time to shield the contents.

"Shut up!" she cried, smacking me across the arm. "It's your birthday? You weren't going to tell me?"

I winced. "It's no big deal," I murmured. "It's just

another day to me."

"What! Oh, no way, Kara," she retorted, "We're going to celebrate! How old are you?" She stripped her bag from her shoulder and tossed it onto her bed. Her brows arched severely, expecting an answer. "Well?"

"Twenty-one," I replied reluctantly, scowling into the box. *Thanks Mom,* I thought bitterly.

"Oh boy!" she squealed eagerly. "I know just where we're going!"

I rolled my eyes and moaned softly.

"Get over it!" she said. "You're going to have fun. You'll see." She dashed to her closet, her blond ringlets bouncing all the way. She tore open the door and began scouring the hangers. "What to wear? What to wear?"

My gaze set back on the contents of the box. There was a flurry of Styrofoam peanuts inside, but a brightly wrapped gift peeked out from beneath the pile. I lifted the present carefully and sat it on the desk. Reaching back in I felt something shoved below the packaging material. Tugging it free, I recognized it immediately. It was a box of chocolate mints. My favorite candy. My father's favorite too. I smiled at the familiar green package, remembering how we would bicker over the last one. *Dad, if you were here now, I'd let you have all of them.* I opened the box, rattling the plastic enough to make Cassie swivel her head in interest.

"What have you got there?" Her blue eyes swept across my hands.

"Mints. Do you want one?" I offered begrudgingly.

She crinkled her nose. "Ew, no. I hate mint," she said. "Thanks though." She returned to her task.

Good. I didn't want to share them anyway. "So, where are you dragging me?" I asked as I bit into the tiny square of minty goodness.

"The Limbo Bar."

I groaned. "I hate bars. I don't drink."

"You'll like this one. It's got karaoke and good music." Cassie snatched a neon pink tunic from a hanger and held it to her chest. "What do you think of this? With leggings?"

"It's nice," I lied. The bold color choice made me squirm.

"What are you going to wear?" she asked as she crouched down. Like a golden retriever with a bone, she began digging through the pile of shoes that littered the floor.

I shrugged and glanced around the room. *The gift! I nearly forgot about it.* I retrieved it, and sat it in my lap. I pried off the curling ribbon and tugged at the paper. Tossing the torn shredding aside, I opened the stark white box. Folded between thin sheets of tissue paper was a navy blue tank top. An intricately crocheted flower spread across the bust. It was my style. Simple, but stylish. A small smile formed on my lips. *I know what I'm wearing tonight.* Underneath the shirt was a messenger bag. It was khaki with teal pinstripes. I rifled through its pockets. Mom was known for hiding goodies in any available hiding spots. Sure enough, the bag produced a gift card, a twenty-dollar bill, and a small velvet box.

"Oooh. What's in the box?" Cassie said over my shoulder. I jumped, not realizing she was so close. Slowly, I lifted the lid, sending it snapping upright. Inside shined a pair of opal earrings. Like two orbs of contained rainbows, they sparkled up at me.

"Pretty!" she approved, before flouncing off into

the bathroom.

I grabbed my cell phone and punched my mother's number into the key pad. It rang twice.

"I take it your package arrived?" her small voice said.

"Mom, you shouldn't have spent so much money on me."

She blew out an annoyed sound.

"I mean it. The opal earrings are beautiful, but I'm sure they were expensive."

"Kara, don't worry about it. It's just money, honey."

"Mom," I protested.

"Don't you like them?" Her tone sounded worried.

"Of course. I just hate it when you spend a lot of money on me."

"Well, I like to spoil my baby. Do you have any plans for tonight?" she asked. "Want to go grab dinner somewhere? My treat."

I hesitated.

"Kara?"

"Well," I started. "Cassie wanted to go out tonight. But I can cancel—in fact, I'd rather cancel."

"No no no. You can go out with me anytime. You go have fun with your friends. We'll get together another night. Go put on your new shirt and earrings."

I gritted my teeth.

"You'll have fun once you get there. You always do," she encouraged.

I blew out my cheeks in frustration, but finally surrendered. "Okay, okay." I smacked my palm across my forehead. "I'll go."

"I'll call you tomorrow, and we'll make dinner

plans. Have fun, and be careful."

"Always."

"Happy birthday, Kara. I love you."

"Love you too, Mom. Bye."

I snapped my phone shut and rested my eyes on the opal earrings. They were stunning. They twinkled at me from their satin pillow. I reached though my hair, removing the gold hoops from my earlobes, and replaced them with the opal earrings. I nearly skipped to the mirror, drawing my hair back so I could inspect them. They flashed a dazzling ray of rainbow light. I smiled once more. *Thanks, Mom,* I thought happily.

****

When we pulled into the parking lot, my eyes landed on the rustic wooden sign overhead. Red letters that resembled crabs read The Limbo Bar. To the right of the broad entry door was an expansive window, allowing passersby a clear view of the shenanigans occurring inside. A weathered bench was stationed beneath it, with years of etched initials and scrawled letters tattooed into the aged wood. As we approached, the overwhelming smell of onion rings and alcohol filled my nose. I wrinkled it in distaste. *I'm going to gag.*

"They have awesome chicken wings here," Cassie said as she reached for the door. When she swung it open, the smell strengthened, but this time I could pick up traces of spicy barbeque. The interior was spacious. Vintage metal advertisements cluttered the walls. A faux palm tree swathed with twinkling Christmas lights and beer cans stood in the corner. The shellacked wood of the bar gleamed under the bright fluorescent bulbs that shined overhead. High-back bar stools were positioned haphazardly along its length. Flickering neon lights illuminated glass shelves, holding rows of shot glasses and bottles of booze.

An attractive redhead was busy hustling orders behind the bar. A karaoke machine was plugged in near the window. A small dance floor, checkered with yellow and red tile opened invitingly at our feet. Several black vinyl booths filled the opposite wall.

Thankfully, Cassie led me in that direction. Slipping into the cushy seat, I felt relieved; the tall backrests seemed to shelter us from the rest of the room. Cassie slid a menu at me, and then signaled for the waitress.

"You already know what you're getting?" I asked, scanning the appetizers.

"Oh yeah. I always get the same thing. Chicken wings with chump sauce."

"*Chump* sauce?" I echoed, giggling.

"Yes. Everything else is too spicy."

I glanced at the wing section. Chump Sauce. Belly Blazer. Tongue Scorcher. Farting Flames? *Wait, what? Farting flames? No, thanks*, I thought.

Our waitress bounded lightly toward us. Her blond hair was pulled into a sleek bun, a couple of pencils jammed into it.

"What can I get ya?" she asked.

"Wings with chump sauce," Cassie answered. "And a margarita."

"Sure thing. And you?"

I glimpsed at her nametag. Nicole. I looked back up at her. Huge hoop earrings dangled at her slender neck.

"Chicken finger basket please," I said. "And

whatever soda you have, just as long as it's—"

"Not diet," Cassie interjected.

We laughed, and Nicole smiled sweetly. "It will be up shortly." She twirled around and sauntered to the bar.

Calypso music filled the air.

"I can't wait to dance," Cassie said, shimmying her shoulders to the beat.

"What are you going to do, start a conga line?" I snickered.

She rolled her eyes but continued to sway to the rhythm. "They start playing regular music around ten."

Before I could check my watch, I noticed Nicole heading our way, balancing two large trays. She nimbly delivered one tray to the booth behind us. She smiled widely at the couple in it, before spinning our way. She pushed a basket of steaming chicken tenders at me and shoved a plate of wings at Cassie, before plunking my soda in front of me, and then easing a wide-mouthed glass goblet onto a napkin near Cassie. Sparkling salt crystals lined the glass.

"Yummy!" admired Cassie, her big blue eyes flashing happily. She peered at me over her giant margarita. "Gonna get my drink on!"

"There you are, ladies. Anything else I can get ya?" Nicole asked.

"It's her birthday," Cassie said as she picked up a stick of celery. "Does she get, like, a free drink or something?"

"Cassie!" I groaned, glaring at her as my blood surged with annoyance. She grinned back at me like a crazy loon.

"For sure," replied our waitress. "What would ya

like?"

"Nothing." I held up my hands in desperate surrender. "I don't drink, but thanks."

"Well, how about a root beer float?"

"Actually," I said slowly, my taste buds already craving the sweet dessert. "That does sound good. I'll take it."

"Coming right up." Nicole breezed through the room and disappeared into the kitchen.

I turned to Cassie, narrowing my eyes at her. "I'm going to kill you, you know that right?"

She waved me away. "Ah, I got you a free float. Be happy." She bit into a chicken wing, smearing sauce across her mouth.

We ate our meal in unusual silence, devouring it quickly, not leaving anything behind. Nicole whisked the empty plates away, refilled Cassie's margarita and plopped a frothy root beer float on the table. I sipped at it, inhaling the spicy aroma mixed with vanilla. Suddenly, the rhythmic clamber of steel drums vanished and some jazzy vocals of a dance song filled the air, instantly filling Cassie's limbs with adrenaline.

"Oh yeah, buddy!" she cried. "Let's dance!" She hoisted her small frame from the bench seat and pulled at my arm. "Come on!"

I sighed, and climbed out of the booth. I smoothed my tank top back into place and followed her to the awaiting dance floor. Cassie was wiggling to the music as I surveyed our fellow dancers. Two drunk chicks ground with each other, while a petite raven-haired boy writhed merrily to the beat. His hair was gelled meticulously as if he were walking against a heavy windstorm. The song blurred into a thumping remix and the boy went wild. "This is my jam!" he hollered as he flailed his manicured hands in the air.

The floor became crowded as songs faded in and out. I became increasingly tired and motioned wearily to Cassie that I needed a break. She nodded in agreement and led me to two empty bar stools. I hiked myself into one, sinking into it with relief. My feet ached, and my head was beginning to throb. I wasn't sure it was because of the loud music, the bright blinking lights, or the strong smell of perspiration and alcohol. Maybe all three.

"I'm pooped," I declared, suddenly realizing I was parched. I swallowed back the dry lump in my throat just as the bartender sidled up to us.

"What are we having, ladies?" the redhead asked, her brows arched severely as she waited for an answer.

"Something with a little umbrella," Cassie requested eagerly.

The bartender laughed and faced me, her green eyes watching me expectantly.

"Just water for me." I smiled meekly, wringing my hands nervously. I felt a twinge of guilt for asking for something so lame. Then, a blabbering brunette stumbled up beside me.

"Three…more…jiggly shooters," she slurred, holding up four fingers. *And THAT is the reason I don't drink,* I told myself. The girl tried to focus on me through slitted eyelids. I'm not sure if she saw double of me, but she gave me a lopsided grin before scooping up her colorful drinks and staggering away.

I let my eyes drift along the length of the bar until they landed on pallid-skinned boy sitting hunched over a beer bottle. His eyes were cast down. His dark hair flopping over his forehead. His jaw was set tight and his lips pressed into a hard line. *Dominic*. My heart fluttered like a loopy sea gull trying to land on a light pole. I clamped my hands tightly in my lap, trying to still my jittery nerves. I watched him quietly for several minutes. He turned to the man beside him. They somehow struck up a brief conversation over the noise. I watched his full mouth move as he spoke. Then he lifted the bottle to his mouth and suddenly I craved to be on the receiving end of those lips.

He patted the man's shoulder and slithered off the stool. My eyes followed him through the crowd. With one hand crammed into his pocket, he sauntered to the end of the bar, toward a beautiful brunette. He stepped up behind her, bending to whisper in her ear. Perched over a martini, the woman smiled salaciously as he murmured quietly. Once she lifted the glass to her lips, I instantly recognized her. The girl I had an unfortunate run-in with on my first day at Belman. I stepped on her toes. Well, not literally anyway, though I came awfully close to it. I nearly scuffed up her two-hundred dollar heels with my twenty-two dollar sneakers. That's like an old beater wagon scraping the side of a limo as it pulls into a parking spot.

My heart sank. *They can't be dating!* Her dark eyes swept across the room, devouring the same man Dominic shared a conversation with earlier. My eyes darted to him curiously. He shifted in his seat, raking a hand through his auburn hair. There was a light dusting of gray at his temples. The sleeves of his plaid shirt were pushed up around his elbows, his khaki pants professionally pressed.

The vixen rose and slowly stalked him like a

hungry lioness, slinking along the crowd until she was beside him. They spoke, both beaming and teeming with lust. She laughed enthusiastically, her white teeth dazzling beneath the harsh lighting. He cupped her cheek tenderly. Light sparked off the band of gold that circled his finger.

He's married.

She raised her hand to meet his, strumming her thumb defiantly across the ring. *She knows, but she's doesn't care.* Slack jawed, I watched as she led him to the dance floor. She danced around him seductively, until he slid his hands over her hips, pressing her against his body. Out of nowhere, Dominic strolled by them, slapping the man on his shoulder as he made his way to the front door.

What just happened? I searched his face, which looked severe beneath the dim lights of the bar. His eyes skimmed the crowd, touching on mine for one heated minute before they quickly darted away, a look of penitence washing across his handsome features. I wanted to go to him. To find out what was wrong, what just happened, and what I could do to erase his look of sadness. I wanted to embrace him. To smooth back his hair, and take his face into my hands and stare straight into those dark portal-like eyes and let them take me anywhere he wanted.

"Kara? What is it?"

Cassie's voice startled me, and yanked me back to earth.

"Huh?"

Her blue eyes followed my gaze, her brows lifted in worry. "Is everything okay?"

I looked around at the crowded bar. There were

dozens of pretty girls mingling through the room. *Was Dominic even looking at me?* I wondered if I had mistaken our exchange, but the weight of those eyes was overwhelming, like when you stand too close to a fire. It feels so good that you don't realize you're getting burned in the process.

"Oh, it's nothing. I just thought I saw someone I knew," I fibbed. "Hey, I'm tired. Can we call it a night?"

Cassie inspected me carefully, pressing her lips together as if she was actually trying to keep from saying whatever was swirling around that head of hers.

"Yeah," she said finally. "Of course." She hopped off the stool and took one last swig of her Bahama Breeze.

I shimmed off the chair and started forging a path through the swarm of frenzied bodies. The thumping bass rattled my brain, which was already buzzing with questions. *What just happened? Was Dominic friends with her? With him?*

The blaring music finally softened, and followed me as I elbowed my way through the herd of swaying couples, until I finally made it to the exit. With Cassie on my heels, I spilled into the cool evening air. I sucked in a lungful, trying to cleanse my insides from the sour aftertaste of smoke and sweat.

My eyes caught movement to my right. It was the vixen again. Her arm was looped lightly through the man's arm as they made their way to a silver sports car. Like a gentleman (that he clearly was not), he gallantly opened the passenger door for her. She lowered herself into the shadows of the car, folding her sleek legs inside gracefully. He rounded the hood of the car before dipping into the driver's seat. My eyes kept flicking from my feet to the car, trying not to look at them, but I couldn't help myself.

The headlights lit up, and the sports car crept slowly out of the parking spot. I continued to cover the oily asphalt, my eyes on them until I stumbled on a patch of loose gravel. *Shit!* I caught myself on a parked truck, thankful I didn't make a complete fool of myself. Flinging my gaze back to the sports car, I squinted against the bright red brake lights. Once the tires rolled onto the main street, it zoomed forward, leaving nothing but the roar of the engine in its wake.

"Come on, Kara. You look exhausted," Cassie urged. "Let's get you home so you can get some sleep."

I nodded my head in agreement, but somehow I knew that my sleep would be restless that night. And it was.

Chapter 12

My entire weekend was restless. My mind rarely strayed from that odd scenario at the Limbo Bar. I struggled with the feelings that Dominic had some role in setting those two up. Like he had played a sneaky matchmaker to an illicit relationship and got off on doing it. I recalled the snarky smile he wore as he whispered to the girl and then the sadness that flashed across his face afterward. That expression haunted me the most.

So when I stepped into class that Monday, I was surprisingly nervous to be near him again. And Cayden for that matter. Our last exchange was tense, and I still wasn't sure how I felt about it. I was flattered of course, but it only complicated things further. I was still trying to tread through my muddled feelings about Dominic, and piling Cayden on top of it all hurt my head.

I opened my textbook and attempted to study to busy myself. As usual, Dominic sauntered through the door a few minutes late. Lucky for him, Mrs. Dixon was running late too. He sank into the desk, and instantly, I felt his eyes on me. I ignored it, focusing on the words before me, but with the weight of his stare upon me, they looked like foreign hieroglyphics.

I squirmed in my chair, my palms becoming slick. I was so baffled by Dominic. I knew that I was attracted to him, but the peculiarities that surrounded him concerned me. My heart and mind were at odds with one another, and I wasn't sure which one to listen to. I was afraid to follow my heart. It was completely clouded by my attraction to him.

I clenched my fists and my jaw, but the unrelenting sense that I was being watched continued. Frustrated, I slammed the book shut and swung my head to face him.

"Can I help you with something?" I blurted out.

For a split second, he looked taken aback. He recovered smoothly by smiling slightly. "I'm sorry; I didn't mean to upset you."

I scowled, my fingers trembling, wishing I could smack the smile off his face. *Don't lose yourself in that smile Kara.* "What are you staring at?"

"You," he said simply, with a non-apologetic tone that made me shiver. My eyebrows shot up in surprise. I didn't know what to say to that. My irritation began to slowly melt away. *Maybe I was wrong about him. I don't know him well enough to judge him.*

We watched each other, waiting, daring the other to speak. My gaze shifted to Mrs. Dixon as she entered the room. She was pushing in a tall metal cart, with a TV strapped to it. The wheels squeaked as she rolled it to the center of the room.

"Good morning, guys and gals," she said. "As I promised on Friday, I will be reviewing the pieces I've missed. Please take out your sketches and have them on your desk. For those of you whose work I've seen, I have a short video about M.C. Escher. If you've never heard of him, I'm sure you've seen his work." She jabbed her pudgy finger at the row of buttons on the TV, flipping the flat black screen to life. I could feel Dominic's eyes still on me, so I took another look at him. He gave me a slight smile, and I wanted to return it, but before I could, he looked away.

Deciding I should focus my attention elsewhere, I settled comfortably into my desk, crossing my ankles as I leaned back. The program was interesting, highlighting Escher's early beginnings in the Netherlands to his rise to fame for his impressive works of realism and mind-boggling infinity pieces. Mrs. Dixon flowed through the aisles slowly. When she finally made it to Dominic, the documentary was ending. She towered over him, scrutinizing his thorn entrapped rose.

"You are a wonderful artist, Mr. Benenati. Don't waste your potential." She walked away, addressing the class as she went. "I'd like you all to attempt the technique Escher made famous. Infinity is a tricky technique to master, but I'd like you to give a whirl. You may either use the rest of the class to work on it, or if need to research the style, feel free to head to the library. There are a few good reference books there."

"When's it due?" someone asked over the sound of zipping book bags and activity.

"Next Monday. That gives you one week." Mrs. Dixon shuffled through a stack of papers, her glasses riding low on her nose. The class nearly emptied, only a few students worked diligently over their sketchpads. I stood, deciding I needed some inspiration and hoped the library would provide some. I glanced over my shoulder and saw Cayden studying his paper. He held a ruler, and appeared to be in deep concentration.

"I'm going to the library. Would you like to come?"

I nearly jumped out of my skin. I turned around,

putting me face to face with Dominic. His dark eyes were hard, like chunks of coal that had just been pulled from a fire. I searched for words, but they were stuck in my throat. His scent nearly intoxicated me. A spicy musk invaded my nose and violated my core. The corner of his mouth quirked, giving a hopeful smile.

"I. Ah, yeah, sure," I stammered stupidly. My ears warmed with embarrassment.

"Here, let me carry that for you." He reached for my sketchbook, brushing his fingers across mine. My skin tingled from his touch, sending little shock waves through my blood stream. His eyes held mine as he collected the book, and I cleared my throat, breaking the exchange.

As I slung my book bag over my shoulders, I caught a glimpse of Cayden out of the corner of my eye. His mouth was set into a hard line. He glared past me, his piercing blue eyes slicing through Dominic like knives. *What is with him? Is he jealous of Dominic?*

"Are you ready?"

No. And yes, I thought. I looked back at Cayden one more time. His eyes were set on me now, pleading with me, as if trying desperately to convey something vital, but I didn't know what. I gave him a little wave before turning back to Dominic.

"I'm ready," I said, lifting my eyes to meet his. He held it for a moment, a sweet smile at his lips until his gaze drifted to Cayden. The smugness was back, as he smirked at him, and I couldn't help but feel small between them, as though I was a pawn. A pawn in a game I knew nothing about…

****

The sky was clear, with just a few clouds stretching

lazily across it. Since classes were still in session, there were only a few people scattered across the courtyard. Dominic and I walked in silence for several minutes. I tried to keep cool, but my heart felt like it was trying to knock me unconscious from the inside out. *I can't believe this,* I thought, looking over at him as we fell into step with each other. *He's here, with me.* The sun basked him in a warm glow, making his skin appear almost transparent. Sensing me watching, he gave me a sideways glance, arching a brow at me.

"Did you have fun the other night?" he asked calmly.

My vision tilted as my heart melted into my toes. *So he did see me.*

"Y…yes," I stuttered, looking down at my shoes. *Why am I embarrassed?* I frowned. *I'm not the one who played matchmaker for a married man.* Squaring my shoulders, I asked, "Did you?"

His eyes tightened and something unreadable ghosted across his features. He ignored my question entirely, by asking, "Why didn't you say hello?" he asked, his tone a bit cutting, and challengingly, as if he were goading me for some unknown reason.

"Why didn't you?" I replied tartly.

He snickered. "You're right. I was just…preoccupied."

I nearly rolled my eyes. *Preoccupied ruining someone's family.* "Were you there with friends?" I prodded.

He shot me a look of spiteful mirth. "At the Limbo Bar, you're always amongst friends." He studied me for a moment. "You don't look like a bar-hopper."

"I'm not," I said hotly. "My friend forced me to

go."

"I knew it," he declared. "You send out a strong 'good girl' vibe."

"Is there something wrong with that?" I frowned.

"No, not at all," he chuckled. "Besides, you know what they say about good girls and closed doors..." His dark eyes flashed playfully.

"No, what?" I feigned innocence. *Ha! Take that! Two can play at this!*

Fleetingly, he appeared flustered, raking his fingers through his fine mop of locks.

My own fingers yearned to entangle themselves in it.

"Never mind," he muttered.

I smirked, feeling giddy for being able to knock him down a peg. "So." I paused to clear my throat, trying to frame my next question.

He watched me with curious eyes, the sun beating gently upon him, making his already pale skin almost blinding. Blindingly beautiful.

His brow lifted.

If one look could melt a person into a pool of quivering, hopeless need, that look would be it. That damn eyebrow arched whenever he questioned, whenever he challenged, whenever he smirked with a seductiveness that was unmatched by any man.

"What does *anima bella* mean?" I bit my lip, suddenly shy and nervous all at once. What if meant something horrible? Like animal-girl...or worse?

He stopped. His normal, intimating expression faded, and was replaced with a gentle seriousness that rooted me where I stood. He suddenly closed the small gap between us, his spicy musk enveloping me like a full-body embrace.

"*Anima bella*," he said in a raspy voice that sent a shiver across my skin, "means 'beautiful soul,' " he answered.

My heart slammed into my chest, and I stared at his lips, desperately wishing I could taste them.

He lifted a hand, and for a moment I thought he was going to bring it to my cheek, but instead he stroked a lock of my hair, then carefully hooked it behind my ear. I resisted the urge to lean into his touch, but was unable to quell the shudder that went through me.

He noticed, his pupils dilated and a smug smirk spread across his face. As if flipping an emotional switch, he dropped his hand and began walking again, leaving me where I stood. The moment was over. I stared after him, watching this mysterious, yet undeniably alluring boy who could easily bring me to brink, only to leave me standing alone, and desperately wanting more.

I caught up with him, and we walked the rest of the way in a comfortable silence. It wasn't until he opened the door of library did he speak again, saying, "After you, *anima bella*."

How could two little words enthrall me so? How could they make me feel vital, and dare I say, cherished? Could it be the significance of their meaning? Or maybe it's the fact that they were emitted by the most beautiful set of lips I had ever seen.

When I stepped inside the library, I was overwhelmed with the scent of ancient books and decaying leather. Although the campus library was up-to-date on the newest technology, it also had an impressive collection of antique books. The first floor was mostly computer stations and magazines. Together, Dominic and I climbed the stairs to the second floor. Rows of countless books welcomed us as we let go of the banister. The smell of polished wood and musky parchment filled my nose.

The second floor was nearly deserted. Aside from the two of us, the only other people there were one librarian restocking shelves and one skinny kid with a head full of cowlicks studying in the corner. I followed Dominic through the rows of towering shelves.

"There should be a book about Escher somewhere in this section." His eyes narrowed at the book spines as he concentrated. I admired his handsome profile. His long eyelashes feathered outward around his deep-set eyes. His fingers lightly brushed along the books as he searched, and I couldn't help but imagine those fingers trailing along my skin. I fought the urge to shiver, shaking my head, ridding the thought from my mind. I followed his gaze, determined to keep my thoughts G-rated. *Get yourself together, Kara.*

I inclined my head slightly, my eyes darting from title to title. Augustus Earle, William Edmondson, Elliot Erwitt...M.C. Escher! When I reached up to pluck it from the shelf, Dominic's warm hand touched mine. Again, a surge of energy pierced my skin. Our eyes met. He felt it too. Our hands lingered briefly before he snatched his away, sinking it into his jeans pocket. He stepped around me and stalked to the nearest table. Confused, I followed him, still feeling the touch of his hand on mine.

I sat down beside him. He appeared tense, avoiding my stare as he flung open the book. He scoured the yellowing pages briskly, his hand clenching into a fist as I scooted closer. I inhaled, taking in his spicy scent. He stiffened when my knee touched his, the muscles flexing in his jaw as he gnashed his teeth together.

"Is something wrong?" I questioned quietly. He didn't look up, but I could see something flare within his eyes.

"Girls like you shouldn't keep company with guys like me," he said through gritted teeth. He adjusted his neck slightly, causing it to crack ominously.

"And what kind of guy are you?" I whispered, pressing my lips together tightly. He stilled, clenching his fists until the veins within them bulged.

His eyes darted to mine, holding me firmly in place as he said, "I'm no angel, Kara Maven."

He stood abruptly, knocking his chair backward. It landed on the carpet with a muffled thud. He glared down at me, as he breathed heavily through flaring nostrils. "It would do you some good to remember that." He turned on his heel and flew down the staircase, leaving me alone and baffled. My eyes were round as I stared after him. *What is wrong with him?*

Once he's out of sight, I turn slowly back around, glimpsing the opened page before me. A never-ending sphere of angry black devils mingling with peaceful white angels loomed up at me. The bat-like creatures mocked me with their ugly grimaces.

An unexplainable fear bloomed within my belly. *This is silly. It's just a picture.* The jarring contrasts of good versus evil, darkness versus light left me feeling uneasy, so I slammed the book closed, satisfied that the eerie monsters were trapped between the thick pages.

Chapter 13

The next day I rehashed my conversation with Dominic over and over in my head. Like a skipping record, his last words played repeatedly, but I have to admit, it was his touch that left a lasting impression.

The way my body tingled, the warmth that spread through me as if I were on fire. I couldn't wait to feel it again. But I also needed answers, and when I saw him again, I was going to demand he give them to me.

When he stomped away from me at the library, he had left me a muddled mess, leaving me self-conscious and in fact, a little miffed.

As I took my seat in Mrs. Dixon's class, my stomach fisted with anxiety. *What if he refuses to talk to me?* The classroom began to fill. Cayden strolled down the aisle and took his usual seat. Mrs. Dixon called the class to order and embarked on a discussion about infinity drawing techniques.

Twenty minutes passed, and still no Dominic. I fiddled with my sketchpad as I waited. Smoothing the tattered corners, and blankly flipping through the pages. My eyes would move from the door to the clock on the wall, repeating the process over and over until Mrs. Dixon said, "Keep working on your infinity projects. If you have any questions, feel free to stop by my office. Have a wonderful Wednesday, you funky monkeys. See you Friday."

I stared at his empty desk. He didn't show, and I couldn't help but wonder if I was the reason why. I stood woodenly, swallowing back a lump of emotion, before I finally walked away. Cayden appeared beside me as I merged into the crowded hallway.

"How's your project coming along?" he questioned with genuine interest.

"Oh, ah. I haven't started it yet," I admitted. My cheeks burned at the realization. I never procrastinated. *What's wrong with me?* "I've researched it though," I added, recalling the creepy eyes of the strange artwork that grinned at me from the library book.

"Have any ideas at least?" His smiled sincerely, making me feel worse. *I've been so in lust with Dominic that I had nearly forgotten about Cayden. Some friend I am.* He was wearing a blue t-shirt with the silhouette of the Belman bobcat swinging a baseball bat. His light blue jeans were loose, and a pair of white sneakers covered his feet.

"No," I answered honestly. "How about you? I saw you working on yours the other day. How's it coming along?" I slipped my hands over the straps of my book bag, squeezing them tightly to keep myself focused on the here and now. Cayden flipped through the pages of his sketchpad and held it so I could see. Endless stacks of books swirled like curling stairwells leading to a nonexistent home in the sky, each intricately designed with realistic leather-bound covers and etched titles.

"Wow," I breathed. "That's amazing, Cayden."

"Thanks," he said humbly, closing the sketchpad softly. "Hey, we have another home game tonight." He watched me with expectant eyes.

"I'll be there," I promised with a smile.

"Great. Well, I had better pick up the pace. I got to get clear across campus for my next class."

"Sure, I'll see you tonight."

"Later," he said as he jogged away.

I watched him quickly close the gap between him and the Furman Building. Then, I headed to my own destination, Ansley Hall, room 401. Professor Milton lectured about Ancient Greece. At times my mind would flounder, unable to grasp his words because it was too intrigued with fleeting images of Dominic. *Does he hate me so much that he'd drop the class?* Frowning at myself, I hunkered down and forced myself to pay close attention. After Professor Milton assigned a slew of reading assignments, he freed us to go. I was thankful to be back in my room. Irritable, I sought refuge in the form of a handful of mints and my downy comforter. Cassie came in the room, finding me tucked deep in the folds of my paisley blanket.

"What's with you?" she snickered, taking in the pile of discarded green foiling. Suddenly her eyes grew wide. "Does Cayden have a new girlfriend or something?"

"No," I sighed. "Why would that bother me anyway? We're not dating." I rolled my eyes at her assumption that I would care.

"Then what?" She flopped down beside me, tucking her legs beneath her petite frame.

"Nothing," I said in a small voice. "I'm just grumpy."

"About what?" she pried.

"Nothing, Cassie. Can't I be grumpy for no reason?"

"No," she remarked plainly, hooking a clump of

curls behind her ear. She wore a delicate pair of pearl earrings. They reminded me of small soapsuds. "But, I won't badger you. If you want to sit there and be a grouch, then go ahead. Doesn't bother me."

I scowled at her as she made herself comfortable (on my bed) by kicking off her shoes and leaning back against the wall. I groaned inwardly. I wasn't about to sit around like that all evening.

"Cayden invited us to his game tonight," I said quickly. The words spewed from my mouth before I could think. She sat up, her blue eyes shining with delight.

"Really? He invited...*us*?"

"Yes." I lied. I just couldn't go to his game alone. I'd look like a girlfriend, cheering from the sidelines. I had to draw the line across our relationship, showing him that we were just friends, and he was not to cross that boundary.

"Wheeeee!" she squealed loudly, bouncing off the bed and darting to the bathroom. "I'm getting ready right now!" When the door slammed shut, I fell into my pillow, and let out a frustrated groan. The soft pillowcase smelled of my favorite vanilla shampoo and I wanted nothing more than to stay buried in it.

I must have dozed off, because suddenly Cassie was shaking me.

"Get up. We're going be late. Are you going to wear that?"

"What's wrong with what I've got on?" I rubbed my tired eyes.

"It's fine. I just thought you'd dress up a little."

"You thought wrong," I said dryly, as I reluctantly hoisted myself from the bed. I took in my attire and was satisfied with it. Stripped of all jewelry, except my new opal earrings, I wore a baby pink t-shirt, my favorite pair of blue jeans, and simple shoes.

"Let's go." Cassie was nearly hopping at the door waiting for me. She had paired a yellow tank top, with white shorts. She wore white flip-flops, showing off her freshly painted pink toes. Her lips were slick with a fruity-smelling lip-gloss.

I trudged past her and out into the hall. She chatted spiritedly as I pretended to listen. *Geez, does she never stop talking?* We came up on the cluster of benches in the foyer, where several girls were perched. They exchanged gossip over opened textbooks and stacks of handwritten notes. My eyes caught an attractive brunette with golden highlights. Her chocolate brown eyes fleetingly met mine. It was the girl from the Limbo Bar. Miss Home-Wrecker herself. She crossed her legs and ignored me entirely. I looked ahead, trying to shake the image of her effectively seducing that obviously older and obviously *married* man.

"Kara, is something wrong?" Cassie questioned.

"No, I'm fine. Just thinking about the game." I fibbed again. I hated lying, but how would I explain everything? The truth sounded like something from a movie.

"Me too," she admitted. "Those uniforms leave *little* to the imagination; you know what I'm saying?" She nudged my ribs with a bony elbow.

I looked at her sideways, grinning at the normalcy of it all. I was on my way to watch a spirited game of America's favorite pastime, with a friend whose ignorance was beyond blissful.

Belman beat the Coastal Cyclones ten to two that

night. And I lost myself in the simplicity of it all. Good girl—one, bad boy—zero.

Chapter 14

By Friday, I felt more like myself. I donned a vintage t-shirt with a pair of snug blue jeans. I took a quick peek in the mirror, sliding a thick leather headband into my hair, before snatching my book bag from my desk, and ducking out the door.

Surprisingly, I didn't dwell on whether Dominic would show or not. Instead, I started brainstorming ideas for my infinity project, when Cayden breezed by me.

"Hey, Kara. Thanks for coming to my game. You must be my good luck charm." His powder blue shirt looked great against his bronze skin.

"It was a great game. You're a natural," I complimented. His eyes swept across the empty desk to my left. I watched him with curiosity, as his features dissolved into seriousness.

"Kara, can I talk to you? About Dominic?"

"What about him?" I asked stiffly, remembering our discussion in the football field. It was obvious Cayden didn't like Dominic or the thought that I was interested in him. Before he could answer, I sensed Dominic's presence. It was compelling and strong, like a giant magnet pulling me toward him. My eyes shifted to the door as he sauntered in with an arrogant stride.

"Speak of the devil," Cayden hissed, before retreating to his desk. I deliberately slunk into my sketchbook, pretending to be engrossed in my work. I heard the chair move beside me. Acting on impulse, I stole a brief peek. Dominic was smiling back at me. I returned it weakly, and turned back to my sketchpad.

"Hey, I'm sorry about the other day," he apologized. "Let me make it up to you."

Intrigued, I turned to face him. *I can't believe I allow one guy to have so much control over me,* I thought. *But there is something about him that I cannot resist.*

"The frat house is hosting a party tonight. I can pick you up early and show you around," he continued.

I was unable to stop myself from frowning. "I don't know." I recalled the last encounter I had with the Kappa brothers. The horrible initiation ceremony I witnessed and the confrontation with that asshole, Troy.

He studied my face. "Come on," he said, smirking. "The guys aren't as bad as you think."

There was something about that lopsided grin that made my reservations about spending the evening with the Kappa knights disappear.

"Okay," I agreed, a smile slowly spreading across my face.

Class went by as though I was in a daze. I was floating on cloud nine and had no intentions of coming down. Dominic even walked me to my next class.

"Is this your last year at Belman?" he asked as we leisurely strolled across the courtyard.

"Yes, my first and last."

He raised an interested eyebrow.

"I spent three years at DGU, and then transferred here." I hesitated, unsure if I should explain why. I looked up at the sky. The sun winked out of sight as it disappeared by a bundle of clouds.

"Do you like it here?" His eyes met mine. The sincerity in them caught me off guard.

"I do," I said, smiling slightly. "Do you?"

He held my gaze as he carefully formed his thoughts. "I do now," he declared.

Three simple words brought my heart rate up several notches. Heat swept across my cheeks as he stared at me intently. *Why do I feel as though he can look right through me, right down to my very soul with those hauntingly beautiful eyes?* Flustered, I cleared my throat, racking my brain for something to say, but came up empty.

"Do you live on campus?" he questioned, breaking the awkward silence.

I nodded, still attempting to find the words that seemed lost in transit somewhere.

"I live off campus, in a frat house on Clover Lane."

"I bet things can get crazy there," I said finally.

"Yeah, but that's what I love about it." He smirked at me, sending a strange jolt through my body.

"You have an awesome car by the way." I tucked a stray strand of hair behind my ear. "What year is it?"

His dark eyes flashed mysteriously as he caught sight of the scar on my wrist.

Instinctively I drew my hand down, and slid my bracelets over it, concealing the thread of puckered skin. It was a move I had only recently recognized I did out of habit. I was ashamed of the ugly scar. A reminder of my weakness. A reminder of the pain I would have caused for my mother if I had indeed taken my own life that day.

In my support group they called it *survivor guilt.*

Apparently it can mean different things to different people. Some people feel guilty because they don't succeed in dying. Some feel guilty for attempting suicide in the first place. For not being strong enough to deal with whatever trauma had left them feeling virtually alone and desperate. Then others feel guilty for the anguish they caused their family. I fit into the third category.

My mom had already lost her husband, and yet I was selfish enough to believe that ending my life would make everything okay. If I hadn't survived, my mother would have been forced to grieve her daughter and the man she so desperately loved. She was mourning enough as it was, and I almost added to her misery.

"Sixty-eight," Dominic answered distantly, drawing me out of my thoughts.

Huh? What did I ask again?

He looked at me, his brows drawn tight over his dark eyes. "The car. It's a sixty-eight."

I flushed a bit, realizing that I had zoned out for moment, recalling my recent "worrisome incident" as my mother referred to it.

He expelled a curse under his breath and ground out a curt, "I'll pick you up tonight at nine."

"Okay," I answered slowly, studying him. *What's with him? Is he already regretting that he asked me out?*

"See ya," he mumbled as he veered away.

I watched him as he shoved his hands in his pockets, walking briskly across the lawn, not even bothering to give me another look as he put space between us. His shadow stretched across the grass as he moved, like a dark figure stalking him, ready to claim his body at any moment. I looked down at my own shadow. It looked pathetically small, but the dusting of flowers across the grass resembled a delicate halo sitting upon its shadowy head. *Looks like an angel,* I thought, grinning to myself before glancing back in the direction of Dominic, my smile quickly fading when I realized he was gone.

****

Somehow, I muddled my way through class, but I kept thinking about Dominic's odd behavior. *What is it about Dominic that affects me so? Sure, he's sexy as hell, but it's more than just that. There's something strong and compelling about him. Something luring me to the edge of sanity...*

Once back in my dorm, I scoured my closet for something to wear. Although he acted odd earlier, I was still excited about our *almost date.*

I heard Cassie come in as I rifled through the hangers.

"You going out?" she asked, prancing up behind me, bringing along with her, her usual smell of fruity lip-gloss.

I grimaced. *There's no use lying this time.* "Yes," I said flatly, shrinking a little as I prepared my ears for the squealing.

"Shut up!" she screamed, her excited expression slacked a little when she said, "With who? Cayden?"

I rolled my eyes. "No," I barked. *Cayden this and Cayden that. That's all she ever thinks about. Although, I am probably the same way about Dominic,* I thought. "There are more guys out there besides Cayden."

"Are there? I haven't noticed." She gave me a wink. "Then who is it?" she asked, as she shucked off her blouse and wiggled into an oversized t-shirt.

"Dominic."

She scrunched up her face. "Who's that?"

"The guy from the parking lot."

"The dude with the badass car?"

"Yes, that's him." I couldn't help but grin to myself. I still couldn't believe it was true. *I have a date with Dominic Benenati. Well, sort of.* I gripped a shirt to my chest, trying to quiet my fluttering heartbeat.

"Wow," she mouthed. "He's hot. Like, rip your clothes off and have sweaty, sticky, amazing sex, hot.

I pressed my lips together to keep from laughing.

"I didn't peg you as a bad-boy banger," she added, touching her finger to her chin thoughtfully.

"A *what?*" I screeched, appalled at the dirty insinuation.

"Don't get your panties in a twist. I just meant, I didn't think you went for bad boys. They cause nothing but heartache, you know."

"Cassie, it's just a date. I'm not signing a marriage certificate."

I dove back into my closet, pulling out a sexy pair of skinny jeans and a white lacey camisole.

I dressed and primped myself, but still had plenty of time to spare before the party. I waited restlessly for the next hour to pass, until finally, I heard the low growl of his car pull up.

"See you later," I called over my shoulder as I stepped into my black flats.

"Have fun." She winked. "Don't do anything I wouldn't do."

I shuffled past her, grinning like a lunatic as I scooted out the door.

Dominic was leaning against the car; the passenger door already open. My stomach dipped and felt as though it had filled with whirling confetti. He smiled when he saw me. His hair, the color of the darkest midnight hour, was shaggy and mussed to perfection. His t-shirt was plain white, but somehow he made it look so cool. He was James Dean reincarnated. *His good looks and bad boy charm should come with a warning label.*

I sank into the passenger seat, allowing him to shut the door behind me. My stomach churned as I watched him round the hood of the car, and then slide into the driver's seat. *He's drop dead gorgeous,* I thought.

He punched the gas, and the beast jolted with a snarl, lurching us forward. My heart heaved into my throat. I gripped the seat beneath me until my knuckles turned white as we whirled toward an isolated collection of historic homes. They had been purchased by some of the college's fraternity alumni to be used as frat houses. Different symbols hung like addresses along the edifices. The car slowed and crept into a paved driveway.

"Here we are," he announced. "Home sweet home."

The house was three stories high, and inlaid with bold red bricks. The design once mimicked colonial architecture, but now that it was home to testosterone-fueled frat boys, it seemed to mock the handsome structures that lined the historic streets of Garet, North Carolina. Plastic lawn chairs doused with colorful spray paint littered the front yard. A handful of frat boys were outside, busy preparing for the party. One was lining a large trash bin with an empty bag, while the others were setting up a beer pong game.

A worn welcome mat greeted me as I climbed the steps. Frayed along the edges, the words had long disintegrated beneath the soles of thousands of passing shoes. Shabby flip-flops and sneakers sat in a heap beside the door.

Dominic pushed the door in, and out wafted the dank smell of stale pizza, sweaty socks, and leather. The air was punctuated with the scent of alcohol. Inside there was a congregation of guys huddled over a large metal beer keg. They were dressed casually. One was even barefoot. Collectively, they hoisted it over their shoulders and made their way past us. Like pallbearers marching the body of a dear friend to their grave, they moved in unison toward the door.

I recognized the cropped short red hair as it passed me. His eyes met mine briefly before casting them down. *Ben.* My stomach sank at the memory of him sprawled across the grass, Troy kicking him ruthlessly. My thoughts were interrupted by a voice behind the refrigerator door.

"We got any pickles?"

I took a deep breath inward, waiting for the boy to reveal himself.

"A-ha! Never mind! Found 'em!" Standing, a boy in a faded ball cap noticed Dominic and grinned.

Thank you, God, it's not Troy.

He slung one arm over the door and lifted the other in the air triumphantly. He was clutching a glass jar of pickles. "Hey, Dom." His eyes quickly pivoted to mine before taking in the length of me. "Who's your hot friend?"

"*She,*" Dominic started, his voice tight with

irritation, "is Kara. And *she* is off-limits."

This revelation caught me off guard. Dominic was claiming me. My heart jumped for joy. My eyes shot to him, but he wasn't looking at me. He was glaring at the boy, who seemed oblivious to the daggers being tossed at him.

With a slight twist of his wrist, the boy unscrewed the lid and peered wistfully into the jar. "Damn. One left." He fished out the lone pickle and bit into it. His eyes moved back to Dominic. "Easy, dude," he said as he crunched away on the pickle. "If you called dibs, she's all yours. Ain't going to hustle in on your game, playa." He winked at Dominic.

They talked about me as if I wasn't there. Feeling a bit awkward, I turned away from them, finding myself facing the living room. It was a mess. *God, this place could use a good scrubbing.* A deflated football lay lifelessly on the coffee table, along with various books and magazines. Crushed soda cans littered the floor, and pinball machine was stationed in the corner of the room. Bright bulbs blinked from it merrily, reminding me of the blinding lights from an amusement park. *Leave it to a bunch of boys to decorate the place like a pizza joint.*

A few party-goers flowed in and out of the front door. I watched as a girl mingled her way through the kitchen. She appeared comfortable there, rifling through the cabinets with ease, as if she'd done it a countless times before. She lined up several shot glasses and filled them with a neon blue liquid. She lifted one to her lips and downed it quickly, sneering as it worked its way down her throat. Dominic strolled over, plucked a shot glass from the row, and emptied it with one clean swig. He lifted another and held it out to me.

"Want one?"

I tucked a piece of loose hair behind my ear and shook my head modestly.

"Not a drinker?" Dominic raised an eyebrow at me. "I should have sensed that."

"You can hardly taste the alcohol." The girl smiled sweetly. "Tastes like gumdrops."

"Don't try to corrupt her," he said.

"I'm not trying to *corrupt* her," she giggled. "I'm just trying to loosen her up. She looks stiff." Sweeping her gaze down the length of Dominic, she purred, "Not at all what you're used to." She rounded the counter and sidled up next to him. His eyes bore into me and I returned the heated exchange, matching him stare for stare until his lips twitched arrogantly. My jaw ticked with annoyance, as I forced myself to break away first.

The girl threw a slender arm over his shoulders and leaned into his ear. "Why don't we sneak away, while your little friend here blends into the wall?"

I tossed one more glance to Dominic before turning away, petty anger collecting within my gut.

"Now, Kimberly. That's not very nice," he chastised. "She's my guest and for tonight, I belong to her."

My heart contracted at the word *belong,* but I refused to face them.

She sighed deeply. "Well, she seems harmless enough. I bet she's never done a naughty thing in her life. Have ya, *sweetie?*"

Ignoring them, I wrapped my arms around myself protectively, wishing I could disappear into thin air.

"That's what I thought," she snorted. "She's lame

Dom, why even bother with her?"

"She's intriguing," he said firmly.

Intriguing? He finds me intriguing?

"The only thing interesting about her is that scar on her wrist. Is she emo or something?"

I glanced down at my hands, catching a glimpse of the ugly thin scar that stretched across my wrist. The dark memory of that day taunted me, spiking adrenaline through my blood. I balled my fists tightly, trying to keep my anger contained. *Emo? She knows nothing of me, and what I've been through.* I whirled around, keeping the flood of tears that simmered hotly beneath my skin at bay. *I will not cry. I'm too pissed off to cry.* Dominic was watching me, studying me, waiting for a reaction, and I wanted desperately to give him one, but I stood fixated in place. I glared at him, noticing his body was strangely rigid compared to the lithe bitch beside him. My heartbeat pounded in my ears as my eyes moved pointedly to each of them.

"That's enough, Kimberly," he said. His voice was subdued, but commanding. "You're insulting my guest, and I won't allow that."

"Whatever." She shrugged, her eyes raking over me once. "Have fun being bored with Miss Tight Ass."

Anger built up, piling higher and higher within me, and I couldn't take it a second longer. Glaring at the stupid smirk that lined her small face, I said, "A tight ass is better than a loose—"

"Kara, come…" Dominic interrupted, rushing forward, still holding the shot of wild blue concoction. He slipped a hand around my waist. "Let me show you around." He looked back at Kimberly, and I followed suit, scowling at her as we walked away.

She gave me the finger, and a final flare of irritation coursed through me. My hands shook. I needed to *hit* something. Not thinking, I snatched the small glass from Dominic's fingers and downed it, hoping it would take the edge off my anger. At first, the thick drink tasted sugary, like melted lollipops, but then it burned and clawed its way to my empty stomach. I suddenly wished I had eaten before I came.

Even though I wasn't a drinker, I still knew it was better to have something in your stomach than just alcohol. My face pinched as the bitter aftertaste stung my throat. Dominic watched me with wide eyes, his mouth parted in surprise. I handed him the empty glass, my veins tingling oddly like I was connected to a morphine drip.

"I thought you didn't drink?" he asked with a smile hinting at his full lips.

"I don't. But it was either that, or knock that bitch into the wall she wanted me to blend into."

He laughed, and for a moment, I lost myself in the sound. It was natural and airy, and I wished he'd do it more often. As his laugh faded, his smile remained, showing a row of perfectly straight teeth, and a tiny dimple I'd never seen before at the corner of his mouth. My gaze lingered on that dimple, thinking, *he should smile more often...it's breath taking.* I was drawn to him, like a moth to a flame, and for the first time in my life, I wasn't afraid to get burned. Everything about him appealed to me. His disheveled hair, his striking eyes, and his lips...whether quirked into a beautiful smile or drawn in a cynical smirk.

Even his distant aura captivated me. The slouch in his shoulders called to me, urging me to knead the muscles within. I pictured my fingertips trickling across his collarbone and down his bare chest. As if caught in a dream, I stared at him, his body radiating an untamed magnetism and I felt compelled to press myself against him.

"I learned something tonight, Kara."

I snapped back to reality and held his gaze, my fingers itching to tangle themselves in his mop of ebony locks. *If I don't put some space between us, I'm liable to do something I'll regret.* Shaken by the questionable need to be near him, I took a step back, but I could still smell him, the potent scent luring me closer. I felt like prey, and he was a skilled hunter. "What's that?" I asked, speaking with an unbearably dry mouth. "Never judge a book by its cover?"

"Or the girl by her lover," he added.

I looked at him in confusion, but he didn't elaborate further. He began to move through the house, setting the shot glass on a coffee table as he gave me clipped descriptions and histories of each room. I followed him, curious and nervous at where the evening would lead. He walked ahead of me, flicking his hand in this direction and that, his words fading into background as I scoured the details of his body. He had a lean build, but firm muscles in his biceps and forearms.

Like a well-oiled machine, he moved with precision. His spicy aroma trailed behind him, like a cloud of heated cinnamon, and I couldn't get enough of it, dragging in deep draws of it into my lungs. A bud of warmth bloomed within my gut, spreading through me as I stared at the delicate skin behind his ears, wishing I could trace it with my tongue.

His tour continued up the stairs to the second floor. The walls leading up the staircase were the same hue as the first level, and aside from a smoke detector, they were bare. The stairwell opened out to a spacious foyer, where it spidered out into five bedrooms and two small bathrooms.

There was up to three twin mattresses in each room, so apparently several "brothers" shared each bedroom. Colorful pennants of rival schools covered the walls. They overlapped one another and dripped to the floor. They were even strung like streamers across the ceiling.

The question of their significance must have been apparent in my bewildered expression, because Dominic wandered over and leaned coolly against the wall, and said, "They're either opponents we've crushed…," he explained. "Or hearts we've broken." His dark eyes swept across the countless flags. I bit my lip at that notion, furrowing my brows in disappointment. *I don't want to be added to that wall of heartache.*

I noticed a bare spot amidst the carousel of nauseating colors. It was a white door to the right of the foyer, which I assumed led to the third floor. Following my gaze, Dominic unhitched himself from the wall.

"Let me show you the third floor." He strolled to the door, opening it with a quick twist of his wrist. My stomach fisted and began to gnaw itself raw as he led me up a narrow staircase. The confining area made me sway slightly. The ancient wood had been sanded to a smooth finish and knots sporadically gouged the slick paneling. My eyes focused on a large clump of twisted fiber. It resembled a warped face. The notch curved into a distorted mouth, gaped open in a desperate scream. I blinked.

Cool it, Kara, it's just the alcohol playing with your imagination, I told myself. I lifted my eyes to Dominic, who was pacing himself for my benefit. His jeans were slung low on his hips; a leather belt circled his slim waist. I followed behind him clumsily, stealing glimpses of his backside as he ascended the stairs. The staircase coiled around until it stretched out into a long foyer. There was one spacious bathroom and three additional rooms. The bedrooms on the third floor were bigger, and by the looks of them, only housed one person each.

"Who's the lucky few who get their own room?"

"The big brothers."

Before I could stop it, a laugh escaped me. *Fraternities and sororities are ridiculous.* "Big brothers, huh? So, let me guess…one of these rooms belongs to you?" I cocked an eyebrow at him.

He nodded as he slowly strutted to the solid oak door at the end of the foyer. He rested his hand on the brass knob. Glancing over his shoulder he said, "The view is best from my room." He pushed the door slowly open with one hand. "You can either believe that and come inside, or you can listen to that angel on your shoulder and walk away now."

Something inside me hollered, *turn around and haul ass out of there*. I smothered that voice instantly, smirking at Dominic as I strolled confidently past him and into his bedroom. His lips pulled upward in response and he followed me inside. I heard the door click closed, but I didn't turn around.

His room was neat, a complete opposite of the filth

downstairs. To my surprise, his bed was neatly made with an expensive looking gray and white comforter. Large squishy pillows lined the broad headboard. A sturdy wooden desk sat in the far corner of the room, where a small beam of light trickled from an iron lamp. A long dresser filled the wall behind me. Ordinary items, like textbooks, and CD's were spread across it.

A stunning jewelry box caught my eye. It was made of glossy wood, inlaid with mother-of-pearl and onyx. I wondered what kind of trinkets he kept in there.

There were two large windows that nearly reached the floor. They were open, allowing the balmy air to drift in lazily. Gauzy curtains fluttered like ghosts in the gentle wind. I approached them, hearing Dominic's soft footsteps trail behind me. I looked out at the expansive lawn and out into the wooded forest that fringed the distance.

The sun had already set and now the moon hung like a gigantic pearl in the black sky. It shined prettily down on the activity below. The front lawn was full of people now. They were chatting excitedly and drinking. Dominic came up behind me and lifted the windowpanes further. I noticed a small ledge jutting out of the brickwork.

Dad would have my head on a platter if he knew I was in here, I thought. My gaze automatically pulled over my scar. I smiled wistfully for a second.

"Kara," Dominic whispered. "What is it that draws me to you?"

I inclined my face to his, absorbing his handsome features. His dark eyes were like steel traps, snaring me into place. As I melted into his gaze, I saw undeniably flecks of scarlet. There was something forbidden and dangerous lurking behind those eyes, but instead of fleeing, I leaned closer, my voice rendered useless.

He lifted his hand to my cheek. Red flags popped up all over the place, and yet I ignored them. His touch sent bolts of electricity through my veins and down into the depths of my core. His thumb stroked my bottom lip once before he clamped his eyes shut, his lips quivering slightly. He slammed his hand hard against the wall, rattling the windows. My heart jumped, but I was scared motionless. When he opened his eyes, they were filled with a delirious rage, as if all he was seeing was red.

"Dominic?" I choked out, my skin prickling with fear.

Get out now!

What the hell is that? Who's talking to me? I searched the room. We were still alone. I felt crowded by him. I tried to take a step back, but my feet felt as though they were stuck in quick sand.

Run! The voice screaming in my head urged again, practically nudging my brain with hard, pointed finger. I winced in pain.

Dominic's stare was relentless while my mind spun with escalating commotion.

The window. It beckons you.

I cupped my ears trying to steady the internal chaos.

Do it. You'll see your dad again. He wishes to see you. Here's your chance to be together again.

My eyes flew open. Frantic to escape the voices in my head, I studied the window frame. *Do it!* The invisible voice demanded. Suddenly, my nerves hardened. I edged closer to the window. I looked down at the ground below. The lush carpet of green looked soft and inviting. I took another step. The humid air swathed my body, relaxing every muscle within me. With my fingers brushing the window frame, I ambled forward, until I was teetering on the gritty ledge.

The night sky welcomed me, hugging me with its tangible warmth and beauty.

Do it!

I lifted my face to the glowing moon and spread my arms out wide. *I can't wait to see you again, Daddy. I've missed you.* Taking a final step, I plunged into the empty air.

Chapter 15

A pair of strong hands crushed my shoulders like a vice, yanking me backward. I fell against the unforgiving wood floor, pain splitting through my lower back. I squinted, fighting back the mounting tears. Dominic shivered above me. His breath was ragged as he smoothed the hair out of my face. Dark circles ringed his eyes like bruises, marring his clear, pallid skin. Comprehension suddenly slammed into me, and a lump of bile rose in my throat. I swallowed it back, my eyes quelling at the bitter taste.

"You did that," I breathed. I dug my nails into the wood and scrambled away from what felt like a bed of red-hot coals. His eyes narrowed, glazing over into hard chunks of black ice.

"You did that," I repeated. "You put those words into my head. I don't know how, but it was you." My hands shook like brittle twigs in the wind.

"You're rambling. You must have hit your head."

"I wouldn't have, if you hadn't lured me out there!" I shouted.

"I think you should leave." His stern voice was commanding.

"With pleasure." I awkwardly lifted myself from the floor, my body smarting with spreading pain.

He made no effort to help me. His eyes regarded me coolly as he said, "Before long, you'll be accusing me of slipping you something and pressing sexual harassment charges against me."

"Go to hell," I hissed, cradling my bruised elbow cautiously.

His lips pulled into a devious grin. "With pleasure," he mocked cruelly.

I let out an exasperated sigh and marched past him. Collecting my composure, I dashed out of the room and down the two flights of stairs. The stench of a bonfire and alcohol burned my nose when I finally made it outside. I pushed through the crowd, bumping into a muscular boy along the way.

"Hey, slow down there, sweet thing," he said, combing his fingers through his dark hair. "What's the hurry?" His gray eyes devoured me, making me shrink back from his intrusive stare. He reeked of alcohol.

"I was just leaving."

"Not before we dance." He grabbed my wrist roughly.

"No, thanks." I tried to wriggle free, but he tightened his hold, making me wince in agony.

"You know you want to, baby. Come here and grind that fine ass on me." He yanked me like a rag doll until I was against his thick body. He had rings of sweat under each armpit and a glisten of perspiration across his forehead. I pushed against him with all my might, but it was like trying to move a concrete statue.

"What are you? Stuck up or something? Move your ass!"

I am not dealing with this right now. Infuriated, I lifted my knee and rammed it into his crouch. He buckled, but grabbed a fistful of my hair along the way.

"You little bitch!" he cried, dragging me to the

ground with him. I shrieked, and he gripped tighter, sending prickles of pain along my scalp. I tried to kick my way free from his crushing weight, but couldn't.

Suddenly, his body was yanked off me. There was a tussle of movement and I turned just in time to see Dominic slamming his fist across the drunken bastards face. It connected with a thud. The boy's cheek oozed blood as his neck snapped backward. Dazed, he flailed his arms wildly around him, swatting at the empty air as he struggled to regain his footing.

"Get the hell out of here before I rip your God-damn head off," Dominic seethed, just as he shoved him one last time.

Like a kicked dog, the boy scampered away with a bleeding cheek and a severely bruised ego.

Dominic swooped down and scooped me into his arms. "I'm sorry, Kara," he whispered. His face was half-hidden in the shadows, but I could see the sincerity in his eyes. "Let me drive you home."

"I'm fine," I sniffled, retching myself free from his lap. I noticed that the crowd had dispersed and we were alone in the front yard.

"You don't seem fine," he shot.

"Why the hell should you care anyway? You're the one who lured me out of a window!"

"Lured you out a window?" He looked around fleetingly, before his dark eyes settled back on me. "Kara, I think that one shot went straight to your head."

"It wasn't the shot! It was *you,* and I know it."

Something sinister flashed in his black-as-night eyes. "That's insane. You need to go sleep it off. Apparently your virgin blood can't handle liquor."

"Fuck you," I spat, as I rubbed my throbbing arm.

"I'm leaving."

"Kara, you can't walk home," he protested. "It's too far and it's late."

"What is it with you?" I threw my hands in the air. "One minute you act like you hate me, then the next you're wooing me with your good looks and charm."

"Wooing you? Is that what I'm doing?" He sniggered; the arrogance of it infuriated me further.

"Don't try to change the subject. You go from conceited asshole to kind-hearted in a blink of an eye. Would you just pick one side of you and stick to it," I begged. "I'm getting dizzy with this emotional tug-of-war."

He looked up at me, his gaze insanely penetrating, but difficult to decipher. I thought for a moment he might beg for forgiveness, but he just set his mouth into a hard line and remained silent.

"Forget it." I turned abruptly and stomped away. *God, he is maddening!* Lost in my thoughts I barely noticed the brawny figure strolling up to me.

"Kara?" the voice called. Startled, I focused on the towering silhouette in the distance.

"Cayden?"

He emerged into the light, his blond hair whipped messily around his face. His chiseled features appeared haggard with concern.

"Oh, thank you, God," I cried. "Can you give me a ride home?"

"Are you all right?" His blue eyes washed over me, inspecting me thoroughly.

"Yes," I lied. "Just ready to get out of here." I glanced over my shoulder and noticed Dominic was gone. *Where did he go?* I shook my head, miffed all over again. "Can we just go?"

"I didn't drive here."

Disappointed, I sighed heavily. "I'll call Cassie. Maybe I can get her to come pick me up." I reached in my pocket and fished out my cell phone. "You need a ride too?"

"Yes, please," he replied.

I dialed her number and waited for her to answer. I watched Cayden survey the area behind me and then with a look of pure determination, stomp his way to the front porch.

"Hello? Hello?" a small voice called.

"Oh," I said, startled. "Hey, Cassie. It's Kara."

"Kara, what's up? Having a good time with Mr. Dark and Mysterious?"

"I'll tell you about it later. Is there any way you can come pick me up?"

"Pick you up? Is everything okay?"

"I'm totally over this frat party and ready to come home." I twirled a stray strand of hair nervously. "Can you come get me?"

"I don't know Kara. *Find Yo' Mate* is on, and I'm really digging this season's bachelor. He's a pilot—"

"Cassie, please," I begged. "Cayden's here, and he needs a ride too."

"Cayden?" Her voice reached another octave with excitement. "Say no more. I'm on my way."

I sighed with relief, knowing that mentioning Cayden would work.

"Thanks, Cassie." I snapped the phone shut and searched for Cayden. He stood at the bottom of the front steps, both hands clenched into fists. Dominic leaned calmly against the railing, his arms folded over his chest. He regarded Cayden with a look of superiority. I quietly made my way up to them, fascinated by their conversation.

"She is different than the rest," Cayden said.

"Why?" he shot, glaring at him. "Because you have feelings for her?"

"When it comes to her, I'll always be a step ahead of you."

"You weren't tonight, my friend. It was my moment of weakness that changed her destiny."

Changed my destiny?

Hearing me approach, both boys stopped talking and turned their faces to me. Too tired to question them, I stood with slouched shoulders; my body still battered from the evenings events.

"Cassie's coming," I declared, my eyes moving from Dominic to Cayden. "I'm going to go wait by the road."

****

"So what happened?" Cassie questioned as I slid into the seat beside her.

"Nothing really. It's just...maybe you're right about Dominic. Maybe he is too intense."

Cayden climbed into the back seat and exchanged a worried look with Cassie.

"Some boys are like spicy chili," she said as she peeked into the rearview mirror.

I rolled my eyes and looked out the car window.

"Everything smells wonderful, looks appealing, and even tastes delicious to the tongue. But then, the true essence burns you from the inside out."

"Absolute poetry," Cayden said. "Your words would make Shakespeare weep."

We all chuckled, and the bleak aura surrounding us slowly began to fade. When we pulled into the boy's dorm parking lot, Cayden lifted himself out the car and bent to my window. I rolled it down and met his steady gaze.

"In all seriousness, Kara, Dominic's got quite a reputation. Don't allow yourself to become just another one of his conquests." He grazed my shoulder with his fingers before stepping away. "Thanks for the ride, Cassie." He gave her a small wave and jogged up the sidewalk and into the building.

Chapter 16

"Come on, it will be fun. Besides, sitting here and pouting all day isn't healthy."

"Cassie, I really don't want to," I said as I tucked my head beneath my pillows.

"Cayden and I think it will get your mind off of things."

"Oh really? You two are discussing my life without me?" I mumbled. *When did they become such good friends?*

"We won't stay long. Come on, Kara. Dominic's probably out having fun right now. So you should to."

"I don't care what that madman does."

"Are you really going to let him win?"

I bit my lip and thought about that. She was right. He was probably wrapped up in the arms of that airhead, Kimberly. I peered out of my mountain of pillows. "Oh, all right. Give me ten minutes."

"Goody!" she squealed happily. "Cayden will be here in five."

"You planned on me going all along?" I asked in disbelief.

"I'm pretty confident in my persuasion skills." Cassie flipped her blond locks and smiled brightly. "Here, I've already picked out your clothes."

I groaned. "Cassie, no. I can pick out my own." I took a weary look at the outfit that lay at the foot of the bed and couldn't hide my surprise.

"Don't worry; I had you in mind when I picked them out. I know better than to try to force you into a mini skirt and heels."

Thank God, I thought, reaching for the clothes. I shimmied into the faded jeans and t-shirt and dragged myself to the full-length mirror beside Cassie's bed. My mouth quirked into a small smile as I admired my reflection. The gray tank top was simple, but slimming. I draped my neck with my charm necklace and slipped into my sneakers.

"I'm ready," I announced, just as there was a knock at the door.

Cassie blew past me and yanked the door open eagerly. "Hey, Cayden," she said in a sultry voice.

Cayden stepped inside, and I must admit, he was quite a remarkable sight. His plaid shirt suited him. It was snug, accentuating the lean muscles in his chest and thick biceps.

Cassie came up beside me and whispered, "That collar is opened just wide enough to make you yearn for more." She wet her lips. "God, I think I'm in love."

Cayden's eyes settled on Cassie. "Wow, I'm impressed you were able to convince her."

"Me too," she replied. "I was about to bribe her with free pedicures for a month."

Cayden chuckled.

"Don't laugh blondie. I never said *who'd* be giving the pedicures." She shot him a playful grin and grabbed her purse from the desk. "Now, let's go have a little fun."

****

"I can't believe I let you talk me into coming here,

again," I said, touching my fingertips to my forehead.

"Oh lighten up," said Cassie. "Have a drink and get your fanny out on the dance floor."

"No, I just agreed to come so you'd get off my back." I settled into a barstool and looked around. The same redheaded bartender was working. She was busy sopping up a puddle of beer until she noticed Cayden. She dropped her rag, and hurried right over.

"A beer and ginger ale," Cayden ordered confidently.

He leaned upon the bar, and gave the bartender a warm smile. She wasted no time in preparing his drink, moving with swift efficiency behind the close confines of the bar.

She returned, and laid out a napkin in front of Cayden. She kept her eyes trained on him, as she scribbled out her phone number, then placed his glass on it. Cayden's flicked a quick glance to the digits. His genuine surprise almost had me laughing.

"Thank you," he said.

"No problem, darling." She flashed a flirty wink.

"Margarita, please," Cassie purred as she bobbed up and down to the beat of the music. Her shiny, off the shoulder shirt sparkled like a disco ball beneath the lights of the bar. "What are you going to have, Kara? A soda?" Cassie asked.

"Yes, please." I shot a quick look at the bartender. She was in no hurry to retrieve our drinks. *I guess you have to be an Adonis in snug jeans to get fast service around here.* "No more alcohol for me."

"No *more*? What do you mean, no *more*?" Cassie asked with narrowed eyes. "I thought you didn't drink?"

"I don't. I mean, I don't *usually*."

"You drank at Dominic's party, didn't you?" She slapped a small hand loudly against her forehead. "Oh boy. What did you do?"

"What do you mean, what did I do?" I asked curiously.

"You're not a drinker, Kara. If you drank even the slightest amount of alcohol, there's a chance it went straight to your head. So what was it? Kiss a boy?"

"Kiss a girl?" Cayden added playfully, his eyes glimmering beneath the bright lights of the bar.

"Throw up on the floor?" she continued. "On someone?"

"What? No." I shook my head. "I didn't do any of those things."

"Are you seriously trying to tell me that the alcohol didn't affect you?"

"It burned my throat and gave me a stomach ache, but that was it."

Cassie studied me with doubtful eyes. "What did you drink? A beer?"

"I don't know what it was," I said with a shrug. "A shot of something blue."

"A shot? You did a shot and remained upright? I'm impressed."

Reluctantly, I recalled that night. The urging voices and the strong longing to see my father again. I retraced the steps that led me to ledge and my breath hitched. "You think it could have messed with my head?" I asked anxiously.

"Well, duh. A lightweight like you, I'm surprised it didn't have you dancing topless."

I forced an awkward laugh, but my stomach flipped

with restlessness. *Oh no. I blamed Dominic for my drunken antics. He'll probably never speak to me again.*

"I'm going to go dance. You coming?" Cassie asked.

I shook my head. "Go ahead, have a good time. I'm not in the mood to dance. I'll just ruin your fun."

"Suit yourself." She slid off the barstool and wiggled her way across the room to the dance floor. Cayden watched her with amusement and then swung his gaze to me.

"If I dance, will you?" he asked.

"You dance?"

"It's more like spasming to a beat." He laughed. "Want to see it in action?" He gestured to the dance floor.

Suddenly curious, I slid off my barstool. "Spasm away," I said, nudging him across the room.

A pumped-up remix blared loudly as we found an opened spot in the middle of the floor. I moved slightly, catching the rhythm with my hips. Cayden didn't waste any time getting his groove on. He wriggled his long legs wildly and swooped an arm around his head like a helicopter. I burst out laughing and caught his swinging hands into mine.

"Oh wow, Cayden. You weren't lying. You look like you're having a mild seizure out here," I said smiling.

He raked his fingers through his hair. "I told you."

The music slowed to a romantic ballad and I realized I was still clinging to Cayden's hands.

"At least I made you laugh, so making a complete ass out of myself was well worth it."

He closed the space between us and placed one hand on my lower back. I gingerly laid a hand on his shoulder. We swayed together as the music played around us. I could feel the muscles beneath his shirt contract as we moved. His sweet scent drifted through the tight space between us. Wisteria in springtime. I inhaled and nestled closer to him just as the song faded, and was replaced by a blood-pounding tune. Jarred by the thumbing bass, we broke our intimate embrace and stared at one another briefly.

"Man, am I pooped," Cassie called above the music. "I need a drink, and this handsome fellow is going to treat me to one." She prodded a spiky-haired boy toward us.

He sported an untrimmed goatee and had deep green eyes. He smiled sheepishly and nodded to us in acknowledgment.

"His name is Jerry—" she said.

"Perry," he corrected.

"Perry, right." She looped a thin arm through his and patted him consolingly. "Couldn't hear you with the music and all," Cassie admitted. "These are my friends, Kara and Cayden."

"'Sup?" Perry asked with a jerk of his chin before they departed to the bar. The duo ordered their drinks while laughing and talking animatedly. Cayden and I found a quiet spot at the bar and sat down.

"Are you glad you came out tonight?" he asked.

I looked up into his shining blue eyes. "Yes. I'm actually having a good time."

"How could you not? I mean, come on. You're with me." He winked and knocked my knee playfully with his. The touch reminded me of our tender dance, and my stomach knotted instantly.

Flustered, I looked away and took a quick assessment of the people around me. Cassie and Perry were working on a pitcher of beer while strangers mingled all around. A slim figure in the corner of the room caught my eye. *Dominic?* I zeroed in on his face, waiting for him to emerge from the shadows. My heart beat steadily, slowly mounting with the prospect of seeing him again. When the man finally stepped under the lights, my heart dropped. Disappointment clearly covered my expression.

"Kara? Are you all right?" Cayden asked, following my gaze across the room.

"I thought I saw Dominic."

He sighed, shaking his head.

"What?" I asked defensively.

"Can I give you some advice?"

"You already have."

"Well, I think it bears repeating."

I met his eyes, keeping my face firm with indignation.

"Stay as far away from Dominic Benenati as you can," he said. "Your heart will thank me later."

I scowled and slide my gaze around the bar, searching for Cassie. *I'm ready to get the hell out of here.* My night was beginning to take a dark turn. I questioned what really happened to me last night. *Was it, in fact, just the alcohol? If so, did I ruin any chance I had with Dominic? What really went on in that frat house?* I found her coming toward me, swaying as she moved. Her eyes were glassy, and a goofy grin was plastered across her face.

"Kara. Kara," she called, bumping into me. She

155

grabbed at my hands and yanked me out of my chair. "Kara. I have to pee, Kara."

"So go pee," I snipped.

"Kara, come with me."

"Oh, all right."

"Thank you, Kara." She patted my face with splayed fingers. "Care-ah. Care-ah," she repeated, as if she was trying out the name for the first time. "Your name is exactly what you are…care…caring. That's you. Care-ah the caring."

I rolled my eyes. "Damn it, Cassie, you are drunk off your ass." I squeezed her hand and tried to steady her.

Perry staggered over. He wasn't much better than Cassie. "Heyyyy, there you are. I thought you were like, gone or something. I looked over and you were like, not there. And then I was like, whoa."

"You're funny," she giggled.

"And wasted," Cayden added, standing from his barstool.

"I'm not wasted, man. I am totally incoherent."

"Exactly." Cayden chuckled. "Come on." He slapped Perry on the shoulder and held him firm. "I think it's best if we all call it a night."

Perry shrugged out of his grip. "You're half right. I'm ready to blow this hole, but I ain't ready to call it a night," he slurred. His green eyes swung to Cassie. "And she's coming with me. Right, babe?"

Cassie nodded so hard, she stumbled a bit. I blew out a disgusted breath and helped her regain her footing.

"Oh no." I gripped Cassie's hand firmly. "You're coming with me," I said sternly.

"No. I wanna go with Terry," she whined.

"His name is Perry, and no, you're coming home with me."

"You're not Kara the caring no more," she pouted. "You're *un care-ah*." She leaned into my face and blew a loud (and very wet) raspberry.

"Kara, why don't you take Cassie to the bathroom," Cayden suggested.

"Oh yes! I have to peeee," she sang as flung her arms out above her head.

"I'll stay here and wait with Perry," Cayden continued, his eyes fixated on me.

I moved my head in a slight nod and began to lead Cassie through the crowd, which was no easy task. She kept stopping and chatting about nonsense to everyone in our path.

As I waited for her to finish explaining why she felt Betty White should run for president, I looked over my shoulder at Cayden. He was leaning close to Perry, his hand squarely on the boys shoulder as he talked.

Perry's eyes were wide as he stared at Cayden, clearly absorbed by his words. He nodded profusely in eager agreement and seemed almost, *mesmerized*.

I wondered what he was saying; wishing the noise of the bar would lower so I could hear. I watched, curious of their exchange as Perry followed Cayden through the room and out the door.

I caught a glimpse of an awaiting taxi through the bar window. Cayden strolled over with his wallet in hand. He murmured a few words to the driver before paying him. I tried to make sense of it all, but couldn't. I tugged on Cassie's hand, weaving our way through the crowd as she chanted, "Put White in the White

House." Finally, we reached the restroom. Cassie disappeared into a stall while I paced the floor, wondering what Cayden had said to Perry. *What did he say? How did he finally convince Perry to go home?*

The toilet flushed, and Cassie spilled out of the stall, tripped over her own feet, and stumbled into my arms. She leaned close to my face, and said, "Thank you for taking me to pee." Her breath reeked a gross concoction of hot wings and alcohol. "You're my best friend."

"Because I took you to the bathroom?" I chuckled. "Sweetie, you need to raise your standards."

She gave me a goofy, lopsided grin. Her bloodshot eyes were hooded from fatigue, and she looked dead upon her feet. I placed my hand on her back, and guided her out the bathroom. Cayden was waiting by the door.

"Where's Larry?" Cassie questioned as she peered over Cayden's broad shoulder.

"*Perry* finally listened to reason and decided to go home," he said. "And I think we should do the same."

Cayden slid behind Cassie's steering wheel while we settled into the backseat. As soon as she sat down, Cassie flopped against me, snoring lightly against my shoulder. I shook my head, and let out an amused chuckle.

Normally drunks annoyed me, but for some reason I didn't mind taking care of Cassie. Maybe it was because she was passed out cold, or maybe it was because my mind was riddled with too many questions to worry about anything else. As Cayden took a sharp corner, she fell into my lap. I smoothed her curls from her face, and found myself recalling the entire night.

How I thought I saw Dominic, and how disappointed I was when it wasn't him. Then there was the strange conversation between Cayden and Perry. I flicked my eyes to the rearview mirror, exchanging the briefest of exchanges with Cayden as he drove us back to campus.

I knew Cayden was different, but this night completely confirmed it. He had a knack for tenderness, for compassion. A niggle of thought worked its way through me. *Cayden is no doubt a godsend...*

Chapter 17

Luckily, Cayden offered to carry Cassie to our room because there was no way I'd be able to schlep her drunk ass by myself. He carefully lifted Cassie from the car and carried her with ease across the parking lot and into the building.

He moved with a graceful air that most men don't possess, gliding lightly through the hallways almost soundlessly. He paused by the door as I unlocked it, gently adjusting Cassie who looked like a ragdoll in his arms.

I pushed the door in, and Cayden skirted around me and placed Cassie in her bed. I shucked off her calf-high boots and pulled the blanket over her. She mumbled and rolled over, her curls toppling over her face.

"Thanks for carrying her in," I said, turning to face Cayden.

"No problem." He drug his fingers through his hair, leaving it in a wild disarray. I couldn't help but imagine him climbing out of bed from a long night of restless sleep…or after a night of rough, passionate sex. I mentally chided myself for thinking something so indecent about Cayden. "Are you ready to play nurse?"

My heart suddenly felt like a cannonball within my chest. "Nurse?" I asked, noticing the unevenness in my voice.

He eyed me for a moment, then slowly answered, "Yeah. She's going to need help recovering from a killer hangover in the morning."

I breathed a quiet sigh of relief. *My imagination is working over time*, I thought. *Cayden knows all we'll ever be, is just friends.*

"Hopefully she'll sleep through the night," I said. I wasn't up for holding her hair back as she puked her guts out. Realizing that I was still holding her boots, I gripped them tighter as I stalked to the closet.

Snatching the door open, I screamed as winged creatures hurled themselves at me. *Bats?* Screeching like wildcats, they flung themselves at my face, scratching and beating me with their leathery wings.

The smell rolling off them was gut churning, reminding me of soiled milk and dank moss. I gagged as they cawed like demented birds. Swarming me like an angry mob of bees, they threw themselves at me, ripping at me with pointed claws.

I protected my head with one hand and swung wildly with the other. My fist connected with one. It screamed, and went sailing through the air.

I shook my hand out, recoiling at the revolting *feel* of it. Like an old damp rag left out to mildew, the creature's body felt limp, and sickly.

I watched in horror, as it shrieked and rushed at me again. When I finally got a good look at it, I gasped and staggered backward, bile rising in my throat. *Definitely not bats.*

There were four of them. Their hands and feet tipped with a single black talon the size of a switchblade. Their skinny bodies reminded me of a plucked vulture. Beady eyes imbedded deep in their skulls peered at me almost lifelessly. As if they attacked simply because it was ingrained in their nature. As if all they knew were destruction, death, and pain. Hooked beaks tore at my hair. Pain pricked at my scalp, and my heart felt as though it was lodged in my throat. I heard a commotion above me.

Shocked, I watched in awe as Cayden smashed a fist into the ribcage of one of the creatures, sending it hurdling through the air. It crashed into the wall, but did not collapse. Instead, it opened its beaked mouth in a deafening squawk before flying out the door.

The others followed suit, their cries rattling the mirror until I thought it would shatter. Covering my ears, I whipped my head to Cassie.

She stirred and blinked her eyes sleepily at me, then said, "Can you guys go screw in *his* room? I'm trying to sleep here."

I opened my mouth to speak, but Cayden interjected.

"You're dreaming," he whispered. "Go back to sleep." He touched Cassie's shoulder lightly and bent to whisper something in her ear. She rolled over, and within seconds, the sounds of her steady breathing signaled that she was in a deep sleep. Cayden lifted his face, and our gazes met.

"Are you okay?" he asked, slowly approaching me.

I nodded, but I was anything but. My heart was still racing as though I had just outrun a tornado. I wavered on my feet, my knees unable to hold me up any further. Cayden caught my arm, supporting my crumbling weight by pulling me into him. My lips parted in surprise, but I was grateful he was there. I sank into him, allowing him to trace comforting circles on the small of my back. My head throbbed and my insides shook from the pulsating adrenaline in my system.

"What were those?" I looked into his face, my brows raised in question. His blue eyes gazed at me with a mixed expression. *Sadness? Frustration? Anger?*

"Hoary bats," he replied, never tearing his eyes from mine.

"Those were *not* bats," I said, shaking my head.

I felt his grip loosen and move to hold fast to my shoulders. "What you saw were hoary bats. They are quite common on campus."

My body was slowly ratcheting down from the high it was on. "But they were bigger than bats. And their mouths…" I shuddered as I recalled the curved bone-like appearance of their beaks, stretched wide open as they hollered above my head.

"Bats are bigger than you think. And you were so startled; I think your mind exaggerated what you saw. I was here, remember? I saw what you saw."

I stared into his eyes, part me wished he would agree with me so I wouldn't feel like I was going insane. But the other part of me prayed that he was right, because if he wasn't, than something from a grotesque nightmare really existed.

Were they truly bats? I had seen bats. I saw them once in Aunt Theresa's attic. They were black. And their wings looked slippery, like damp leather. That's what I saw tonight, I thought. *A black, winged animal. They must have been bats…*

"It's been a long night, Kara. Go get some rest."

I inhaled his sweet scent of wisteria, and suddenly became utterly exhausted. I could barely keep my eyelids open, as I took his large hands from my shoulders. I held them, the warmth of his fingers spreading through me, relaxing every muscle within my body.

"Thank you," I said, just before my mouth stretched into a long yawn.

Cayden's lips quirked into a small smile. "You're welcome, but what are you thanking me for?"

"For protecting me from monsters." I climbed into bed without undressing, sinking into my plush pillow.

His eyes grew round, and his jaw ticked just slightly. "That's what I'm here for," he said, his eyes darkening to a steel blue.

I smiled at him from behind the folds of my comforter. "Good night, Cayden."

"Good night, Kara. Sweet dreams."

I closed my eyes and barely heard his movements as he let himself out. I fell asleep easily, and was pleasantly surprised to have a dreamless sleep that night, considering the nightmare that had just occurred.

Chapter 18

I found my way to the clearing behind school grounds, determined to finish my infinity project. I needed to work on it alone, away from Cassie and her non-stop, jabbering mouth. The sky was almost completely clear. A few stray birds soared recklessly after one another as I scoured the field for a cozy spot.

I settled into a nook of thick oak roots and pulled out my sketchpad. I studied the drawing, indecisive on where to begin. *More shading or more detail?* I worked diligently until I was satisfied with it. I checked my watch, surprised to find that I had been working on it for so long.

Leaning back with a satisfied sigh, I took in my hard work. Infinite scales tipped and dipped their way across the page. Not one balanced; each held another scale within its tray, keeping it askew. Reflecting on the image, I thought of my father, and my gaze instinctively swept across the ugly scar on my wrist.

I closed my eyes and tried desperately to keep the memory from overtaking me, but it was too late. There I was again. Alone, kneeling on the cold bathroom tile of my old dorm room. Holding a dull kitchen knife, I stared blankly into the reflection of the blade.

Eyes, blood-shot and sore, stared back at me, full of boiling rage and sadness that could not be tamped down any longer. I hated the world and myself. I despised God for taking my father away from me. Hell-bent on releasing myself from the pain, I dragged the sharp blade across the tender skin of my wrist.

I cried out and curled my hand around the bleeding wound. Blood quickly collected between my fingers, spilling over my knuckles, and weaving warm, scarlet trails down my arm. Drops of blood dripped like tiny rubies, splashing carelessly onto the white tiles.

My roommate Jen called for me, throwing the door open with a start. It knocked me to the floor, blood smearing across the tile like paint on canvas. Vaguely, I heard her on the phone, frantically describing my wound. Her voice became distant, as vertigo set in. I tried to blink it away, but the spinning would not relent. Jen came back with a towel.

"Oh shit, Kara," she exclaimed, guiding me into a seated position. I pressed my back to the wall for support as she pressed the towel firmly to my wrist. I hissed and breathed through the pain. A storm of footsteps thudded through the hallway and into the bathroom.

"Thank god," Jen said, moving aside so an EMS worker could kneel beside me. My vision spotted white, and then all went black.

I felt a warm hand on my shoulder. My eyes flew open and looked into the face of a handsome man. *Dominic?* His smile comforted me, and I began to relax under his touch. Something heavy was placed into my hand, and automatically my fingers curled around it.

Everything is going to be all right now. You are not alone. I'm right here and you will soon be reunited with your father.

I licked my dry lips and moved my head in a slow

nod.

There's only one way to make that happen. And you know what that is, don't you?

I looked down and saw a large knife gripped tightly in my hand. The blade was as long as my forearm and it gleamed dangerously in my lap. I nodded mechanically as I lifted the knife and rested the serrated blade against my wrist.

Do it!

I plunged the metal deep into my skin, crying out as pain tore through my shredded muscles, quickly spreading throughout my entire body. I stared at the gaping hole, tears springing to my eyes when I realized what I had done. *I did it again. Oh God, no! I did it again!* I tried to scream, but my sobs choked me until all that came out was a pathetic whimper. Blood trickled its way across my skin, leaving bright red paths down the length of my forearm.

Two strong hands covered my wound, squeezing with such pressure that I became woozy. Heat sizzled across my skin, as though I was leaning against a hot stove. *Fuck!* I looked up, meeting a startling pair of crimson eyes. They burned with intensity, nearly reaching inside me and touching my very soul.

Dominic. I struggled to pull my arm free, but he held firm, unyielding even a fraction of restraint as I fought as much as the pain would allow.

"Be still. I am healing you." His voice commanding, and I froze at the finality of his tone.

"What just happened?" I asked, wincing as he adjusted his fingers. The burning sensation continued, intensifying at the heart of the wound and feathering out through my veins.

"You had a little accident."

Right, an accident. I looked up. The sky was painted with dark streaks of gray and flecked with twinkling stars. "How long have I been here?" My heart pounded with rising panic. My ribs felt like they were squeezing my insides like a vice.

"I'm guessing a few hours," he replied.

A few hours! My stomach twisted until I felt I'd vomit. *What the hell happened?* My eyes darted around the field until landing on something shiny in the grass a few feet away. My mind bumped and clanged like a caboose slamming into a stalled train car. Yanking my arm free, I stared into Dominic's tense face.

"You!"

His nostrils flared and the creases in his brow deepened.

"You did that!" I shrieked hysterically. "You made me do it!"

He only watched as I ranted, his face unreadable. My breath came out in short pants, my body shaking from anger, fear and desperation.

Am I losing my mind? I laid my hands on my head, clutching my hair. The pain in my wrist pulsated, but it was just a dull ache now. I wretched my fingers free from my hair and searched for the bloody mess that was supposed to be there. Instead, I found my old scar solidly etched into my skin and beside it, was a fleshy thread of pink, circling my wrist like a delicate bracelet. *What the hell?*

"How did you…why did you…?" A swarm of questions berated my mind, but I didn't know where to start. I watched Dominic climb solemnly to his feet. "Are you trying to kill me? Or just drive me mad?" I demanded.

"I'm not *trying* to kill you."

"Oh, that's right. I'm the one doing the killing, so that makes you an accomplice."

His eyes blazed as he took in a sharp intake of air. "You're babbling," he sneered. "You lost a lot of blood. I should get you back to your dorm."

"I'll be damned if you're taking me anywhere," I said. "You're a lunatic."

His nostrils flared as he growled through gritted teeth. "I'm trying my best to stay away from you." The hard planes of his face were severe and deeply shadowed. He swore, and closed his eyes for a beat. My heart raced as I watched him quietly work through something.

When he finally opened his eyes again, he swung them to me, pinning me into place with unnatural force. They were disturbingly candid, unsettling eyes, and yet they were undeniably beautiful. "But it's impossible when you let your demons control you."

Chapter 19

"Now you're the one babbling," I said.

With a sigh, his shoulders slouched, and his sharp features softened. Slowly, he made his way across the grassy lawn, watching the ground as he took long, but unhurried steps. He stopped at the edge of the forest.

The moon was hidden amongst the pine trees, only its gentle glow outlining his silhouette in the darkness. He appeared almost ghostly standing there. Not quite human, but not at all like a threatening monster. He was hauntingly beautiful and as always, strangely compelling.

"Dominic," I started carefully. "What are you?"

He snickered arrogantly. "What do you think I am?"

"I don't know," I confessed. If I hadn't thought it would sound foolish, I would have guessed the devil himself. "All I know is…you're different."

He laughed. "Different?"

Bars of moonlight spilled across the forest floor. He weaved in and out of the trees, winding like a snake through the pooling light, only to disappear again in the shadows.

I searched for him, turning my head sharply to the left and right, trying desperately to catch a glimpse of him. "I'll figure it out, you know," I said squinting into the darkness.

Suddenly he was in front of me. I gasped. His face just inches from mine, pallid skin reflecting a gentle silver beneath the moonlight. His warm breath puffed lightly across my already tingling flesh.

"I doubt that," he mocked smugly. His dark eyes flashed, the red flecks swirling ominously throughout the black orbs.

"Your skin is hot," I pointed out.

Something eerie flickered behind his eyes, but I refused to let it affect me. I licked my dry lips. "The lunch lady," I began cautiously. "You hooked her up with a dealer." I studied his features, but there was no movement. Not even a subtle flinch.

The minutes stretched on until he finally muttered, "She ultimately made the deal, not me."

"You convinced that girl to sleep with a married man," I continued. "Why?"

He shrugged nonchalantly. "Her soul is black. She would have done it anyway." He reached down and picked up a broken branch.

I shuddered at his callousness. "That's no reason for you to get involved."

"Oh, but it is," he said slyly, arching that damn eyebrow at me, goading me to react as he toyed with the jagged limb, breaking off wispy leaves and letting them flutter to the ground.

"Why?" I searched his eyes, praying I'd find some shred of humanity, but instead I found indifference. "What does it matter if she screwed him or not?" I asked. "What, do you get off on sick shit like that or something?"

He chuckled more out of annoyance, rather than humor. "Look, why don't you go back to your dorm?

171

Back to your simple little life and forget about what you saw."

"No," I seethed through tight teeth, shaking my head violently. "What are you?" I demanded. My sanity depended on his answer, and I wasn't leaving until I heard it, good or bad. I glared at him, my hands trembling as the adrenaline spiked within my veins.

He regarded me with impassive eyes, idly snapping off twigs. The sound crackled through our silence as he broke off pieces one by one until I couldn't stand it a moment longer.

"Answer me!" I shrieked. "What the hell are you?" My face flushed with fury, and I was on the brink of completely losing it. "You let me carve open my wrist! You had..." I could barely spit the words out; my voice was teeming with bitter rage, and I could feel the heat rising up my neck and touching my ears. "You had me out on a fucking ledge on our first date! You tried to kill me!"

His dark eyes blazed with anger, and he hurled the dead limb through the air. I recoiled as it zipped through the air at an unnatural speed. He tore through the empty space between us, stomping with maddening fury. My heart pounded painfully in my chest as I watched him quickly close in on me.

Oh, shit.

He loomed over me, and I felt trapped, stifled by his close proximity. I lifted my gaze hesitantly, frightened to make eye contact, and noticed the red flecks in his eyes were more intense then I remembered. He was so close. And for the first time, it was too close.

"Just the fact that you even stepped out there, means that you've considered it." His voice was low and hypnotic. It was as though he was trying to coax the truth from me, and I did my best to resist. I tore my eyes from his, staring off into the desolate surroundings, my eyes welling with frustration and resentment for the boy who lured me blindly into his beautifully twisted world.

"Kara," he said sternly, seizing my shoulders, his grip like an iron wrench, pinioning me into place.

For a fraction of second, I searched his eyes, noting the severity of his face before shaking myself free. *Distance. I need distance.* I staggered to the nearest tree and leaned into it for support, pressing my back against it. *Get it together, Kara. If he senses you're weak, there is no telling what he'll do.* I watched as he scrubbed the back of his neck, closing his eyes as he let out a deep sigh. He stayed that way for a moment, as if he need time to figure everything out.

When his eyes fluttered open, his gaze shifted to mine, resignation clearly all over his face. He shoved his hands into his pockets, then once again, he began to close the space between us, crossing the grass without a sound. My heart felt as though it was trying to hammer its way out of my chest. *This boy is not natural; there's something ethereal about him.*

"Why would you want to commit suicide?" The words sliced the air, folding me in half as if I had been punch in the gut. I closed my eyes, wishing he would just go away. I hated him for figuring it out, and I hated him even more for asking me about it.

It was supposed to be a secret. A fact so hideous, I buried it deep inside, hoping it would eventually diminish, like a lost memory, never to return.

Forgetting momentarily about Dominic, I allowed

myself to picture my father's face, his kind hazel eyes, and his hearty laugh. *Daddy.* The thought of reconnecting with him became overwhelming and soon, the whisper of possibility began creeping across my sanity once again. The will to die, greater than the will to live.

"Kara. Don't," Dominic begged.

His words startled me, and my stomach heaved me back into reality. I doubled over with the sickening embarrassment. *I am loved. My mother loves me. She needs me. I care enough about her to stay alive.* I recited the mantra I was forced to write during my first support meeting. It seemed silly back then, and I remember balling up the paper I had written it on, and tossing it in the trash as soon as the meeting ended.

Back then, I was above treatment. Above needing encouragement from strangers who walked the same dangerous path I did. But damn if it didn't help. Even though I threw away the paper with the mantra, written in my own angry handwriting, I still remembered the words as clearly as if they were a beloved poem. I often relied on those words to save me from a disastrous downward spiral.

I am loved. My mother loves me. She needs me. I care enough about her to stay alive.

"Kara," Dominic said again, startling me. "Answer me!"

"Yes, damn it! Yes. I've attempted suicide," I screamed. Aside from Jen, Becca, my mom, and my support group, no one knew that sick side of me existed, but now, it hung in the air between Dominic and me, exposed in all its twisted glory. "I just wanted to be with my dad again," I whispered, pressing my back deeper into the trunk of the tree, ignoring the jabs from the rough bark. I felt the burning of my inner rage well and spill over, and I cried until the hot tears ran cold.

I slid down the tree until I was crouching on the balls of my feet. I pressed my face into my hands, my head aching from crying.

Through my fingers, I saw his shoes step in front of me. He knelt, bringing with him that tantalizing elixir of heat and spice. I could feel his intense stare invading me, boring so deep, violating my soul. *Please don't look at me with pity*...

With a feather light touch, his brushed his fingers along my cheek. It was a touch so tender, so loving, I nearly chalked it up to my wild imagination until he said, "Look at me."

I lifted my face, and stared into his crazy-beautiful eyes. They seared into me, as if siphoning out information about my past—about *me*—leaving me raw and exposed.

"You know that's not how things work, don't you?" His voice held an edge of sorrow, as his thumb brushed over my bottom lip, his eyes following his moment. I quivered beneath his touch, my mind boiling over with confusion.

How can he turn so quickly, like a flipped switch? What's more—how can I? Conflicted, I shrank away from his warm fingers, but instantly wished I hadn't as I watched his eyes flicker with sadness. He expelled an exasperated breath.

"Fine," he muttered, lowering his head and raking his hand through his inky hair. He was unable to mask his uncertainty as he framed his next words. No longer were his features stern and sharp, but now they were conflicted and fragile. My stomach roiled with anxiousness as I waited for him to speak. *Come on. Say it.* My fingers twitched with the urge to touch him, to let him know it was okay. Slowly I reached out to him.

"I'm a demon." His words dripped with sheer abhorrence.

Disgust clawed at my throat, the bile collecting and burning until I swallowed it back. "A demon?" I echoed, pulling back my hand and fisting it in my lap.

"*Part* demon." He lifted his face, and met my stare. "My mother was human. My father is a demon."

I collapsed into the dirt, clinging to the tufts of grass to steady myself. The ground was damp, cooling my clammy palms. I shook my head as though I could erase his words.

"My true title is Damamah," he explained, "a whisperer."

"A whisperer?" I repeated, my gaze fixated on the grass because I could not bear to face him. Not yet.

"The nudge of temptation that lures you into committing sins."

"Why would you want to help people commit sins?" I finally looked at him. The moon's rays reflected off his creamy skin, and his eyes, now dark as night were like hollow caves, begging to be explored. *How can something so beautiful, be so dangerous?*

He stood, jamming his hands into his pockets again. I peered at him, wondering if he kept his hands in his pockets to keep from touching me.

"Demons do not possess free will, Kara. It's my lot, and I must obey."

"So you," I said unsteadily, "*work* for Satan?

Convincing innocent people to commit horrible crimes?"

"The people I persuade are far from innocent," he said as he paced back and forth. "And yes, ultimately Satan is reigning master over all demons."

Satan? I shuddered. *What have I gotten myself into?* I remained quiet for a long time as I tried to make sense of everything. It sounded totally implausible, and yet it was the only explanation he offered.

As I thought about Ms. Colleen, the vixen, and even myself, walking blindly toward the window ledge, a sickening realization washed over me. *He's a demon,* I thought. *A real live demon, feeding off sin and destruction.* I stared into his eyes and swallowed before I whispered, "You're the devil's wingman."

A sly smile formed on his lips. "Something like that," he said. "I've never met him. He's like one of those big-time CEOs that never learns the names of his employees." His eyes danced with sour mirth.

"It's…" I searched for the right word. "*Wrong.*"

He looked at me sharply, his smile diminishing instantly. "Quit being so righteous. You know nothing of the world around you, so don't cast stones at things you don't understand."

Again, anger surged through me. I am far from a self-righteous person, but I do know right from wrong. And what Dominic did was *wrong.* "Attempting to quote the bible, are we?" I asked coldly. "You won't burst into flames for doing that?"

Dominic laughed heartily, and then looked at me pointedly. "That only happens when my kind steps inside a church."

"Really?"

"No," he answered dryly, pinching his brows tight over his dark eyes. He crossed his arms and leaned against a tree, appearing relaxed, the familiar air of arrogance shrouding him once more. "We can enter most holy ground, but humans like to think they're safe *somewhere*."

With a flick of his wrist, he gestured flippantly around him. "Simple humans. It's amazing they have lasted so long. They just keep persevering through wars, disease, and poverty." He touched his chest with his fingertips. "If I had a heart, I'd be touched." He rolled his eyes and unhitched himself from the tree.

He's absolutely infuriating! "Your mother was a human," I pointed out, finding myself torn between wanting to wrap my hands around his throat and wanting to wrap my arms around *him*.

How could he make me want to choke the life from him one minute, and cover his face with kisses the next?

The corner of his mouth inched upward, his eyes glimmering alluringly. "Recessive gene," he replied while examining his nails impassively.

And we're back to wanting to kill him again. "You're unbearable. Take me home."

His intrusive eyes sank into me, his expression suddenly softening. I wanted to stomp away, to leave him standing there like the idiot he was, but I didn't. I couldn't. I just gazed at him, wishing I could forget about his lopsided grin and his oddly stunning dark eyes.

"Kara," he said with a sigh. His features were drawn, his eyes tight with concern. "I'll only end up hurting you. I care about you too much to risk that."

Did he just declare something to me? Did he mean

to?

He stood in front of me, and I resisted the strong urge to lace my fingers in his.

I was positive I misunderstood him, but to be sure, I asked, "You care about me?

"More than I should."

Acting on a whim, I brought my hands up and pressed my palms against his cheeks. They burned like a fever. I wasn't sure if I'd ever get used to that.

His black eyes latched onto mine. I waited as he struggled with something internally, pain and confliction clearly written across his face. Eventually, his expression shifted, the hard planes of his features softening into a sweet smile. As our faces drew closer, my breathing became ragged with anticipation. When he wet his lips, it was nearly my undoing. My chest heaved with expectation, trembling each time his breath crept across my skin. I looked into his eyes; the crimson specks were recessing, like a fading tide within a murky sea of black ink. They were hypnotizing.

"If I am under a trance, don't ever rouse me," I murmured.

His eyes glimmered just before he pressed his warm lips to mine. Our mouths moved together in perfect unison, as if they were molded to fit one another. The kiss deepened, and together we were swept away by our unraveling emotions, pawing at one another as though each other's breath was the only oxygen we had.

When we finally parted for air, we both stood staring at the other, panting. Dominic took my hands, his touch warming me like a soothing balm. He cast his eyes down to our intertwined fingers, his long lashes fanning out over his high cheekbones. "My fraying willpower makes it hard to walk away from you."

"Then don't," I whispered.

"I hope I don't do anything we'll regret." His face looked pained, and I ached because of it.

"I trust you with my heart."

"You shouldn't," he said, his voice strained as he hung his head, his raven hair dangling over his forehead like weeping willow vines. I pushed them back, letting my fingers trail down his sideburns and across his lips.

He enveloped my hand with his, pressing my fingers to his mouth, kissing them tenderly. My body reacted.

The same tingling sensation tickled its way through me, just the way it did when we first touched that day in the classroom.

Twining our fingers together, he led me back toward campus, stopping to retrieve my sketchpad and book bag and asked, "The scales…"

"The sign for Libra," I hedged, watching him closely.

Dominic raised his eyebrow in interest.

"My father's sign."

He shook his head knowingly. "It's late. I'll take you home." Up ahead I saw his mean machine, and although my dorm wasn't too far, I was happy he offered to drive. It was dark, and the past few hours wore me down to a frazzled shell of myself.

I watched as he folded his elegant frame beneath the steering wheel. With a slight grin, he jammed the key into the ignition. The metal monster roared to life, its grumbling filling the tense silence between us. I was almost sure he regretted our kiss, until his hand reached out across the space, seeking my own.

I clung to him, the warmth of his palm calming me. I smiled at our joined fingers as he pulled into an empty parking slot. With the car still rumbling angrily, he turned in his seat to face me. Even under the stream of harsh security lights, he looked beautiful.

"If you were smart, you'd stay away from me," he said.

"Then consider me stupid," I replied stubbornly, jutting my chin out defiantly. "Because I can't do that."

He gazed at me quietly with hooded eyes. I wanted to lose myself in those disturbing, yet striking eyes. They were hypnotic. If he told me to walk blindfolded in traffic I would…and that scared the hell out of me.

Chapter 20

I couldn't wait to get to Mrs. Dixon's class the next morning. After the night before, my heart felt full, knowing Dominic's true feelings for me. I dressed to impress that day. Pulling on a snug pair of jeans and a sexy button-up blouse, I smirked at myself in the mirror. I left my hair loose, letting it fall naturally to the middle of my back. I lined my lips with gloss and headed out the door.

I skidded to a stop when I rounded the classroom threshold, my chest thumping with anticipation. Dominic was already there. *He's early.* I gazed at him, my heart filling with pride that I could finally call him *mine.*

Still unsure how I managed it, Dominic's heart belonged to me. It wasn't just my heart but *everything* I had that belonged solely to him. He must have sensed I was watching, his eyes immediately found mine and a sweet, lop-sided grin filled his face. I rushed to him, eager to close our distance.

He caught my face with his warm hands and peered into my eyes. "Tell me it's not insane to have stayed awake half the night thinking about you, and the other half sleeping, dreaming of you."

"Not at all," I whispered. "That's exactly what I did too."

He grinned and gently turned my arm over. "How's

your—"

"It's fine," I interrupted, pulling my hand free and tucking it behind my back. I couldn't bear to see the guilt in his eyes when he looked at it.

"Kara, even if you *could* hide it forever, I'll still remember what I did."

"It's not your fault."

"It *is* my fault," he said tersely, slamming his fist into the desk. It shook and rattled loudly, causing me jump. I ignored the curious looks being thrown our way, but Dominic gave the crowd a harsh stare, sending them scurrying back to their own business.

"I'll always have to live with the memory of watching it happen, over and over in my head." His eyes looked pained as he sank into his seat.

I reached out for him, but he caught my arm, turning it over gently and strummed his fingers across the scar. I shuddered at his tender touch. "This might as well have been tattooed across my heart."

My eyes welled with emotion; the grief in his eyes overwhelmed me. "Dominic, don't do this to yourself. You can't help what you are." I laid a hand on his shoulder, feeling his soothing warmth through the fabric of his shirt.

He kissed my palm softly. "I don't deserve you."

"Good morning, movers and shakers," announced Mrs. Dixon as she entered the classroom. I hurried to take a seat beside Dominic.

"Ready to turn in those infinity projects?" She smiled at the class and motioned for us to pass them up front. The sound of rustling book bags and notebooks filled the air. I reflected on my drawing for a moment, confident that it should draw in an easy A.

I glimpsed Dominic's work amongst the flow of projects that swept toward the front of the room. It was beautifully drawn, but just as haunting as his last sketch. Thick strands of chains poured from the top of the page, pooling into endless stacks of linked wedding rings.

"Dominic. That drawing. It's amazing," I said, my voice full of astonishment.

He smiled shyly. "I had some pretty amazing inspiration." He stretched his lean arm out to me and I met it halfway. The heat of his fingers sent a small current of electricity through me. I smiled, and released him as Mrs. Dixon called the class to order.

Overwhelmed with the feeling I was being watched, I glimpsed over my shoulder and noticed Cayden glaring at Dominic. His blue eyes shone with alarming intensity. The muscles in his jaw clenched, and his nostrils flared angrily. His eyes swung to me and I gave him a slight smile. He didn't return the gesture; in fact, he averted his eyes and ignored me for the rest of the class.

****

"Want to blow off your next class and come over to my place?" Dominic asked as we merged into the hallway.

My heart squeezed at the notion.

"We can do whatever you want. I'll even watch a chick flick with you."

I giggled and took his hand. "We don't have to do *anything*. I'm happy just being with you."

He squeezed my hand and led me across the parking lot.

My heart was giddy as I buckled myself into his

grumbling monster mobile and soon we barreled through the quiet streets.

The frat house was surprisingly quiet.

"Everybody's either in class or at some sort of practice," Dominic informed me. "Want to watch TV?"

I glimpsed the couch and saw scattered chips and peanuts across the cushions. Empty soda cans teetered on the armrests, and an unknown stain covered one of the pillows.

"Uh, no offense, but I'm scared to sit on that."

He chuckled and nodded his head in agreement. "Guys are filthy pigs, what can I say?" He wove his fingers through mine. "If I promise to be gentlemen, will you come up to my room?"

I hesitated for a fleeting minute. My mind raced with the prospect of being alone with him. *Alone...in a room...with a bed.*

The thought was a little intimidating. "I'll be on my *best* behavior," he assured me. "I promise."

I smiled up at him, and said with false confidence, "Let's go."

He led me up both flights of stairs and through the corridor to his bedroom. Stepping inside, I felt a strange dip in my stomach. The windows were just as I remembered. Transparent curtains blew in the wind, reminding me of the horrible incident that nearly took place.

"Don't even *think* about it," he admonished gently as he closed the door behind him.

"I'm sorry, I didn't mean to. It's just being here again—"

"Kara, I mean it. If you let your mind go weak, there's a chance we'll do something we'll both regret."

His face fell into serious angles. "But only one of us will be around to feel the remorse."

Understanding washed over me and I shivered at the thought. *Let my mind go weak.* That's what I did last year. I let my mind go weak, and I tried to kill myself. My heart ached at the memory, but I couldn't dwell on it. Not now anyway. Not with Dominic standing next to me. That could prove dangerous.

Dominic quietly moved in front of me, pulling me close as he snaked his arms over me. They were strong, protective arms and they fit around me just right.

"Don't be frightened. It's just easier, for me, if you keep the thought of suicide from your mind. Resisting the pull of sin is nearly impossible for a whisperer. It's our nature to convince mortals to seal their sin. You have no idea how hard it was for me to alter your destiny, *twice.*"

"So why did you?"

He gave me a long look, and then reached his hand to my cheek. His touch was like warm honey, spreading slowly over my body. "Because I could not bear for you to leave this earth without me."

My lips parted in surprise and before I could say anything, he bent and left a chaste kiss on my cheek. His face lingered close to mine, his hot breath charging my body with a tingly current. Reacting on carnal impulse, I crushed my lips eagerly against his. Our mouths molded effortlessly into one another, synchronizing into a passionate exchange of sweet tastes and cravings for more. I felt his body react to our kiss, fueling me to deepen it. A low grumble rattled his vocal cords when we finally released each other.

"What are you trying to do to me?" he panted.

I smiled up at him adoringly. "Sometimes, a peck just isn't enough."

His lips lifted into a beautiful smile. "Kara Maven, you have a hold over me that trumps all others. You make me feel invincible and completely weak all at the same time."

He cupped my neck, his thumbs stroking my cheeks as we kissed again. When he pulled away, he bent, trailing feathery light kisses along my jawline and chin. I quivered when he lingered at the hollow of my throat, his tongue flicking out, tasting me. The wet sensation against my flushed skin caused me gasp, and I yearned to feel it again.

His hands glided over my hips, stopping to rest on my lower back, his fingers digging into me as I leaned into him, intoxicated by his spicy scent. Growling hungrily, he gently arched my back and continued his assault on the sensitive areas of my neck and down to the open collar of my blouse. I felt his nose skim the center of my chest before the heat of his lips seared my skin. Tangling my fingers in his hair, I moaned softly, aching for more. Lifting his head, he snared me in his smoldering gaze.

"Forgive me if I lose myself in your heartbeat," he whispered, his voice thick with lust. "Feeling it race reminds me what I would have lost if I had let you seal your sin. It is vital that I keep this beating as long as possible." He paused, swallowing hard as he splayed his palm over my heart. "If anything should happen to you that is the day my own heart will cease beating."

Overwhelmed with emotions, I covered his mouth with mine, devouring his soft lips, and plunging my tongue past his teeth. He moaned against my mouth, nudging me, walking me backward until I felt the bed behind me. He leaned back, his eyes set on mine, silently asking for permission. I hooked his belt loop with a finger, and pulled him closer, answering him by planting a solid kiss on his lips.

He smiled, and wrapped an arm around my waist, gently lowering me into the soft mattress. He covered my body with his, as I tugged at his earlobe with my teeth, which sent him groaning into my hair. His skin becoming hot with excitement. I felt his fingers slip between us and work at the buttons of my jeans.

I reached for the hem of his shirt and pawed it feverishly. Reading my hurried signals, he pulled his shirt up and over his head with one fluid motion. His pale skin was flawless, as though he was carved from polished oyster shells.

Straddling my thighs, he unfastened each button on my shirt slowly, until finally it fell open. His mouth puckered sexily, sucking in a sharp intake of air as he took in the sight of me. His eyes lingered on my lacey bra, my chest heaving beneath it with arousal.

Bending at his waist, he pinned my arms to the bed as he planted light kisses across my stomach and up my ribcage. I moaned with building desire, feeling his body tense, as he grew stone still. His lips pulled away from my skin, but I could still feel him breathing hard against stomach. His hands contracted into fists, clutching my fingers so tightly it hurt.

"Dominic? What's wrong?"

He remained silent.

"You're scaring me," I whispered.

He lifted his face, our gaze meeting across my chest. His handsome features were tight with angst, as his eyes flooded crimson. I watched in horror, recalling the first time I had seen the blood red flecks. I was in this room, creeping toward the ledge, with his voice pushing me closer. I pursed my lips, not knowing what to say or do to help him through it.

He sighed deeply, closing his eyes once again before lifting himself off me. "I'm sorry, Kara," he said, reaching his fingers in the pocket of his jeans and pulling out a set of keys. "Here, take my car back home."

He bent, leaning close to my face as he folded his fingers over mine, placing the keys in the palm of my hand. "I have to go, I'm sorry." We kissed, then he pulled his shirt back on quickly, ducked out the door, and disappeared.

****

That night as I crawled into bed, I thought about what almost happened, my skin flushing with the memory. I touched my lips, still able to taste his kiss. I almost let myself go, almost let Dominic claim a part of me that I had carefully guarded, fortified with isolation and a thick layer of insecurity. My vulnerability.

I frowned, recalling the way his body suddenly tensed, as though someone had walked in and interrupted. I couldn't explain what happened, why he left in a hurry, or why his eyes flooded with something volatile. However, there was one thing I was certain of. I never wanted anything or anyone as bad as I wanted Dominic Benenati.

There was something about him that filled the hole in my heart. That made my bleak existence brighter. For the first time in over a year, my will to live was greater than my will to die.

Chapter 21

I slept well into the early afternoon, when a knock at the door startled me awake.

"Coming," I called as I slid off my bed. I opened the door, surprised to see the face smiling back at me.

"Mom. Hi." She looked pretty. She wore a breezy purple tunic with slimming black Capris. Her brown hair hung in gentle waves.

"Hey, I'm here to make good on my dinner offer." She glances at her watch, and says, "Or more appropriately, lunch offer. You didn't forget, did you?" Her caramel eyes appeared hurt.

"No," I started, fumbling over my words. "Well, kind of," I admitted, biting my lip. Immersed in all things Dominic, I had totally forgotten about my belated birthday dinner.

"What? How could you forget? You don't already have plans, do you?" A slight frowned pulled at her lips.

"No."

"Good." She smiled and peered past me, quickly taking in the room. "Where's your roommate? Would she like to join us?"

"I'm sure she would, if she were here. Lucky for us, she's student teaching at Pineville Elementary."

"Don't you like her?"

"Oh sure," I said. "We've become surprisingly

close in such little time. It's just; she goes a little nuts with birthdays. She'll have every waitress in the restaurant singing me 'Happy Birthday.' "

She laughed, which surprised me. I hadn't heard it much since Dad died, so hearing it again made me smile.

I stepped aside and watched her inspect my small space. Her familiar scent of tea olive wafted through the air as she moved about the room.

"Are you happy here?" she questioned quietly. Her hands clasped in front of her.

"Yes," I replied.

I crossed the floor and stepped into the bathroom long enough to change into a comfortable t-shirt and slim jeans. When I came out, she was facing me. Her eyes sparkled with an odd combination of contented sorrow. Her features softened and she smiled wistfully. "Then that's all that matters."

"Mom. I just can't do it. I can't come home, and face those memories. Not yet."

She nodded and held up a small hand in protest. "I know," she whispered. "Trust me. If I could escape the memory, I would."

Not knowing what to say, I was relieved to hear footsteps in the hall. Flicking my eyes to the door, I saw his familiar tousled hair.

Dominic looked stunned as he skidded to a stop. "Hello," he said. My heart swelled with happiness just by looking at him. His dark eyes met mine briefly before settling on my mother.

"Mom, this is Dominic," I said smiling. "Dominic, this is my mother, Hannah."

"Nice to meet you, Mrs. Maven."

My mother inclined her head in acknowledgment. "Same here."

"Kara," Dominic began. "I just came by to explain about yesterday, but I can come back later."

"No," I said quickly. "I mean, please, stay."

My mom shot me an amused look. "Yes, in fact we were heading out for a belated birthday celebration. Would you like to join us?"

"Whose birthday?" he questioned, swinging his eyes to me. My mom strolled over and looped her arm through mine. "Kara's."

I smiled meekly, feeling awkward as he stared at me.

"I didn't know it was your birthday," Dominic said. "If I had known—"

"It's no big deal." I felt the heat spread through me as my cheeks flushed with embarrassment. I hated being the center of attention, which is why birthdays were more annoying than festive to me. "Can we just go?" I asked impatiently.

"Of course, honey," my mom said. "Just lead the way."

****

Lunch with Mom and Dominic started off smoothly. The conversation was casual and Dominic was charming as ever. He easily won over my mom, and impressed me with his impeccable manners. *Why does he keep this side of him carefully hidden*? I wondered.

My mom looked over her steaming cup of black coffee, and asked, "Would you like dessert, honey? After all, it is your day, might as well indulge yourself." She flagged down the waitress before I could even answer.

As I ordered a slice of cheesecake, I noticed Dominic looking uncomfortable. His face was tense, and his eyes distant.

Once the waitress left, I leaned over and quietly asked, "Dominic, are you okay?"

"Fine," he answered through gritted teeth. His hand flexed into a fist so tight the veins beneath his skin bulged. He acted as though it was a great effort to keep from pounding a hole in the table.

I placed my hand over his balled fingers. His skin seared like a bonfire. My impulse was to snatch my hand back, but I held tighter. "Are you sure? You feel feverish."

He flinched and suddenly stared at me with intense scarlet eyes. I startled at the sight, withdrawing my hand instantly. His jaw line set sternly, and he quickly stood from the table. He looked over at my mother.

"It was nice to meet you, Mrs. Maven," he said stiffly. "I apologize, but I must go." He turned to me. "Kara," he started to say, until his face colored with weary distraction. I watched his features pull into sharp angles before he shot me an apologetic look. "Sorry."

He turned and flew through the restaurant as though he were on a terrible mission. However, his odd behavior seemed lost on my mother. She smiled and leaned across the table, gathering my hands in hers.

"Kara, that boy is totally smitten with you."

Heat crept across my cheeks.

"Look at you." She laughed. "I think the feeling is mutual."

"He's a great guy," I said, unable to contain the grin that spread across my face.

J. M. Davis

"Are you two exclusive?" Her eyebrows lifted expectedly. "Oh, what am I saying? I saw the way he fawns over you. It's obvious how he feels about you."

I was slightly shocked by that.

"You be sure to take things slow," she warned. "A boy that oozes that sort of passion is bound to move fast."

"Mom," I groaned, pulling my hands free and pressing my face into them, trying to hide from the impending sex talk.

She frowned. "I just don't want you to get so wrapped up in him that you lose sight of who you are. I remember what young love feels like. It's strong and all-consuming."

I looked at her through my fingers. "Please, Mom don't do this. Not here."

"I just want you to be careful, Kara. Don't let your heart rule your head." She watched me, waiting for a response that I couldn't give her. I was speechless, because that's exactly what I've been doing. Allowing my heart to override all sensibility within my head, but the truth was, I had no plans on changing any of that. When it came to Dominic, all I needed to do was *feel*.

"Well, all right," she said with a nod.

We gathered our things and headed to the register. My mom began digging around her purse for her wallet when the cashier said, "You're all set. The dark-haired fellow took care of your check before he left." The woman behind at the counter grinned at us broadly.

"Oh," Mom breathed. "Well, that was unexpected."

"That's Dominic," I said with a smile.

Chapter 22

The next day, Dominic caught me by surprise as I was heading back to my dorm.

He fell into pace with me and said simply, "Hey." He looked down at his shoes as he walked.

"Hey," I mirrored, taking a long sideways glance at him, studying him before I continued. "Thank you for paying for lunch yesterday."

"You're welcome. It was the least I could do." He shoved his hands into his pockets and kicked at a rock. I watched it ping across the lawn.

"So are you going to tell me what that was all about?"

He turned. His features were ratcheted tight with apprehension, like a child being forced to apologize for something weren't sorry for. "Do I have to?"

"Yes."

His shoulders sagged a bit as he said, "I was summoned." I could feel him staring at me, but I pretended to not be affected by his words. When I didn't respond, he continued by saying, "I can't control it, you know?"

"Control what?"

"The voices. When they call, I must go."

I nodded, slowly comprehending what he was saying. Not matter what he's doing, what *we're* doing, once they summon him, he must go. I swallowed as I let that information sink in.

He stopped short, grabbing me around the waist, and pulling me into him. "Listen to what I am saying, Kara." His dark eyes clamped me into place like a vise. "When the voices of the sinners whisper, I am required to answer." He glared at me, taunting me to react to his words.

"I know," I said simply.

"And that doesn't bother you?" He searched my face for proof, not believing my words.

"I care about you, Dominic." I inclined my face to his. "And all that comes with you. The good and the bad."

"What if the bad outweighs the good?" he asked through lowered eyes.

"It doesn't." I wrapped my arms around his neck, feeling the warmth that radiated from his skin.

"You don't know what it's like to hear you say that." He pressed his forehead against mine, holding me as though he never wanted to let me go. I inhaled his spicy scent, like warm cinnamon, then felt him fumble for something in his pocket.

"I've got something for you," he said, pulling away. He took my wrist in his hand, his fingertips brushing along my scars before he draped a delicate silver chain across my skin. I leaned away from him, watching his deft fingers work at the tiny clasp. When he was through, he laced his fingers through mine.

My lips parted in admiration. A beautiful silver bracelet clung to my wrist. Two tiny charms hung lightly in the air. A lock and a key. I looked up at him, confused by the meaning.

He smiled faintly. "A lock. Because I have been

bound." He kissed my palms lovingly, making my insides melt into my toes. "And a key," he said in a hushed tone, "because you are unlocking everything I have come to know. All that has ever held me down…Kara, you're the key to freeing me."

"Oh Dominic, I love it," I gushed. The sun glimmered off it prettily. I looked up into his handsome face. Shadows ringed his eyes, intensifying his bold gaze.

"I am poison, but *you* are the antidote."

My breath caught at his touching words. *Oh my God, is this really happening?* My heart swelled and nearly leapt into my throat. *Kara Maven has tamed the hellion that is Dominic Benenati.* My eyes welled with overwhelming happiness.

"Don't ever leave me," he whispered his raspy voice raw with emotion. "A life without you would be worse than a thousand lives in hell."

"I'm not going anywhere," I assured him, pulling him close.

"Promise me," he demanded.

"I promise."

"Would you mind sealing that promise?" His dark eyes flashed.

"With what?" My mind wandered relentlessly with the prospects, imaging a blood oath, or worse.

"A kiss will do." His sweet lips quirked into a smile, before pressing them against mine. When we parted, Dominic stared into my eyes, his face alight with an excitement that could have almost been labeled as giddy. "Can I show you something?" His mood was infectious, and I couldn't help giggling at him.

"Sure." I loved this side of him. The playful and

loving side that only I got to see. He acted almost human. His lips broke out into a lopsided grin as he practically hauled me across the courtyard.

"Ow," I mewled softly, my wrist smarting from his grip.

He frowned slightly. "Oh, right. Sorry. Mortal legs mean mortal pace." He slowed for a minute, giving me a sly sideways glance. It was apparent that something was stirring in his thoughts, and I wondered what plan he was brewing.

I didn't have to worry long. Before I could react, he moved in front of me, and crouched. Cupping the back of my thighs, he threw me effortlessly over his shoulder.

Chuckling, he sprinted toward the secluded patch of forest behind the campus.

"Dominic!" I shrieked, pounding lightly on his backside. The firm backside that I wished desperately to sink my nails into…

"Put me down this instant!" I felt laughter roll through his entire body. His strong hands held fast to my legs as they dangled over his shoulder. I kicked playfully, trying to wiggle free from his hold.

One of his hands released and I wondered what he was doing, until I felt a smack against my butt cheek. The sting of it spread across me, but it wasn't unpleasant. I sucked in a deep breath as my stomach dipped with sudden desire.

Feeling bold, I bit my lip, and swatted at his rump in retaliation. I felt his body go rigid. I worried I crossed the line, until his hands slowly slid up my thighs and kneaded the delicate spot under my backside. I gasped and grew limp under his touch. After several heat-charged moments, he gently lowered my feet to the ground. His eyes were carnal and devoured me hungrily.

"You started it," I said quietly, never tearing my eyes from his.

"That I did," he said, slowly nodding. He pushed my hair from my shoulder, his eyes following his movement. I shivered as he traced a lazy finger along my collarbone. "And I shall finish it as well." His dark eyes flicked to mine.

My insides nearly exploded. *How can he make one simple sentence sound so damn hot?* My breath quickened, and my senses seemed to heighten. The aroma of heated cinnamon—his delicious aroma—filled my nostrils.

I inhaled deeply, wishing I could bathe myself in it. I could hear his shallow breaths and see the vein that ran along the delicate flesh of his neck pulsate. I licked my lips as I stared at his mouth, my body humming with anticipation.

"I wanted to show you," he said softly, "where I come to escape."

My mind jerked into awareness. *Oh, right. There's a reason we're out here.* My heart stalled momentarily, and then righted itself back into a steady beat. "Escape what?" I asked, my voice cracking.

"The voices." He pulled his eyes off mine, and took in the scenery around us. His face was placid, and the serenity of it was beautiful. Like a motionless lake. Pristine and flawless on the surface, but what lay beneath was a complete mystery.

"I thought there was no escaping the voices?" I questioned, searching his face as he stared out into the wilderness.

"There isn't. But they're harder to hear way out here."

"Really?"

"Well, not really." He strolled a few steps away from me, watching his feet as he walked. He crouched, eyeing the dusting of purple flowers before him. He plucked one from the grass. It looked delicate, fragile in his hands. I wondered if that was how I looked when he held me.

"They always beckon me, no matter where I am, or what I am doing," he continued. "But, out here, they seem so distant. Like I can forget about the voices and who I am, and just be me. Just be Dominic. Not Dominic the demon or Dominic the Damamah."

He sighed and looked wistfully over at me. His lips pulled into a smile that didn't reach his eyes. He looked sad and lost. But what could I do? I couldn't sever the ties to his demonic nature. If I could, I would have sliced through them with my teeth if I had too.

I tore my eyes from him and finally took in our surroundings. *No wonder he loves this place. It's lovely.* The clearing we were in was lined with thick oak trees. Wildflowers sprinkled the grass, marking the only hint of color among the canvas of green before us.

Overhead, the trees opened up just enough to allow patches of blue sky to peek through. The sun's soft rays filtered through the canopy of leaves. Somehow, through the dense trees, a gentle wind blew past us, keeping the heat at bay. He watched me silently as I absorbed everything.

"It's beautiful here," I said.

"Do you hear it?" He cocked his head in a way that

made me want to run my tongue along his slender neck.

Shaking the thought away, I looked at him, puzzled. "Hear what?"

"Silence. And for once, that's what it's like in my head. No voices. No thoughts of sin…nothing."

I frowned. *I have sinful thoughts whirling in my head right now…*

"I said I didn't hear thoughts of *sin*. What I want to do to you may be devilish, but it's far from sinful." He gazed at me, his mouth quirking into a lusty smirk.

My knees felt like water, but my insides erupted into flames. "Can you read my mind?"

He shook his head, saying, "No. I only hear thoughts of sin." He started to slowly close the gap of space between us, his eyes wandering leisurely down the length of me. "But I'm an expert at reading body language. And yours is calling to me loud and clear."

Heat crept across my cheeks, and my pulse quickened. He stopped in front of me, our bodies mere inches apart. Tucking the small flower behind my ear, he smiled, his fingers entwining in my hair.

His gaze ran from my neck, slowly over my chin and across my mouth before fixating on my eyes. He leaned into my face, his nostrils flared as he inhaled deeply.

"You smell so sweet; I can hardly wait to taste you."

My lips parted in surprise, and then curled into a delighted grin. His eyes, deep as the darkest point of the night sky, pinned me into place. I concentrated on breathing as he slowly dipped his head into my neck, planting light kisses along my throat. Moaning, I entangled my fingers through his hair. The trail of his breath on my skin ignited my desire even further. *I want him so badly it hurts.* He seized my hips with both hands, pulling me against him. Setting his mouth on mine, he kissed me eagerly, his hot lips branding me as his once more.

He reached up, placing a hand on each side of my face, deepening our kiss until I felt as though I could no longer breathe. Forced to part, we stood panting as we stared at one another. His fingers curled into my neck.

"Demons can possess a human's body, by force," he said, his voice hoarse and sexy. His dark eyes glimmered as he narrowed them at me. "I want you to give me yours freely."

"It's yours. It's always been yours, and it always will be yours," I whispered.

His eyes welled with happiness, before he crushed his lips against mine. His fingers looped into the top of my jeans. The warmth of his fingers prodded me to fumble with his belt, eager to shed him of his clothes.

He groaned against my mouth, sliding his fingers under the hem of my shirt, kneading my skin roughly. I gently sucked his bottom lip, savoring the taste of him before I shucked off his shirt.

I took a moment to appreciate his amazing body. His flat stomach was etched with taut muscles. The sharp angles of his abs curved down and out of sight, hidden by his denim pants. Together we worked at the buttons of my shirt. I trembled as his hands slid the fabric off my shoulders, dropping it to the ground. *Dear God, I feel as though I'm going to explode!*

I watched him, too afraid to blink for fear I'd miss something, as we sank into the grass. It was soft, so I didn't object to laying down in it. *Who am I kidding? If it were a bed of nails, I'd still gladly lie across it for him.* He unbuttoned my jeans and slid them off painfully slowly. He tossed them aside as his full mouth parted, his eyes exploring my body with a hunger that made me swell with pride. I had never been looked at like that.

As if I was the reason he existed, the reason he lived and breathed. His fingers danced along my arm, down to my wrist and across my stomach. I watched his hands as he ran them over my breasts. Those long fingers, perfect for piano playing, tickled across my skin and left my body singing for more. He inched closer; our bodies were so close I could feel his rapid heartbeat against my chest.

His hand found my backside, the gentle strokes practically had me purring as he finally covered my body, pressing my back into the earth. I don't remember him removing the rest of his clothes or mine, but I do remember the growl against my ear, like a jungle cat claiming his mate, as we merged into one being. Pain sliced through me as my body was forced to accommodate him. I cried out against Dominic's ear, and dug my nails deep into the tight muscles of his back.

He pulled back and touched his forehead to mine, his hot breath ghosting across my face when he asked, "Do you want to stop?"

I shook my head.

"I don't want to hurt you." He placed a tender kiss to the tip of my nose.

"I have never wanted anything so much, Dominic," I said. "I'll be fine, please, just don't stop."

"Unfortunately, *anima bella*, pain and love usually

go hand in hand," he murmured, just before sinking deeper into me. I bit my lip to keep from whimpering, and soon the agonizing pain gave away to a gentle ecstasy that had me soaring. From that moment forward, I truly belonged to Dominic. My mind, body, and soul were his to possess. Forever.

****

As we lay in the grass, Dominic traced lazy circles on my shoulder, my head on his chest, listening to his heartbeat. We watched the clouds for a while, both silently basking in the afterglow. The ache between my legs was a constant reminder of Dominic. Our lovemaking was what I considered the most phenomenal clashing of bodies, mortal, immortal, cosmic, or earthly. Dominic claimed me, and I claimed him. His touch might as well have been tattooed across my soul because he was that permanent, that eternal.

I lifted my face, our gaze meeting instantly. His usual pale skin was flushed, his skin still sticky and glistening with perspiration. His scent was stronger, spicier, and heady.

"Isn't it funny, how people fall in love? I asked. "How they can be miles, states, even countries apart, and yet still they find their way to each other."

His fingers continued to move across my skin, stroking my arm and elbow. "Do you know how I found you?" he questioned, his voice low and silky smooth.

Intrigued, I shook my head modestly, my heart pounding as I waited for his answer.

He brought his hand to my face and caressed my cheek lovingly before gently pinching my chin. "Your soul called to me."

"My soul?"

"That's why I call you *anima bella*," he said tracing a finger down my cheek. I smiled at the memory of when he first called me by that name. How tender the moment felt, and how special he made me feel.

"Souls and hearts either radiate darkness or they radiate light," he continued. "Those with blackened souls will always choose to sin, without or without the help of a Damamah."

"Do Damamahs have souls?"

"No." His eyes swept past me, becoming distant and troubled. "Unless they are half breeds."

"Half mortal, half demon," I offered.

He nodded, then swallowed, the muscles in his jaw flexing as he waited for my next question.

"So which soul do you have?

His eyes closed as if my words were painful. "It's dark," he whispered finally.

My heart and stomach sank in unison.

"But," he continued, his gaze shifting back to me, "when I met you, I felt it spark, as though it was brought into the light." His eyes flickered with a lightness that only enhanced his beautiful features. "My soul connected to yours, like a long lost puzzle piece. Your soul cast a light on my blackened soul."

His words filled my heart with happiness and a love that I had never felt before. It was intense, overwhelming, and profound. I stretched my neck, touching my lips to his. A low rumble vibrated the back of his throat. I could feel his heart quicken beneath my fingertips. Slowly, our kiss heated, reigniting my need for more. I tenderly encouraged his lips to part. His tongue flicked against mine. The sweet taste of his lips slowly morphed into a spicy aphrodisiac. I needed more. I needed *him*.

I sat up, shifting so I could see him entirely. I marveled at the perfection of his naked chest. He gave me a lopsided grin, as he guided me over him. Taut muscles rippled in his arms as he set me across his hips, my legs straddling him.

I settled into the warm apex of his body and felt his fingers tickle across my thighs. I bent, my bare chest grazing his as I kissed his full lips, smothering his soft moans.

Closing my eyes, I dissolved into my body's throbbing need. His touch became hot, searing me like branding iron, marking me as his. I sat back, rocking deep, eliciting a sigh from Dominic as his eyelids fluttered closed.

I stared as his long lashes, smiling, waiting for him to open them again. When he did, I held firm to them as he devoured me with those dark, keen eyes. They were like a black hole, sucking me into an unknown oblivion.

Pulling me into him, he whispered, "I love you," against my lips. Our connected bodies forged a bond that would never be broken, a love that was built on the foundation of our darkest moments, and our deepest fears.

Our two souls, once broken and crushed, were not shattered. Instead, they hardened, like precious diamonds. Unbreakable and beautiful.

Chapter 23

Dominic and I became inseparable over the following weeks. He'd walk me to class, which earned me quite a lot of stares. Girls would take me in, their faces colored with jealousy. They probably wondered what I had that they didn't. In fact, I often asked myself the same question. He'd open doors like a gentleman and even shared snippets of his past with me. During one evening stroll, I learned he was an only child, like me. His mother died during childbirth and his father never married. I felt even more connected to him after that. On the way back to my dorm one afternoon, he reluctantly explained his role as a Damamah.

"It's my job to ensure that hell stays full," he said matter-of-factly.

Full of occupants, I thought darkly. "Are there more like you? More Damamahs?" I asked.

"Many. We're everywhere humans are."

"How do you decide…" I gnawed at my lip, pondering how to form the right words. "Which person does what sin?" I said finally.

"I don't. It's not like I randomly choose people and then force them to commit a sin. Everyone is tempted with evil. If a soul is weak, then my influence will provide the necessary courage to go through with it, to seal their sin as we call it."

"So, you're the little devil on people's shoulders?"

I asked in amazement.

I thought about the disturbing image at the library. Tranquil angels mingling with winged demons. Their bared mouths and glaring eyes haunted my dreams, but yet looking at Dominic with his crooked smile, it was hard to imagine him as something so vile.

"I despise that old wives tale," he said. "Can you really see me in red spandex, carrying a pitchfork?" He flung his arms out, his eyebrows lifting in question. I inspected him. He looked amazing in his dark denim jeans and cool vintage t-shirt.

"Well, actually…" I let my voice trail off alluringly, a smoldering smirk pulling at my lips.

He let out a hearty laugh, tossing one arm over my shoulder.

"So how is the sin chosen?" I questioned, still intrigued by our conversation.

"It's whatever the person has in their thoughts," he explained. "I can't put ideas in your head. I can't persuade you to do something that is completely out of the realm of your desires."

I pursed my lips together thoughtfully. I recalled teetering on the narrow ledge of the frat house. The voice in my head that subtly urged me to jump. Knocking the memory from my mind, I scolded myself for rehashing that dreadful night.

"Take Cassie for instance," he said, sweeping his dark eyes to mine.

I felt my face slack at the mention of her name.

"Relax; I can't persuade Cassie to do anything. Her head is full of rainbows, gyrating boy bands, and fluffy unicorns."

My hand flew to my mouth, muffling my giggles.

"The most outrageous thing I could convince her to do is flash truckers on the highway." He gave me a quick peck on the cheek. "And that's hardly a sin," he added.

We found ourselves at the door of my dorm room. I pressed my back against it, frowning pathetically, hoping he'd agree to stay a little longer.

"I guess...I'll see you tomorrow," I said slowly, obviously stalling.

He raked his fingers through his black hair, looking at me through hooded eyes. "If not before," he murmured. "I hope to star in your dreams tonight."

I smiled. "You always do."

He took my hand, lightly kissing my palm, then pressed his lips against my scars, lingering there as though his lips could heal. He continued to trail airy kisses up my forearm, even planting a few on the crook of my elbow. I never knew the skin there was so sensitive. My hungry loins became instantly ravenous. He lifted his head, leaning in close to my face; I could feel his hot breath against my cheek. I inhaled his spicy scent and like an addict, I needed more.

My veins pulsated, practically singing for him. He pinched my chin tenderly with his thumb, tilting my face to his, then took his time trailing his mouth across my cheek, until finally he crushed his wet lips against mine.

A fever slowly spread through my veins. The flow of ecstasy. I grew limp in his arms as his hands slipped up the hem of my shirt. His fingertips skimmed across my skin, spiking me to the very core. I squirmed from the mounting need within me and deepened our kiss. All too soon, he pulled away.

He pressed his forehead to mine, and closed his eyes, panting heavily. When he finally opened them, he peered at me through a thick fringe of dark lashes. *Damn those eyes, and matter how strange they are, they're absolutely beautiful to me.*

"God, I wish I could crawl inside of you," he whispered, sliding his fingers through my hair and lacing them behind my neck.

I smiled and found myself wishing for the same thing. At one time, I would have thought that to be bizarre and slightly creepy. Now I wanted nothing more than to share the same heartbeat with Dominic.

"Even this close, you're too far." His voice was low and raspy with desire. He reached for my hands, bringing them to his lips. "Until tomorrow, my love."

"Tomorrow can't come soon enough."

He kissed my knuckles tenderly before turning swiftly and disappearing down the empty hall.

****

And as it turned out, tomorrow came all too quickly and with a vengeance. It was twilight and I was wandering the back lot of the library parking area. I stayed late studying and sleepily searched for my vehicle. Finally spotting it along the last row, I sighed with relief. *Thank God.*

It sat between a moped and a peculiar looking vehicle. The closer I got, the odder the car became. It was blood red and hovered just inches above the pavement. Its scooped hood and flared headlights gave the car an angry appearance. The chrome grill seemed to grimace eerily at me as I scurried around it.

Just as I reached for my keys, the car door popped open. I jumped at the sound, dropping my bag on the ground, spilling my books across the asphalt.

Against my better judgment, I dropped to my knees and began shoving my belongings back into my bag. The car door slammed, and with it, my body went into panic mode. My pulse quickened and the hairs on the back of my neck stood erect. The smell of charred copper wafted through the air. I quickened my pace, frantically shoving the last of the books into the bag.

The ominous sound of crunching gravel froze me into place. Uneasiness marched up my spine like an army of hostile ants. The footsteps stopped. I stared down at my trembling hands, too afraid to lift my eyes.

"Miss Maven," the bass-soaked voice rumbled.

Shocked to hear my name, I looked up with a jerk. A man with a chilling sneer loomed above me. His skin, a sickly gray, looked unnatural and tightly drawn over his bones. He wore expensive tweed pants and polished wing-tipped shoes. His eyes were entirely pitch black. Like tiny eight balls, they rolled over me leisurely.

"So this is who he defied me for." He spoke mainly to himself.

My mind flew into a frenzy, spinning at a dizzying rate. I flattened my palms across the pavement, trying to steady my tilting vision.

"A pitiful creature. Though beautiful, you are so...helpless." His mouth slowly manifested into a terrifying grin. His teeth were like a deadly row of sharpened razors. The dull security lights sparked off them, causing me to flinch.

"Who are you?" The words somehow escaped my dry lips.

"Like you haven't already guessed," he admonished sternly.

I shifted from my knees to my feet, attempting to stand, but a strong force pressed against my shoulders. I struggled against it feebly, gasping at the weight of it.

"Stay as you are," he commanded. "I merely wanted to see the girl responsible for defiling my son, and the appalling debasement of my family's principles." Like a hungry shark, he circled me. "I sent those demons as a warning to you, Miss Maven," he said, drawing out the "miss," reminding me of a snake hissing in the grass. "You'd be foolish not to heed it."

Demons? What demons? My breath hitched as I recalled the night after Cayden, Cassie, and I went to the bar. *Those weren't bats after all...*"Dominic will have to cast me away, before I ever leave his side," I said, my voice not as demanding as I hoped.

His eyes narrowed, and his lip trembled in sinister sneer. "If your fragile existence means anything to you, you'll stay away from Dominic."

And with that, the crushing pressure lifted. I was able to stagger upright, as he turned on his heel and strolled back to the strange car. Before sinking into it, he regarded me once more with those his alarming black eyes and said, "Oh, and should anyone ask, tell them Vasuth Serrule spared your feeble life today."

I watched in horror as the lengthy antique car slithered away, leaving a cloud of dust in its wake. I threw myself into my car and slapped the locks shut.

I sat there quaking like a frightened rabbit that had just outrun a fox. My heart beat frantically and my thoughts whirled like a poor shack in a tornado.

, I envisioned myself zooming down the interstate, back to the sanctuary I called home. Mom would make me some chicken noodle soup and everything would be fine. *But everything won't be fine,* I thought. I had to tell Dominic about his terrifying father and his unexpected visit. With a shaky hand, I dialed Dominic's phone number. He answered on the first ring.

"Kara? What's happened?"

Vasuth left me rattled. Even normal functions were a struggle as my throat felt constricted, making it hard to breathe. "Your father," I wheezed through quick and shallow intakes of air. The line went dead, and within minutes, someone knocked on my window.

"Oh shit!" I hollered, panic spiking through my veins.

"It's just me," Dominic said, staring at me as though I was a terrible accident. The kind that you don't want to see, but it's nearly impossible to look away.

I unlocked the door, and with it, a flood of tears ran down my face.

"How'd you get here so fast?"

"Demon speed," he said, opening the door. "Demon, remember?" He gestured to himself, his brows lifting from his dark eyes.

"How could I forget," I said drily.

He slid in the passenger's seat and scooped me into his lap. "I'm so sorry, Kara."

"Why would he want to hurt me?" I sobbed.

"What did he say?"

I recounted the visit and shivered as the image of his black eyes rolling over me with repulsion lingered in my memory.

Dominic pursed his lips tightly.

"And he sent demons, as a warning…" I continued.

"Demons? You never told me—"

"I thought they were bats," I said waving him off. I recalled their shrill screams and their bony bodies. Their dull skin reminded me of dried blood on an old towel. Dark, and almost crispy. My scalp prickled, remembering the jolt of pain like sizzling forks being pressed into my skull as they yanked at my hair.

"Bats?" Dominic's brows pulled together in thought. His eyes darted around, and then settled on me. "Hellions," he breathed. "They are meager creatures; they have no great strength."

"Oh?" My eyebrows shot up. "Well, they scared the hell out of me." I slid out of his lap, falling back into the driver's seat.

"I didn't mean to imply that you shouldn't have been scared. That's exactly what my father was aiming for. I just wish I had known about it." He scowled.

Crossing my arms over my chest, I frowned back at him. "I thought they were bats!" The memory resurfaced. I thought about Cayden, and how he insisted that they were just bats. His words, *I was here, remember? I saw what you saw,* played in my head. I thought they were some sort of mutant killer bats, and I was partially right. When I thanked him before he quickly left, little did I know that he actually did, protect me from monsters that night...

"Kara, what is it?" Dominic asked, interrupting me from my dark thoughts.

"Cayden was there too."

Dominic's eyes blazed as he clenched his jaw tight. "Cayden?" he spat through gritted teeth.

"Cassie drank too much that night, so he carried her in for me. I went to put her boots in the closet and out swarmed these flying bird-like things. They were hideous." I shuddered at the memory of their beady, yet cruel eyes and the instinct within them to torture me. "Cayden told me that they were bats. And the more I thought about it, the more he had to be right. At the time, I thought monsters didn't exist." I caught his eyes; the fire within them extinguished and was replaced with sadness. His face was placid, as he remained quiet for a long time.

"I have to talk to my father," he said finally. "Explain why I showed mercy."

"Why you showed mercy?"

"I didn't allow you to seal your sin that night on the ledge. Instead of allowing you to jump, I intervened. And then again in the field. I even healed you. Interfering with a decision to sin is strictly forbidden," he explained.

My wide eyes regarded him a sickening realization. *I'm in love with a demon.* Though I had known it all along, nothing else had penetrated me to the point of absolute clarity until now. My heart felt heavy, like it had been filled with lead weights. My throat felt as though I were drowning, inhaling gulps of water instead of air.

"I must speak to him, explain everything." He brushed his warm lips against mine and climbed out of the car.

"I want to go with you," I blurted, the words tumbling out before I knew what I was saying.

Dominic leaned down, his black brows knitted tightly. "Absolutely not." His mouth was set in a frown.

I clambered out of the car and stared at Dominic from across the roof.

"Dominic, I demand that you take me," I said,

stamping my foot into the pavement.

"Did you just stomp your foot at me?" he asked, almost laughing.

His smile nearly distracted me, but I ignored it. "If I'm going to be the topic of conversation, than I think I have a right to be there."

"Kara, where do you think my father lives?" he asked pointedly, arching a severe eyebrow.

"It doesn't matter. I'm going with you."

"You're unbearable," he sighed.

A ghost of a smile hinted at my lips at the echo of my own words.

Dominic took off toward the small forest that lined the school campus. I ran to keep up, my lungs burning as I pressed harder until I couldn't go another step.

"Dominic," I breathed, my limbs were on the verge of collapse. "I can't go any further."

He stopped short. Worry creased his forehead as he took me in. Not even a bit winded, he quickly came to my side. "I'm sorry. I forgot how slow mortals can be."

I arched an irritated brow at him and leaned into my knees, struggling to control my haggard breathing. "Excuse me for being human."

His lips inched upward in amusement. "Can you continue if we walk? I'd like to be as far away from campus as possible."

"Why?" I asked in confusion. "What exactly are we doing out here?" My insides churned as I waited for his answer.

He gave me a pointed look with eyes as hard as obsidian. "I need to summon hell's doors." His tone took on a darkness that made me shiver.

It was my bright idea to tag along, so now I have to

suck it up, I thought bitterly. I nodded, catching my bottom lip with my teeth.

"Are you frightened?" he asked.

"A little," I admitted, wringing my hands nervously.

His brows pinched together as he frowned at me. He ran his warm fingers down my cheek tenderly. "I'd never let anything happen to you." His voice was comforting, and somehow I knew he meant it. He threaded his fingers through mine, and led me further into the dense woods. The moon winked above us, casting a silvery sheen on the trees. We walked in silence, each lost in thought until finally, he stopped.

Almost completely shrouded by darkness, he crouched to the ground. I watched, slack jawed, as he reached into his denim vest and withdrew a small dagger. *Does he always carry that around?*

The polished blade was slightly curved, and etched with scalloped carvings. The handle was fashioned into a flared serpent's head. A single ruby fused into its eye socket. Gripping it solidly, Dominic fisted the dagger and drew it down.

Chapter 24

He rammed the knife straight into the soft dirt, slicing the blade through the thick layer of grass, notching out a large square. When he was through, he sank to his knees. With his palm open to the moon, he drew the sharp edge of the knife across it. Like tiny teeth, the serrated blade ripped open a small gash. I gasped, covering my mouth with trembling fingers. The pooling dark blood contrasted eerily against his pasty skin. Slowly, it crept down the creases of his hand until tiny garnet beads beat lightly onto the damp grass.

"With thy blood, grant to thee, access to the Underworld passages."

Suddenly the earth began to shake violently. My arms flailed as I struggled to stay upright. The ground moaned as it heaved outward of the hacked square. A small metal building lifted from the ground. Clumps of grass and soil rained down as it rose higher and higher.

Dominic remained motionless, with his head lowered until the anguished cries of ripping roots were over. I gaped at the tower before me as Dominic climbed stoically to his feet. With a look of approval, he sank the dagger back inside his vest and turned to face me.

"Is that an elevator?" I said, my voice resonating off the rusty metal. The smell of dirt and cold steel filled my nose as I stared blankly at the contraption.

Dominic gave me an impish grin. "We've had it since its invention. There used to be just stairs," he said as he jabbed his pale finger at the button.

The doors groaned, as if in pain, as the heavy rod-iron gate lifted. *An elevator to hell? What next? An escalator to Heaven?*

Dominic stepped inside and watched me expectantly. My feet felt like cinder blocks as I moved toward him. I crooked my neck to inspect the ancient looking machine, from top to bottom. Aged vines coiled and snarled around it like snakes. Coppery patches of rust ate away at the chewed metal.

I stepped inside. It was cold inside the elevator. I shivered as I examined the panel of buttons. There were four levels.

"No emergency phone?" I mused darkly.

"Babe, where we're going, *no* one can save you." His lips quirked into a sinister smile as he poked the first button on the panel.

Like steel jaws, the iron gate lowered menacingly over us, and slammed closed with a final clank, entrapping us within the belly of the hell's elevator. We began to sink into the earth, the metal moaning, and twisting as it plunged deeper. Dirt sprinkled though the slats of metal, dusting me with a fine brown powder. Dominic looked unscathed. He still looked cool in his denim vest and the white shirt beneath it, was just as pristine as ever.

Kara, listen to me," he said, his tone unabashed with a chilling seriousness. "Stay close. And do not say anything while we're down here. The inhibitors of the Underworld are cunning, and they will coerce you into saying something that is binding according to Underworld Laws. Dealings with darkness *always* come with a price. Remember that." I chewed my lip as I let that information sink in.

The elevator finally came to an abrupt stop. I tottered ungracefully. Dominic reached out, steadying me by grabbing my elbow. His eyes were keenly alert and faintly glowing a deep crimson. The metal gate lurched and rose slowly. Dominic stepped out and reached his hand back for mine. I shook the dust from my hair and wrapped my fingers tightly around his. The warmth comforted me slightly, until I looked around.

The walls, as expected, were layers of blackened earth. Roots twisted everywhere, like creepy tentacles. Dominic reached into his pocket and pulled out a single match. He struck it on the rusty steel, igniting it in a small bundle of flames. Although small, the light emitted a powerful glow, allowing me to see the endless corridors that branched outward. I followed Dominic through the darkness, squinting through the rolling heat that licked at my face.

The narrow hall finally opened up into grand stateroom. It was deeply shadowed and smelled dank from years of decay. Ancient lanterns hung from the low ceiling and black mold dripped like spilled blood down the corners of the room. The match slowly died between Dominic's fingers. My eyes darted wildly as they tried to adjust to the darkness. Dominic squeezed my hand reassuringly.

"It's all right," he said. "I'm right here."

Suddenly, one by one, the lanterns caught fire with a deafening boom. I hollered in fright, nearly climbing into Dominic's arms.

"It's okay. I'm right here," he said, rubbing calming circles between my shoulder blades.

I took a hesitant look around. Bolted securely to the wall were several steel cages. They were slick with mildew and worn with age. Bile burned at the back of my throat when I saw it. A gaunt figure lay crumbled on the floor of one of the cage. It heard us and crawled to the far corner of the cage, cowering pitifully against the metal bars. Sickly yellow skin stretched thinly across its jutting bones.

"What is that?" My voice barely came out as a whisper.

"A tortured Soul. It's enduring its punishment."

"For what?"

"Disobeying orders."

"Whose?"

"Dark officers. There are many ranks within the Underworld, Kara." His eyes were grave as he said, "There is far more to this world than you can possibly imagine."

Before I could question further, the Soul turned its head, startling me silent. It had no eyes, just hollow crevices where they should have been. Dried blood lined its face like old tears. Lips, parched white with hunger, suddenly gaped open and let out a horrific cry. I covered my ears, wishing I never insisted on coming here.

"Quiet!" Dominic yelled with authority. "I am not here to deliver cruelty. Drawing attention to yourself will only cause you further misery. I suggest you take your punishment in silence."

The Soul slowly closed its mouth, smothering the shrill scream. I gripped my racing heart, desperate to flee from this horrible place.

My eyes skimmed the room further. Exquisite tapestries that nearly reached the dirt floors draped the walls. They reflected skewed scenes from the Bible. Eve making love to a giant serpent. Noah's ark, filled with dead animals, floated upon a blood-red sea. The city of Sodom was no longer portrayed as vile. Here, it was lavishly etched into a glorious kingdom. I shuddered as we marched past the disturbing images.

"I see you're admiring the tapestries," boomed a foul voice. I noticed Vasuth striding through the poorly lit corridor to my right. I clung to Dominic, dread seeping into my veins. As he approached, his teeth shined brightly beneath the glare of the lanterns. "Each one has been hand-sewn from the intestines of the weak."

My stomach hurled in a violent wrench, nearly dispensing my lunch onto my feet. I gagged, as Dominic stroked my back, his eyes fixed on his father.

"Was that necessary?" he questioned, his voice tight with anger.

Vasuth's nose and eyes flared at once. "Same can be asked of you, *son*. Is it *necessary* that you bring this *girl* here? What do you wish to accomplish by bringing a mortal to the Underworld?

"I wish to explain why I showed mercy."

"Your explanation is futile," he barked. "But may prove to be entertaining." Vasuth crossed his arms and motioned flippantly toward Dominic. "Proceed."

"It's very simple, Father," Dominic began. "I love her." His voice was like stone. His declaration sent my mind reeling; though I had heard it before, hearing him announce it to his father seemed permanent. Seemed real.

"Don't be a fool," Vasuth hissed. "You're not capable of such a thing. Demons only feel lust. You're confusing the two emotions."

They only feel lust? Then, what about Dominic's mother? Did Vasuth not love her? I wondered.

"Do the girl a favor and free her," Vasuth said, suddenly looking mildly amused as his eyes leisurely drifted over me. "Of course, you could have your fun, like you always do, until you grow tired of her company." His gaze fastened to mine like a hungry leech. "Heed my warning; he will grow tired of you."

My throat felt like it was seizing. The temperature seemed to be rising to unbearable degrees. Perspiration trickled down my back, though Vasuth and Dominic appeared to be more than comfortable.

"That's enough," Dominic snarled. "I know my feelings, Father, and they are strong for her."

The humor vanished from Vasuth's face. "You know there are consequences for interfering with a sinner's destiny, Dominic. The only reason you're not imprisoned next to that pathetic Soul over there, is because you're my son. If you care about the girl as much as you say you do, you'll stay away from her. Our world is not for the weak, and this *mortal,* is just that. *Weak.* You'll break her sanity and her heart."

His ominous eyes glared at Dominic. His lips twitched, hinting at a snarl before speaking again. "Forget about *love.* It's a useless emotion that preys upon the vulnerability of humanity. Now take her away." He dismissed us with a flick of his hand. "And don't bring a mortal back in the Underworld unless they plan on staying," he added.

Dominic flinched, but remained silent. Vasuth watched impassively as we solemnly climbed back inside the elevator. The gate like an iron trap lowered and encased us within its steel gut. The earth around us grumbled, like a tired old man waking from a nap.

Layers of dirt flaked off like sheets of cake, landing heavily at our feet. The elevator emerged with a final upheaval and anchored itself into the thick roots of surrounding trees.

The gate, strangled with twisting vines, released us from its prison, spilling us back out into the black forest. We watched the elevator sink back into the earth. The jagged layer of grass wove back together seamlessly, putting the ground back to the way it was. I looked over at Dominic timidly; he had been stone silent for the entire ride back.

"Dominic, say something, please."

His eyes latched onto mine. His features collapsed into a pitiful look of pure torture. "Kara, we can't be together."

It was as though someone smashed my knees with a hammer. I nearly crumpled where I stood. "Why can't we? We love each other. Dominic, why does anything need to change?"

"My father is right. I'm from a world you know nothing about, a dangerous world that you have no business being a part of. You'll only get hurt."

"I'm strong enough to try," I whispered.

He drew his lips into a hard line. His silence was unsettling. I fidgeted where I stood, my ribs compressing my heart in a wrenching grip.

"Demons do not possess free will," he said finally. "I will always be a Damamah. A whisperer. Could you live with that? Knowing that I lure people into committing sins, could you continue to lie with me? Knowing that I whisper words of encouragement into the ears of thieves? Rapists? Murderers?" His black eyes searched mine, his handsome features twisted in torment. "No, you couldn't. And I won't ask you to try."

I just stood there, stunned silent at his words. I loved him wholly but would my conscience eventually overrule my heart?

"Then..." I paused; my mind was a frantic mess of disparity. "Turn me into a demon."

His dark eyes widened. He appeared physically sickened by the thought. He stared at the ground, his jaw clenched, accentuating the sculpted planes of his face.

"Kara, you don't know what you're asking for," he spat through gritted teeth. His fists balled tightly at his sides. When he finally looked up at me, his eyes had changed. The red speckles had absorbed into a pool of black, causing them to look like hard obsidian.

"Yes, I do," I said stubbornly. Of course, I really didn't. How does one become a demon? Is it even possible? Does a demon bite you, and drain you of humanity, like a vampire sucks blood? Does Satan him transform you through some elaborate ritual? I had no idea, but for Dominic, I was willing to find out.

He gave me an icy glare. "Why would you want to be like me? I'm poison."

"But I am the antidote, remember?" I said through welling tears, throwing his intimate words back at him.

He flinched, his eyes tightening as though he'd been hit in the stomach. "Demons don't do anything but devour souls."

"I don't care. I don't care about anything, except being with you. Even if that means turning me."

"You'd give up your free will?" he demanded, his eyes boring into me angrily.

"I have no free will when it comes to you. Every part of me belongs to you, don't you see that?" I reached out for him. He backed away, as though I were diseased.

"Demons are born, not created," he growled.

I felt deflated. There was nothing left to offer. It was over. I couldn't become a demon, and he wasn't capable of pretending that that side of him didn't exist. His partial humanity wasn't enough to cancel out the darkness.

"I love you, Kara. So I have to protect you. Even if it's from me..." He looked sorrowful and my heart nearly disintegrated within my chest.

"No, Dominic. Don't do this." My voice grew shrill and frantic. "I won't live without you," I whispered, "I can't."

"You have before," he said as he turned away, "and in time, you will again."

And just like that, he faded into the darkness. I sank to the cold ground, wailing into the bleak emptiness that surrounded me.

Chapter 25

I don't know how much time passed, and I didn't care. The moment Dominic walked out of my life, time seemed to just, stop. I sat there, alone, within the dark recesses of the forest. My chest felt ripped apart, the raw edges tingling with jarring agony. My vision blurred from countless tears, but I looked wistfully in what I guessed was the direction of Dominic's house. I wanted desperately to tear through the trees and fling myself at his door, but I didn't have the nerve or the energy.

The night air grew damp around me, and droplets of dew collected like sparkly gems on the leaves. Overhead, the crescent moon emitted of a pastel glow, barely lighting the sky. I finally dragged myself upright, dusting the dirt from my knees.

I had to get myself back to campus. I forced my feet to move, but I felt as though I was standing on a shoreline, with the continuous waves ripping away the sand beneath my feet.

Holding my head, I waited for the vertigo to pass before I started my trek out of the woods. As I walked, I hugged myself, recalling my last moments with Dominic. Tears streamed down my face, as I struggled with suddenness of it all. Life as I knew it was over.

Everything that mattered to me was gone. I had nothing to live for now. On trembling legs, I tried to concentrate on my direction. I had to find my way through the thick trees. I ambled my way through the underbrush, retracing our steps with a hazy mind until finally I reached the edge of the forest.

The lights of the campus shone like beacons, but they still seemed so far away. I simply could not go on. My legs gave out beneath me, scattering me across the grass. Groaning, I reached into my pocket and pulled out my phone, and punched in Cassie's number, pursing my lips as I waited for it to ring. It went to voice mail. I snapped the phone shut, cursing silently as I started toward the direction of campus.

Suddenly the phone rang loudly, echoing off the tall pine trees. I jumped and fumbled to open it, nervous that the noise would draw attention to me. *What do you think is out here? A lunatic wielding a bloody ax?* Actually, with what I learned from Dominic, my world wasn't as simple as I thought it was, and that terrified me. With shaky hands, I snatched the silver phone open.

"Hello?" I half-whispered, half-shrieked.

"Kara? What's wrong?" Cassie asked, her voice full of concern.

"Can you come get me?" My eyes ached. I squinted them shut and massaged my sockets, ignoring the dirt that stained my fingers and palm.

"Where are you? What happened?" Her tone was shrill. I heard racket in the background, so I figured she was getting dressed.

"I'll tell you when you get here. I'm in the back lot, behind the library."

"Don't move. I'm on my way." Cassie hung up, leaving me alone with my thoughts and the eerie silence around me. I rushed across the field, to the empty parking lot. The pavement was glossy with moisture, brilliant security lights reflecting off shallow puddles. A few minutes later, I noticed headlights swing onto the road. *Thank God.* Cassie's car slowed to a stop beside me. I yanked open the door, and scrambled inside.

"Thanks, Cassie."

"Geez, Kara, you look like hell. What happened?"

"Dominic," I started with a trembling voice. Tears erupted viciously, streaming down my cheeks and onto my lap.

"Oh Kara," she murmured apologetically. "I'm so sorry." She rifled through the glove box and handed me a napkin. I pressed it under my nose, trying to gain control over the hot flood of tears. The car suddenly accelerated, turning sharply and heading back toward the dorms. Cassie didn't speak the entire way. She let me weep in peace, only offering a meaningful pat on the shoulder from time to time.

I was thankful to slink into the shower that night. I turned the dials and let warm water spill over me as I sank into the tub. Hugging myself, I let the sound of water mask my tortured sobs. I stayed that way until the water finally cooled, evicting me from my seclusion.

I dressed quickly and ducked under my fluffy comforter. Cassie gave me a knowing nod and remained quiet as I curled up into a tight ball. I closed my tired eyes and prayed for a dreamless sleep.

****

The next day went by in a blur. I don't remember anything that happened, or if I even made it to class. I just remember when I finally dozed off that evening the image of Dominic filled my dreams. His pale skin was a deep crimson. Two horns protruded from his forehead, curling menacingly into sharpened points. I laid beneath him, completely enthralled and stark naked, my skin slashed into ribbons. Bright red blood dripped from his black fingernails. I screamed into my sweat-soaked pillow, thrashing wildly in my sheets. Two arms circled me, attempting to hold me steady. My eyes flew open, my breathe hiccupping loudly as I searched the blue eyes before me.

"Kara. It's okay," assured Cassie, shushing me gently and stroking my hair lovingly. "It's okay." I folded into her, allowing her to comfort me. "Dominic is crippling you. You need closure, honey, so you can start to move on."

"Maybe I don't want to *move* on," I shot.

"I know," she started carefully. "But…maybe it's for the best." I stiffened and drew upright to glare at her. She held up her hands in surrender, and said, "Just hear me out." I scowled at her, but she continued anyway. "The way he'd looked at you…it was like….he *owned* you. His love may have been too intense for you, Kara."

I scowled at her.

She sighed. "I planned on going to a study group tonight." She regarded me with narrowed eyes. "But, I think I might cancel." Cassie was like a Labrador retriever, undeniably loyal. But I couldn't let her ditch studying for me. Besides, I wanted to deal with my heartache alone. Like I had always done.

I held up my hand in protest. "No, don't do that. I'm fine."

"You don't *look* fine," she rebutted.

"I'll be okay," I urged. "Really. Go. I'm just going

to back to sleep anyway. No need for you to stay for that."

"You sure?" She arched an eyebrow at me doubtfully.

"Yes," I said, sinking back into my pillow, just for good measure.

"Okay. I'll probably be back late. We're cramming for midterms." She gave me another thorough once-over before standing and gathering her books. "Get some rest, Kara. Each day is bound to get easier."

I forced a slight smile and waved goodbye. As soon as the door clicked shut, tears pricked at my eyelids, but I was too exhausted to cry. Alone with the silence, I realized that Cassie was right. I needed closure. And whether Dominic liked it or not, I was going to get it. *Tonight*. With my newfound determination, I jumped out of bed, dressed quickly, and scooted out the door.

****

My eyes stung and my head throbbed but I finally reached the frat house. As I drew closer, I noticed a few brothers mingling around the front yard. One boy noticed me, and moved closer. He nonchalantly looked over his shoulder several times at the others.

They had flipped on some music and started a game of corn-hole, ignoring his slow progression toward me. His hair was dark and his eyes, even from a distance, stared at me with startling force. *Dominic*?

My heart nearly leapt into my throat. I picked up speed, eager to wrap my arms around him. Then, I recognized him. The drunken boy from the frat party. Panic seared through me like a lance. My eyes darted to the group of guys. They were whooping and hollering like monkeys, far too engrossed in their game to notice anything else.

"Hey there, sweetie," the boy said casually. "Looks like me and you have some unfinished business." He lumbered toward me, his mouth set in a fierce grimace, and his brows pulled angrily over his gray eyes.

I backed away clumsily, my limbs filling with wet sand.

"Come to Daddy…"

I turned to run, slipping on a wet patch of dirt. Heaving myself forward, I somehow recovered my posture and pumped my legs as fast as they would go.

"Get back here, you little bitch," he shouted as he burst into wild pursuit. He caught up to me within seconds, clamping his hand like a wrench over my shoulder. With brute and bitter force, he hurled me to the ground.

I landed hard on the unforgiving earth, my head cracking against the packed dirt. I wanted to check myself for wounds, but my reflexes automatically guarded the rest of my body.

He stood over me, snickering arrogantly. "Where's your prick boyfriend now?" He looked around dramatically, his collared shirt damp with perspiration. "Doesn't look like he's here. He won't mind if I take a hit. Us frat brothers share everything, even little whores like you."

"He'll kill you," I said firmly.

He snorted as he fumbled with the buttons on his cargo pants.

A voice drifted through the trees. "He won't have to." Cayden materialized out the shadows, his features hard and his mouth pulled into a grim line. "I'll do it for him," he snarled.

"Cayden!" I let out a heavy sigh, my shoulders sagging with relief.

"Oh really? Mr. Goody Two Shoes knows how to fight?" the boy questioned with a condescending tone.

"Fight?" Cayden chuckled. "No, I don't fight." He balled his fists at his sides. "I battle." Then he struck the nearest tree, the bark exploding where he hit.

I flinched, staring at the hole in the tree trunk. Cayden's blue eyes flashed with frightening finality.

The boy paled. "Look, man, I don't want any trouble." His hands surrendered in the air, crudely leaving his pants unzipped. I averted my eyes, thankful Cayden had come when he did. I swallowed, shuddering as I thought about what might have happened, if he hadn't.

"There won't be any," Cayden continued, his eyes holding firm to the boy. "As long as you keep your filthy hands off her."

He nodded eagerly. "You got it, man," he said backing away.

"Remember this for next time." Cayden stared at the boy with contained rage. "An eye for an eye, and a tooth for a tooth. If you even *think* about going through with your sick intentions, you'll never be able to piss standing up again." The air was thick with tense hostility, and though Cayden remained remarkably calm, something beneath his eyes said he was anything but.

The boy swallowed, nodding woodenly once more before scuttling off, his pants nearly falling around his knees as he ran.

Cayden watched him until he was out of sight,

before sinking down beside me, his forehead creased with concern. "Kara, are you all right?"

"Thanks to you, I am." I clutched at my chest and my heart beat violently against my ribs. "Not to sound ungrateful, but what are you doing here?"

"One of the frat brothers is on the ball team, remember? I was here to see him."

Oh, right. Ben. I didn't want to relive that memory, so that explanation was enough for me. I just wanted to get the hell out of there.

I attempted to stand, my knees quaking like a house of playing cards. Cayden must have sensed my fragile state and fluidly rose to his feet, offering his hand. I took it willingly, needing the extra support. He closed his fingers. Like a catcher's mitt, his thick hands made mine look childlike. I stood on wobbly legs, my mind still reeling with what just happened.

"Cayden," I murmured over the singing cicadas in the grass. "Thank you so much, for being in the right place at the right time." I looked up at him through weary eyes, suddenly exhausted.

"Anytime," he replied modestly. "Let's get you back to your dorm. I'm sure Cassie has worried herself sick by now."

My mind fluttered to my friend. She was probably cramming for midterms, something I should have been doing. Her statement "*Bad boys. They cause nothing but heartache*" rang annoyingly through my head. The hole where my heart used to be reminded me of the harsh truth behind those words.

Cayden led me to an impressive, silver sedan, parked haphazardly across the lawn. I sank into the lush leather, the fabric squeaking gently beneath my weight.

Cayden immersed his brawny body into the driver's seat. He looked even more strapping behind the steering wheel. The car smelled of freshly oiled leather mixed with a lingering scent of wisteria. I looked over at him, and smiled faintly at myself. I just endured a turbulent storm of emotions and chaos. Yet, somehow, here was Cayden. My silver lining.

Chapter 26

The sleek car moved quietly as it maneuvered smoothly over the roads. Cayden rounded the dorm parking lot, found an empty slot, and pulled in. The engine's slight hum suddenly vanished.

"Kara," Cayden said carefully. "Mind if we take a walk?"

"I'm really not up to it." *In fact, the only thing I am up for is a hot shower and time alone,* I thought. "Maybe later, okay?"

"It can't wait."

"Cayden, what's going on?" I asked. I didn't like the pained expression in his face. My stomach churned as I wondered what was wrong.

He unfolded his frame from the car and waited for me to join him. I sat for a moment, collecting my thoughts, before stepping out onto the pavement.

"What's this about?" I demanded, slamming the door shut behind me.

He ignored me and started to stroll across the parking lot, in the direction of the ball field. Sighing, I pushed forward. He slowed his pace, allowing me to catch up.

"It's none of my business," he started.

I gnashed my teeth together. I hated discussions that began with "It's none of my business," "I hate to pry," and "Don't get upset."

He scrubbed his neck roughly. "Kara, I don't know what your relationship with Dominic is, but you should be mindful of the company you keep."

I stopped dead in my tracks. My heart nearly crumbled at the sound of his name. "You were right Cayden," I seethed through gritted teeth, balling my hands fiercely at my side. "It's none of your business."

I knew I shouldn't have snapped at him. He didn't deserve it after just saving me from that despicable piece of shit, but my wounds from Dominic still ran deep. Just the mention of his name was still enough to turn me into a useless heap.

"Kara, please." He held up his hands defensively. "Hear me out."

My stomach scrunched tightly like a fist. "Leave it alone, Cayden. You don't know me well enough to tell me how to run my life." I whirled around and marched away. He caught up with me easily, grabbing my elbow. I spun around irritated, stamping my foot in the dirt.

"Leave me alone!" I snarled.

"He's not what you think."

"Oh really? And what exactly *is* he? Are you going to tell me he's bad news? A bad influence, maybe?"

"Kara, just listen," he pleaded. "Come with me to the ball field. Please."

"What?" I snapped. "Cayden, now is not the time to swat a few balls."

His blue eyes held mine, pleading. He looked conflicted, like he was wrestling with something internally.

"Please," he repeated quietly.

After a long moment, I finally said, "Fine." I flung

my hands outward and stalked toward the baseball field. The stadium lights were off, but a few security lights dimly glowed around the diamond. The smell of freshly cut grass and dusty clay assaulted my senses.

"Well?" I crossed my arms over my chest and glared at him.

"Actually, it's probably easier if I *show* you," he said as he shed his shirt.

Show me? "Cayden, what the hell are you doing?"

Slowly, he turned around. My eyes drifted across his taut muscles. They flexed with each graceful movement.

"Do you see those scars?" He craned his neck and regarded me wearily.

Squinting, I leaned forward and noticed a constellation of freckles scattered across his tanned skin. Then, I found them. Identical scars punctuated each shoulder blade. I examined the left one closely. The half-moon shape was slightly raised and silvery. My gaze swept to the right. It was the mirror image of the other. Normally, I considered scars blemishes. Ugly reminders of yesterday's wounds, or in my case, last year's weakness.

However, these scars were different. They were almost beautiful. Like tattooed artwork, they were elegantly etched into Cayden's perfect canvas. I felt my anger slowly evaporate. I slowly lifted my hands over the scars. I could easily conceal them beneath my thumbs. I flicked my eyes to his, waiting for permission. He moved his head into a slow nod, so I traced the crescents with my fingers and felt him shudder beneath my touch.

"What happened?" I asked as I gently probed the

puckered skin.

"Stand away from me," he demanded.

My head snapped up. "What?" I snatched my hands back.

"Step back, Kara." His voice was commanding.

Slightly hurt by his tone, I backed away. Cayden started shifting his shoulders as though he was trying to shimmy into a wetsuit. The strength in his back rippled beneath the surface of his skin. An enormous pair of wings sprang outward, nearly knocking me to the ground.

I clambered backward, gasping at the sight of them. They looked as delicate as ancient parchment, and just as thin. Iridescent shades of nudes and pinks swirled seamlessly together. As if sewn with magical golden thread, the wings sparkled in the sunlight. Like a billowing cape around his strong frame, they stretched out wide.

An arsenal of bombs exploded within my chest. *Cayden's an angel!* With the grace of a swan, Cayden folded his wings silently behind him.

"Are you repulsed?" His voice was straightforward.

"No."

"Do you know what I am?"

"Yes," I whispered, astonished. "Everything I once knew as myths…they are all true."

"There is always a grain of truth behind every myth, Kara. We are mentioned in every aspect of the mortal world. Fairytales, folklore, art, music, even history lessons. We're hardly a secret."

Suddenly my legs felt like water and I swayed, flailing my arms to catch myself. Cayden was beside me faster than my mind could register his movement. His hands circled my waist, supporting my crumbling weight. I leaned into him, inhaling his sweet scent.

I looked past his face and gazed at his wings. The sheer skin, like a gauzy curtain, stretched tightly over what looked like golden bamboo rods. The dainty frame looked as though it were fashioned with godly precision.

"Why...are you on earth? Are you like, my guardian angel or something?"

He smiled warmly. "No. Your Guardian is Blain. He's been assigned to you since your birth."

"Can I meet him?"

He shook his head. "Guardians remain unseen. Knowing their image would only hinder their work."

"How so?"

"If you were to see or feel his presence, you would know that you're in some sort of danger. Instead of allowing him to Guard, you could possibly interfere with his efforts, causing grave consequences."

"Oh," I said in a small voice. "I see."

"I hear he used to be quite busy in your adolescent years," Cayden added, his eyes were full of mirth now and I began to relax, allowing him to hold me steady.

"I was a bit clumsy," I muttered.

He laughed, then fingered a loose strand of my hair before hooking it behind my ear. All amusement vanished as he narrowed his eyes at me. "Although, there was a recent incident that had him worried. Thankfully, intervention wasn't necessary."

My eyes caught his. They were hard, like cut sapphires. Fleetingly, I felt compelled to ask him to elaborate, but I bit my inner cheek instead. I knew what incident he was referring too. *My attempted suicide,* I thought. Heat crept up my neck and across my cheeks. I had always been ashamed of my dark past, but somehow with Cayden knowing about it, I felt even worse.

"I'm an Angel of Vocem," he stated boldly.

"Angel of Vocem?" I echoed, my head full of rattled bewilderment.

"Angel of Voice. I am the tug in your gut when something doesn't feel right. Your conscience leading you to reason."

The image of a talking cricket popped into my mind. "Like the bug with the top hat and cane?

Cayden let out a hearty laugh, and although I wanted to join in, I couldn't. Instead, I remained transfixed, and gazing as his wings contracted and mingled with his body's natural rhythm, moving fluidly and evenly. They were very much an extension of him, just as his arms and legs were. I felt the weight of his stare settle on me, and our eyes met.

I covered my mouth and spoke through parted fingers. "I'm sorry. I was staring."

"It's all right. I understand. It's overwhelming, I'm sure." He tenderly clasped my hand and held it to his chest.

"Do you live in heaven?" I asked.

He moved his head into a slow nod. "I do."

"Where is it? Is it as perfect as they say? Gold streets and all?" The questions just kept tumbling out. I couldn't contain my fascination, or curiosity.

Cayden's lips quirked upward. "Something like that. Would you like to see it?"

"Ah." I shot him a long look. "Don't I have to be

dead to go to heaven?"

"Usually," he answered. He cocked his head slightly and regarded me carefully. "But, as my invited guest, we'll keep your heart beating this time." He winked and spread his magnificent wings. The sound was like a beach umbrella springing open. Then, he slowly reached one hand out and placed it above my heart. His fingers splayed softly against my collarbone. I watched, pursing my lips to remain quiet as he closed his eyes and lowered his head. His blond hair dangled above his forehead.

"Angels of Powers cast over this body. Enter wherein to seal her lungs and veins. Protect her mortal body and allow her to enter into Heaven unscathed. By the Mighty and all that is Holy, blessed be to me and this journey."

"What are you doing?" I asked suspiciously.

"Placing a protection prayer over you," he said. "You can't enter Heaven without it."

"Where exactly is Heaven?" My nerves began to shake in their nonexistent boots, and I considered changing my mind.

A smiled tugged at his lips. "The sun," he answered.

My mouth dropped open. "The sun?" I echoed lamely. "That's impossible."

"Is it?" he asked with a trace of amusement.

"Yes," I began. "Scientists say it's a ball of gas and fire."

"Scientists *think* it's a ball of gas and fire. However, they have never been close enough to test that theory. That's all science is anyway, just a bunch of theories bound together with a thread of coincidences."

I stared at him in disbelief. "You're serious?"

He nodded. "Let me show you."

Growing increasingly uncertain, I scrambled to make sense of things. "Wait. The protection prayer…what exactly is it protecting me *from*?" My palms grew slick, and I wrung my hands nervously, trying to dry them.

"Since we will be in such high altitudes, I have to ensure that you don't asphyxiate from lack of oxygen or that you don't suffer from embolism."

"Do I even want to know what that means?"

"It's the formation of gas in your fluids. Your blood and other fluids will begin to bubble, which is deadly to mortals. That's why astronauts wear those pressurized suits."

"That brings the old saying, 'making your blood boil,' to a whole other level," I said dryly. "So do you rely on the protection prayer too?"

"No," he said, batting his wings once. "Earthly affairs do not affect me. Angels don't need to breathe, and our temperatures stay constant. Human sickness cannot inhabit our cells or blood."

"Oh," I squeaked. I had nothing to say to that.

He snaked one strong arm around my waist, pinning me tightly against him. A glittering vapor circled us, pulsating like water, caressing my skin like a cool mist.

"What is that?" I asked, watching in awe as the air danced around us.

"Shroud of invisibility." He lifted one arm over his head. "So no one can see us do this!"

Suddenly, we launched into the sky. My stomach melted into my toes as the ground disappeared beneath our feet. My breath caught in my throat as we soared upward. My legs dangled helplessly as his wings beat quietly against the air, sending us farther and farther up. It was nothing but open sky and traces of gray clouds as we whirled through them. I tried to fight the urge to look down, but I couldn't resist.

My belly somersaulted several times before lurching into my throat. *Oh!* Earth was merely a speck of color, like a seed floating amidst a sea of murky water. My head felt like a sandbag teetering precariously on a staircase. I gripped Cayden's neck so hard my knuckles bulged. As the oxygen thinned out, my mind smeared with foggy images. I felt as though I was looking through a glass bottle. Distorted and hazy, the space around me seemed to tilt and sling wildly, like a slab of clay on a whirling pottery wheel.

"The vertigo will pass," he assured me.

I buried my face into his chest, desperately trying to steady my spinning head.

"Take a look around," he whispered into my ear.

Easier said than done, I thought. Reluctantly, I pried my face away and took a weary look around, feeling him charge through the empty sky. It was punctuated with sparkly stars and the odd smell of salt and burnt metal. We arced slightly, aligning our course with a bright orange ball in the distance. Like a smoldering tangerine in the darkness, it illuminated the never-ending abyss around us.

I watched it, hypnotized by its beauty as it glowed invitingly before us. *That solves the mystery of why people say they see a bright light when they die*, I thought. My eyes ached, as though they that had been raked with sand straight from the Sahara desert. The heat became increasingly stifling; compressing my chest so severely I felt it would collapse in on itself. My bracelet stung my skin, nearly branding me forever. Which would have been poetic actually, since Dominic was the one who gave it to me, and just like a brand, he too was eternal.

"Didn't your mother ever teach you to *not* stare at the sun?" he scolded. "Avert your eyes."

I did as I was told, pressing my chin against my sticky shoulder. I felt him lunge with determination, plunging us further into the orbit of the deathly heat. My blood seemed to churn like thick lava through my veins. I clung to him as we hurled toward the bright inferno. Like dragon tongues, countless flames licked outward at us and without hesitation, Cayden barreled through them.

Chapter 27

The searing heat extinguished instantly, a soft glow of light enveloped us as Cayden lowered me to the ground. He regarded me with caution as he waited for my reaction. I slowly spun around myself, gaping at the awe-inspiring view. My skin felt charged, as if I was standing on a circuit of electricity. I looked down at my feet; they stood upon bricks of glistening gold. Shimmering palaces, lightly dusted with crushed diamonds, twinkled prettily in the distance.

"Is it what you imagined?" Cayden's silky voice gently stirred me from my daze.

I shook my head slowly, absorbing each beautiful detail before finally saying, "Doesn't even come close."

His hand found mine, and he led me through the splendid streets. Doves as delicate as snowflakes perched upon swooping branches of sparkling trees. Several angels floated past us, watching me carefully through sharp eyes.

Their wings, like delicate lace, moved like flower petals in a gentle wind. Their lovely faces were enchanting. My eyes lingered on their hair. One had flowing tresses the color of antique roses. The other had feathery white hair, tipped with a turquoise that could rival a mermaid's tail.

"Our time here is limited, Kara," Cayden interrupted. "The protection prayer is fleeting and cannot be renewed."

"I want to see my dad," I said, looking into his sparkling blue eyes, pleading with him to give me just one minute with my father. "Please, Cayden. Let me see him before we leave. Just let me tell him that I love him." My lips trembled as I whispered, "Just one more time."

"Kara, you must know that this is your last visit. Are you prepared to say good-bye for a second time?"

"I never got to say it the first time," I said firmly, feeling my nose start to tingle from my encroaching emotions. "I was too deep in denial to allow myself to come to terms that he was sick, let alone gone for good." Tears pricked at my eyes, and I quickly blinked them away.

"Very well." Cayden lifted his arm and whistled a melodious tune. A dove fluttered down and landed softly on his fingers. The bird's wings were downy and the color of freshly fallen snow. He brought the dainty bird close to his face. "Randall Wayne Maven," he instructed precisely. The dove cooed before stretching its wings and flittering gracefully away. "The dove will find your father and summon him to us."

I stood gaping at him, astonished, and slightly amused. "So instead of phones, you use doves? Interesting. Will they peck out a text message too?"

"Funny," he replied flatly, his lips twitching in amusement.

A dull haze crept over the sloping street. I watched it soar past the stunning palaces with rhythmic vibrations. As the object approached, I detected a familiar presence from within it. I looked hard into the center of the trembling mist.

An image slowly took form. A man with thick dark hair and intelligent eyes stared back at me. I knew the curves of his face. His strong chin and broad forehead. The space around him seemed to flicker with energy.

"Daddy?" I breathed. *Oh God, I've missed him so!*

"Kara," the voice called, cradling my ears like a fluffy blanket. His watery image slowly solidified until he looked like himself again. I ran toward him, and then stopped suddenly. I wanted desperately to touch him, but I was worried that, like a mirage in the desert, he would disappear.

I also feared that I wouldn't be able to let him go. My father and I were incredibly close, and going on without him the past year has proved to be an enormous and nearly impossible task.

Sensing my apprehension, he opened his arms out wide and smiled sweetly. I needed my daddy. I needed to feel his strong embrace again. Just one more time. It was always like a shield, protecting me from the world. I flung myself around his neck eagerly, cherishing the feel of his arms around me again.

"I miss you so much," I mumbled into his chest, tears welling in my eyes.

"I miss you too, princess." He stroked my hair and hummed quietly as we rocked back and forth.

"I don't want to leave you," I said through my sobs.

"You'll be here, soon enough. Then we will have forever together." He smoothed my hair from my face. "First, you have a few things to accomplish, like, graduation."

He tweaked my nose and smiled. "And succeeding in a career. Starting a family. Knowing the joys of being a mother. A grandmother." He lifted my chin gently. "Becoming bingo champion at the senior center," he added playfully.

Good old Dad. Heaven hadn't changed him at all. I smiled and sniffed loudly.

"Kara, it's time to go," Cayden interjected.

No! I can't leave him. Not yet...

My dad pulled me close, giving me one of his famous bear hugs, and I wept again. The tears were relentless, coming so violently my throat became hoarse. I held him as tight as I could, memorizing the way he felt, and praying the memory would last.

When I felt him pull away, I whimpered, clinging once more to his waist, like I had done so many times as a child.

He tenderly untangled me from him, and lifting my chin, forcing me to look up into those familiar hazel eyes "I'll be waiting for you, kiddo. Until then, know that I love you and I'm always just a heartbeat away."

"I love you, Daddy," I whispered.

He kissed the center of my forehead, then studied my face. His eyes filled with restrained emotion, but he gave me a comforting smile as he handed me over to Cayden.

I refused to go gracefully, clutching his hand as long as possible, before my fingertips finally slipped away. I wiped my face with the back of my hand as I watched my father wave goodbye, slowly dissipating into a glimmering mist. *I love you, Daddy.*

Cayden gripped my waist and raised one arm over his head. "Ready?" he asked. I nodded woodenly, still too caught up in my emotions to speak. He expanded his magnificent wings, and in a flash we were off, speeding through the vast space that seemed to stretch on for eternity. I recalled the last moments that I shared with my father. Devouring the details, I was actually happily content.

I knew my father was living lavishly, in a body that would never ache or age. I cast my eyes to Cayden. He was staring straight ahead, maneuvering us through the shroud of darkness.

"Thank you," I said. "Thank you for allowing me to see him one last time."

He smiled down at me briefly, before setting his eyes back on the open sky.

"For you, I'd do anything."

I didn't know what to say to that, so I pressed my lips together and looked out across the space around us. The wind cut across my face, almost making me lose my breath. I gasped, realizing my chest was beginning to tighten.

"Cayden," I choked, my insides burning as streaks of labored breath scraped across my throat.

Cayden looked down at me, his eyes rounding a bit before he surged faster, his wings beating so quickly they were a blur behind him.

My vision grew spotty, and just before I let it claim me, Cayden said, "Kara. Stay with me." His grip grew stronger around me, rattling me a bit. "Kara, keep your eyes open," he urged.

The strange smell of outer space began to diminish, and the air started to warm. I inhaled, this time taking in a big gulp of air. It stung my chest, but at least I could breathe again.

We landed softly, and Cayden kept both hands on my waist, eyeing me intently.

"Are you all right?" he asked, his face colored with worry.

I nodded slowly, assessing myself carefully. My chest ached, and my legs were shaky, but I was relieved to have my feet on solid ground again.

He released me, and I wobbled slightly.

"I'm good," I reassured him. Feeling about as graceful as a bear in high heels, I balanced myself with outstretched arms. I started to move, steadying myself after each step, my body still unwinding from our flight. "I wonder if this is how stewardesses feel all the time."

"I doubt it," he chuckled. "Their version of flying and mine are a little different."

He fell into my pace, offering his hand whenever I started to stumble.

"I walked better when I was in Heaven."

"Your body is still adjusting to the overturn of gravity and oxygen. You didn't need it while on Heaven's ground because of the Protection Prayer."

I recalled the pristine loveliness of Heaven. The pure elation I felt when I felt my father's arms around me again. "I look forward to living there…"

His blue eyes caught mine, flashing with a sudden sadness that rattled me.

"Someday," I mumbled quickly, averting my eyes from his intense gaze.

"That will be a long time from now, Kara." His tone was even, though his face was colored with panic.

"I know, Cayden. I was just saying it was a beautiful place and when the time comes, I know I'll be happy there."

He turned away from me, his jaw flexing with

some underlying emotions. I wondered what he was thinking.

"Will I be an angel?" I questioned, catching my lip with my teeth. I worried that I had asked too much. "My father. He wasn't one, was he? He didn't have wings."

"When a human dies, their spirit resides in Heaven for eternity. They do not become angels. Angels are born, from angel parents."

"Of course. Like demons..." I breathed, remembering my heated exchange with Dominic.

"There is only one exception to that rule," Cayden informed me. "Any human murdered by a demon is automatically granted angel status."

That certainly seems fair to me, I thought. My mind swirled with questions, but all the newfound information proved to be too much for one night. I was suddenly exhausted, my eyelids growing heavy with fatigue. Finally, we reached my dorm and I sighed with relief.

"Have good night, Kara." His voice was low and soft as silk.

I looked up, into his eyes and smiled. "Good night, Cayden," I said quietly. "Thanks again for letting me see my dad one last time."

"It won't be the last time," he replied in a soothing tone. "Someday, you'll have forever to spend with the ones you love. I hope I'm there to share it with you." He pressed his lips to my temple before disappearing down the empty hall.

****

The coming weeks proved to be exceedingly difficult. Dominic never came back to Mrs. Dixon's class. Evidently, he dropped the class, though he remained in school. I caught glimpses of him on campus, which pierced my gut and renewed old wounds. Cayden continued to be supportive. Sensing my sadness, he would attempt to cheer me up.

"Want to go play putt-putt?" he asked one sunny afternoon, as we meandered slowly across the courtyard. It was the perfect day to play. The weather was warm, and clouds stretched across the brilliant blue sky like pulled taffy.

"Thanks, but no."

"Come on, it will be fun. There's a batting cage there too, I can get some practice in. You wouldn't want to deprive a ball player a chance to practice, would you?" He cocked a blond eyebrow at me.

I laughed meekly. "No, I guess not."

"Come on, I'll even buy you a hotdog."

"Oh, boy. Now you've made it worth going for," I said laughing.

Cayden appeared to be offended as he hugged himself and said, "Ouch that hurt. I thought my company would be enough." Then he chuckled, his eyes shining in the sunlight.

I nudged him playfully as we made our way across the parking lot. He dug out his car keys from his pocket and pressed the unlock button. The lights flashed on his car, making it easy to locate in the parking lot.

As I rounded the back of it, the sun sparked off the chrome insignia on the trunk. It was an incredible car, and I couldn't help but compare it to Dominic's mean machine.

Cayden's car was sleek, pristine, and aerodynamic. Dominic's was a tough, grumbling metal beast that reeked with attitude.

Lowering myself in the comfortable leather, I let my eyes run over Cayden as he adjusted the mirror and snapped his seatbelt into place. He turned, beaming at me brightly. Excitement rolled off him like water.

"Are you ready for my mad putt-putt skills?"

"You're such a weenie." I giggled.

And with that, he put the car into gear and we sped toward Captain Spanky's Fun Park.

****

It was a typical putt-putt course. Neon octopuses hung from fabricated caves. Fish sculptures slathered with blinding paint emerged from teal pools. An oversized treasure chest full of shiny plastic rhinestones beckoned to us at the final station. It sat at the end of winding green turf and all we had to do was sink our painted golf balls into the hole that sat directly behind it. It took me five tries. Poor Cayden struggled, swinging his club a total of nine times before he found success.

"So where were those mad putt-putt skills you were going to show me?" I teased.

"I thought I had game," he said laughing. "But you definitely put me to shame." Using his golf club, he playfully "knighted" me, touching me on each shoulder. "I dub thee Princess Putt-Putt."

"Why thank you," I chuckled as I curtsied. "Now, I do believe you owe me a hotdog."

"I'll even spring for a vanilla shake too," he said, giving me a wink.

We ate over pleasant conversation, but my mind kept finding its way back to Dominic. I was nervous to bring him up, but I had questions only Cayden could answer.

"Can I ask you something?" I lifted my gaze from my half-eaten hotdog to Cayden's blue eyes.

He studied me as he finished chewing before saying, "Sure, anything."

"The inner voice thing. That's you and Dominic, isn't it? The angel and the devil on people's shoulder?"

"That's right," he said carefully.

"Why didn't you reveal yourself to me before?" I knotted my fingers in my lap. "I mean, why now?"

Cayden's mouth parted in surprise. "Kara, I'm not like your Guardian Angel. I wasn't assigned to you, and neither was Dominic. Angels of Vocem and Damamahs have the ability to sense a mortal's intentions within their range of..." He paused, searching for the right word.

"Hearing?" I offered.

"Well, yes, I guess that's one way to describe it." He appeared uncomfortable, shifting in his seat before continuing. "We live our days amongst mortals, waiting and listening for the opportunity to either help, or hinder a sin."

I sat motionless, absorbing his words completely before saying, "So no matter where I go, there will always be a Damamah and an Angel of Vocem to guide me. But it won't always be you and...." I couldn't bring myself to say his name, so instead I swallowed it down, letting it burn as it buried itself within me again.

I noticed Cayden's eyes swing to the batting cages, sensing his reluctance to elaborate further, so I just let it go. I forced a strained smile and said, "You ready to get some *practice* in? That is what we came for, right?"

His eyes found mine, a smile pulling at his lips.

"Of course. And I'm hurt you would insinuate anything different." He stood and deposited our garbage in the trash bin, and dug deep into his pockets, withdrawing a handful of shiny quarters. I followed him to the batting cage and stationed myself beside it, watching him shove a helmet on his head, before crouching in his usual stance. Primed and ready to rumble, he adjusted the bat in his hands, waiting for the balls to start flying. A loud knock startled me, as the pressure released from the machine's engine. A whirl of white flew toward Cayden. He swung the bat, connecting it with ease.

Over and over, the balls sped toward him, and again and again, the bat cracked across each one. When the noise of the contraption faded, he flung the bat over his shoulder and regarded me with an air of playfulness.

"You want a turn?"

"Me?" I pointed at myself. "You're looking at a gym class reject. I'm terrible at sports."

"Come on, I'll teach you." He smiled broadly and I couldn't help but return it. There was something attractive about his boyish charm.

"No way," I said shaking my head. "I'm going to get socked in the face with a ball."

"Not with me guiding you," he said, gesturing for me to join him.

I sighed heavily as I stepped inside. I looked nervously around the small, caged arena. Cayden crammed a helmet onto my head and handed me the bat. I held it awkwardly as Cayden inserted the necessary amount of money and came back to stand behind me. I could feel him smile.

"What?" I asked pointedly.

"Nothing, it's just your stance. How do expect to

hit the ball like that? Here, let me show you."

He slid my fingers lower on the bat. I studied the smooth wood grain finish, my fists tightly wrapped around the grip. I felt his body move behind me. He lightly arched my back and lifted my arms.

"Open your legs wider. Plant them firmly into the ground," he instructed. The sound of the machine kicked on. The buzzing of the mechanism hummed, like a busy Laundromat, before spitting out a zipping baseball. I felt Cayden's arms flex around mine as we swung the bat in unison. It connected, sending a vibration through the wooden bat and down to my fingertips. After the last ball was tossed, my tingly arms shook with fatigue.

"My arms feel like wet noodles," I said, laughing.

Cayden took the bat from me, his gaze holding mine as I rubbed the life back into my arms. Then, he dipped his head, and pressed his lips against mine. The moment our lips touched, I was blinded by the image of Dominic. His jaw was set tight, and his fiery eyes blazed with disapproval. I pushed Cayden away, blinking at him. "What are you doing?"

His eyes were fixed on me, his face etched with disappointment. "I'm sorry, I thought…"

"Thought what?" I demanded. "That you could just kiss me, and I'd be okay with it?"

"I thought I could make you forget."

"Forget about Dominic?" I asked in disbelief.

"It's hard to see you obsessing over him. I want you to love me, the way you love him."

I stared at him, while internally, I grappled with my feelings. Cayden made me feel peaceful. Content. Dominic made me feel *alive*. Like I was on the verge of something great. They were two very different feelings. And two very different men. Resigned, I slouched and turned away from him.

"Cayden," I started. "I want to, believe me. It would be so simple to be with you. But I love Dominic."

"You mean, you *loved* Dominic," he corrected.

"Yes, I *loved* him," I agreed, turning to face him again. I gazed at him firmly, pleading for understanding. "I love him still," I said quietly, the weight of my words hanging in the air.

"He walked away from you, Kara. He left you alone. Yet, here I am. Standing right here, asking you to just give us a chance."

"Cayden, please—" I pinched the bridge of my nose, and closed my eyes, wishing I could disappear.

"Don't you feel *anything?*" he asked, taking a step toward me.

My mouth felt dry as my stomach started tying itself into knots. I lifted my face.

"Kara, I know you do." He moved to stand in front of me. "I can sense it." He placed his hand lightly over my heart, and I swallowed hard, not knowing what to do.

"A seed of tomorrow," he said. "It's there. And I will tend to it daily, watering it with my love and shining my light of hope on it until it blooms."

Warm tears rimmed my eyelids. My gut felt laden with lead. *Cayden is here, right now, when Dominic is not.* He was offering himself wholly to me, promising me a future that Dominic couldn't.

"Kara, I loved you before I even laid eyes on you," he said, his eyes resigned, but holding steady to mine.

"What do you mean?"

"Your father talks about you incessantly. The girl he describes is smart, beautiful, strong, and vivacious." He snickered softly, shaking his head a little, as he looked off in the distance, as though recalling a memory. "I was *in love* with you before I even saw you." His gaze shifted back to me. "And you're every bit as wonderful as he said you were."

I absorbed his words. *My father talks about me.* My stomach somersaulted and sank simultaneously. I missed him terribly. The familiar ache returned, wishing I could see him again.

"Come on, we should probably get going," Cayden urged, taking my hand, distracting me from my thoughts.

The drive back to campus was peaceful, but mentally I struggled with my thoughts. Although I could no longer claim Dominic as mine, he was still very much a part of me. Cayden was an amazing guy, supportive and easy to be with, but I wasn't in love with him. Needing to distance myself from him, I was relieved when we pulled into the dorm parking lot. I needed to be alone. I needed to sort things out, and being near Cayden wasn't helping.

"Thanks for today. I had a lot of fun," I said before I climbed out of the car.

"I'm sorry I had to ruin it," he replied gloomily.

"You didn't ruin it, Cayden. You just have to realize that I'm not over Dominic, and I'm not sure I ever will be." I shut the door, and bent to look through the window. "I've never loved anyone like I love him."

"That's what scares me," he said, giving me a half-hearted smile before pulling away.

****

That night, I lay in bed, trying to sort out my feelings. Although Dominic had walked away from me, I was still fiercely loyal to him. My soul was still reaching out to him, shining a beacon of light on his, guiding him back to me. Before my body surrendered into a fitful slumber, I came to two definite realizations. Loving Cayden would be simple. But not loving Dominic was impossible.

Chapter 28

I woke up to ear-piercing screams ringing off the walls. It wasn't until my throat felt hoarse, that I realized they were coming from me. Cassie launched herself onto my bed. Her sleep mask sat crookedly against her forehead. Her blue eyes regarded me with gut-wrenching pity. "Oh, Kara. You need to put an end to this," she murmured, as she touched my wrist. "This has been going on for weeks now. Seeing him around campus is too difficult for you. After midterms, you should go home for a while. With me going back to Georgia, I really worry about you being here alone. Are you exempting any of your midterms?"

"All except Drawing. But all I have to do is turn in my portfolio."

"Well, maybe you could turn it in early? Enjoy your break *away* from Belman. Time away might be just what you need."

I nodded in agreement, watching Cassie climb her small, pajama clad body back into bed. Tucking herself beneath her pink blanket, she looked over and smiled warmly. "Night, Kara," she whispered.

"Night." I snuggled back into my pillow and somehow fell back to sleep. Dominic didn't haunt my dreams anymore that night, and somehow, it left me feeling even emptier. As least when I dreamed about him, he still seemed close, even for just a moment.

I woke up in the morning, ready to tackle the day head-on.

"When are you leaving for Georgia?" I asked Cassie, as I loosely braided the length of my hair.

"Right after my last class." Her voice was bouncing with excitement. She gave me a long look, her bubbly expression morphing into a troubled appearance. "Are you going home?"

"Yes, so you don't have to worry about me."

"Good," she sighed. "Well, let me give you a hug now, because I don't know if we'll see each other before I leave." She stood and skipped over to me, throwing her slender arms around me.

"Text me when you get there, so I know you made it safely," I instructed.

"I will." She pulled away and smiled. "Enjoy your time alone." She squeezed me once more and left.

Throwing on some dark green jeans and a breezy tank top, I was out the door before nine o'clock. After meeting with all my professors, I successfully exempted each midterm. My grades were acceptable, and I was grateful that I was able to pull off what I did. Mrs. Dixon took my portfolio early but wouldn't grade it until everyone else turned theirs in. After agreeing to email me my final grade, she wished me "a happy break" and bid me farewell. As I walked away from her, I couldn't help but think, *a break is what I need to try to forget about Dominic, but I'll be damned if it will be happy.*

****

"Cayden, I'm going home for a while," I hedged carefully.

"You're coming back, aren't you?" His face slack

of all emotion.

"Of course," I said with a hint of annoyance. "This is my final semester. I'm not going to mess that up."

He breathed a sigh of relief. "Can I call you?"

"I'd rather you didn't." I watched with a surge of remorse as disappointment spread across his handsome face. "I just need some time, Cayden. You understand, don't you?"

"Not really. I thought we had something great going. Is this about the other day?"

"No." I averted my eyes and frowned.

"Kara," he said, his eyes searching my face ruthlessly.

"A little," I confessed. "I'm just confused, Cayden. I don't know what the hell I'm doing anymore. My mind and emotions are going in different directions; I don't know which way is up."

His eyes tightened and his lips twitched before saying, "All you need to do is *feel*." He stepped up against me, and lifted my hand to his chest. His heart thumped steadily against my palm. "My heart is yours, Kara. Now, all you have to do is decide what feels *right*. What feels easy and natural."

Being with Cayden is easy and feels as natural as breathing. My thoughts turned to Dominic, my pulse surged a bit harder as I recalled his hauntingly beautiful eyes. I closed my eyes, and could almost smell his intoxicating spicy essence.

But I'd rather be alone with my memories of Dominic, than in a relationship with Cayden, pretending that what I felt for him no longer exists.

I can't do it, I thought. *I won't.*

"I just can't turn off my feelings for Dominic. I

love him."

"He's evil, Kara, and you're good. The two extremes can't coexist in harmony."

"It does within Dominic."

"How can you love someone who beckons innocent people to commit sins?"

"It's not his choice. He has no control over that."

He scoffed mockingly. "Kara, did you know he was in the shadows that night at the frat house?"

Like a boulder on a paper airplane, my heart sank. "What are you talking about," I asked in a small and shaky voice.

"When I found you with that vile—"

"I know what night you're talking about, Cayden," I snapped. "What the hell are you trying to tell me?"

"Because he was thinking about it, Dominic was there."

"He wouldn't have allowed that to happen," I said shaking my head roughly.

"I was there to interfere with the boy's emotions," he explained. "That's the only reason it didn't."

"No!" I screamed, balling my hands into tight fists. "He would *not* have let that happen to me. He loves me!"

"Whenever *any* sin is considered, we are both there. In some form. That night on the ledge. That was *me*." His eyes were pained as he grasped at his chest, clutching it as if he were trying to rip his own heart out. "That was *my* voice in your head, begging you not to step out onto that ledge."

"I will never believe that Dominic would hurt me." My face was tense with anger.

"You said it yourself. It's not his choice. It's the

blood that runs through him, Kara. He is what he is. A demon."

"That's not all that he is. His mother was human," I said defensively. "I know that side of him is stronger than his demon side. His love for me proves that."

"That makes it even worse!" he shouted angrily. "That means he has *partial* will power. It's his choice whether he uses it or not. And clearly—"

"Clearly, he used it when he saved me from the ledge."

"He put you *out* on the ledge!" He threw his hands despairingly in the air.

"We are done here," I said firmly, turning on my heel.

"Kara, please," he called.

I stomped away from him, my mind practically folding in on itself with grief. I refused to believe that Dominic would purposely hurt me. If he *were* there that night, he would have put an end to it. *Wouldn't he?* I thought about the countless kisses we shared, and the passion behind them. *Of course he would.* I realized then, I was in love with a memory. A shadow of my past. But it was all I had. For the first time since my father died, I had the will to *live*. And not just out of *survivor guilt,* but because I wanted to experience *true love*. Wholly and irreversibly. They say, "Its better to have loved and lost, than never to have loved at all" and until I met Dominic, I never thought that to be true. Now I know it is. Although life without him was pure hell, the joy he brought me, if even for only a little while, was worth it all.

According to Cayden, Dominic lurked near sin. So to see Dominic again, I simply needed be there too. My breath hitched as understanding hit me like a freight train. As I made my way back to my empty dorm room, I hatched a plan to do just that.

****

I unlocked the door to my dorm hesitantly. Cassie should have been gone by now, but what if she had forgotten something? When I swung it open, an empty room stared back at me. Cassie had packed up most of her clothes, but left everything else as it was. Her bed was made, but her CD collection was still scattered across her desk. The silence was disturbing, but I closed the door anyway.

I crossed the floor to the bathroom. My knees felt gummy, like they were sculpted out of silly putty. Flipping the switch, I squinted against the intrusive overhead lights. With a shaky hand, I opened the medicine cabinet. My fingers brushed across the line of medications, sending a bottle of cough syrup clanging into the sink. I jumped and gripped my chest. It felt oddly hollow. I didn't realize I had been holding my breath until my lungs felt as though they were about to burst. I let out a ragged breath and plucked a bottle of sleeping pills from the stack. *Am I really about to do this?*

I looked down at my bracelet. The lock and key charms dangled in the air, and I thought of Dominic and the beautiful words he said the day he gave it to me. *A lock. Because I have been bound. And a key, because you are unlocking everything I have come to know.* My heart swelled at the notion of seeing him again. Touching him again. I nearly shivered recalling his long fingers, which with one caress could elicit chills and comfort all at once. And those eyes. Those damn, hauntingly beautiful eyes that saw the ugliness within me, the tainted, artificial strength I paraded around in, and yet loved me anyway.

I'm not committing suicide, I reminded myself. *I'm just luring Dominic to me.* All I had to do was *think* about it, consider it so passionately that I teetered on the brink, and Dominic, the whisperer, would appear. As a Damamah, he would be obligated to use words of persuasion, encouragement, and possibly even seduction to ultimately shove me over the dark edge. But I was certain this time would play out exactly as it had before. Instead of whispering wicked thoughts into my head, his love would prove victorious over his otherworldly duties. He would not allow me to seal my sin, I just *knew* it.

I popped the lid off and stared down at the little pills. I imagined myself downing the entire bottle easily, my body slipping dangerously into a deep sleep. *I swore I would never do this again,* I thought, suddenly feeling out of breath. Panic flared within my chest, my mind screamed at me, *Say the mantra! Say the fucking mantra!*

I dumped the contents of the bottle into the palm of my hand. A few pills fell to the floor with a gentle pinging sound. I lifted my palm to my mouth. I looked around me, expecting Dominic to be standing there. He wasn't. I focused on my thoughts, so sure that I hadn't been thinking hard enough to warrant a visit from my Damamah. *Dominic. If you can hear me…please come. I need you.* I stared down at my hand. The pills suddenly looked like a handful of blocks, boxy and painful to swallow. Again, I saw myself choking them down and falling limply to the floor. Out of

267

desperation, and half-crazed with love, I expelled a quivering breath. *Dominic will save me.* I tossed my head back, and parted my lips. Using my hand as a funnel, the pills tumbled into my awaiting mouth.

Chapter 29

My shoulders shook violently and along with a stream of saliva, the partially dissolved pills poured from my mouth. Through blurry eyes, I realized I was face down on the bathroom floor. I touched my cheek. It was tingly, and I could feel the imprint of the tile. "What happened?" I groggily asked myself aloud.

"*You* decided to be an idiot—that's what," a cool voice scolded.

My head snapped upward. "Dominic!" I breathed. My head and my heart pounded. *It worked!* Exhilaration unfurled within my belly, and my lips threatened a smile until he scowled at me. I felt the eager butterflies dissolve and fade away as quickly as they came.

"Kara, what the hell were you thinking?"

"Obviously, you know what she was thinking," answered another voice.

Shielding my eyes, I squinted into the narrow hallway. The bathroom light seemed unnaturally harsh, or maybe the residual sleeping pills were taking effect. "Cayden?"

"Who else?" He leaned against the doorframe, his eyes washing over me with sadness. Pity. It stung deeper than I expected.

I hugged myself, casting my eyes down the length of me. Suddenly aware of my dismal appearance, I wiped my chin and attempted to stand. They immediately reached out to me, offering help, but Dominic was the first to pull away. I noticed that Cayden was wearing his baseball gloves, which confused me, but my head was so cloudy with the lingering traces of drugs, I couldn't ponder much of anything. His strong arms sat me upright. He tried to steady me, but I yanked myself away, smoothing my hair as I looked wistfully over at Dominic. His jaw was fixed tight, and his dark eyes devoured me without mercy. Rage rolled off him like bubbling lava down a volcano.

"I'll ask again," he snarled. "What the hell were you thinking?"

I opened my mouth to speak, but the words faded before they had time to form. My fingers itched to reach out to him, but I feared if I moved, it would only anger him further.

"I just wanted to see you again," I said hesitantly.

His eyes softened, but his mouth screwed into a rigid frown. "Kara, don't do this," he pleaded. "You heard my father. I'm not capable of love."

"I don't believe that!" I said hotly. "You love me, I know you do."

He scoffed, shaking his head in disbelief.

"Three times!" I continued. "Three times, you saved me from sealing my sin. Doesn't that show that you are capable of love?"

"This time technically doesn't count," Cayden interjected. "Your intentions of malice weren't pure."

I looked sharply at Cayden. "What?"

Undoubtedly realizing he was interfering with a sentimental moment, he retreated a few steps and looked away, the muscles clenching tightly in his jaw.

I turned back to Dominic, who only snorted and said, "What the winged bastard is trying to say is, because your suicide attempt was a farce, my influence didn't matter. Neither did his. Your heart and soul has to *want* it. It's only then, when your mind can be convinced."

"But you still came." I looked over at Cayden, who ignored me. His eyes focused ahead of him on the wall, his arms crossed over his chest. "You both did."

"We answer every call of sin," Dominic said. "We don't know your heart's true intentions until we read it."

I swallowed, hesitant to ask, but too curious not to. "And what did mine say?"

Dominic's fiery gaze held me as he said, "That you don't want to die, but you're willing to come close to it for love."

I felt my nose twitch with impending emotions. My lids felt heavy from the collecting tears. "I would. Oh God, for you Dominic, I would. Without so much as a second thought. I love you."

He snarled, which should have send me recoiling, but instead I tested a couple steps toward him. He remained where he was, careful not to reveal a thing. I wondered if he wished to meet me halfway, or bolt from the room.

"I have demon blood coursing through me, Kara. With it, I am bound to this life. A loveless, ugly life of duty and sin."

I shook my head. "No. You're half human," I whispered. "And it's beautiful."

His gaze latched fiercely onto mine, like barbs

snaring me into place. I caught a glimmer of hope behind those ebony eyes, so I clung to it, trying my damnedest to coax it further by saying, "Dominic, don't give up on me. I love you too much to lose you."

His mouth shrank into a tight frown, and his nostrils flared menacingly. I felt like a maimed animal being circled by a vicious wolf. I held my breath as I watched him move, slowly covering the space between us. The severity in his face disappeared with each step, until finally, he stood in front of me. I closed my eyes in rapture, treasuring the intoxicating aroma of him. *God how I've missed this. Missed him. Missed us.*

I opened my eyes to find him watching me with that same intense stare that we shared on the campus lawn. The same pull of crazy attraction, like strong magnets drawing us together until we could no longer resist it. We touched. The length of his body pressed against mine, sending a jolt of pleasure through me. He cupped my face, his palms warm against my cheeks. Unable to keep my tears at bay, they slipped across my skin, leaving warm trails behind them. I leaned into him, covering his hands with my own. *I love him. More than life itself, I love him. He is worth living for.*

"My father fell in love with a human once," he said finally, taking a ragged breath. I looked up at him. He gave me small smile, as if this fact had renewed his hope. He rubbed his thumb across my tear streaks, drying them as he said, "I love you, Kara."

My heart swelled with happiness. "I love you." I laid my hand upon his chest, feeling his coiled muscles flex beneath his t-shirt.

His eyes shined, like sparkling obsidian as he bent and pressed his lips against mine. They were warm, just like I remembered. And they were eager. A growl rumbled deep within his throat, vibrating against my fingers. I moaned against his lips as he invaded my mouth with a maddening skill that left me weak in the knees. Blazing heat seared through me, like crackling electricity along a livewire. Dominic's kiss was like no other. It enflamed me. Like gasoline on a roaring fire, it engulfed me with a fiery desire that refused to be doused. Lost in one another, we barely noticed the figure approaching us.

Cayden cleared his throat loudly.

We parted, but only after Dominic scattered a few tender kisses across my forehead and nose. I smiled up at him, happy to be back in his arms.

I finally shifted my gaze to Cayden. His face was taut with resentment as his blue eyes drilled into me with repugnance.

"So is *this* your decision?" he asked.

"Cayden, my feelings for Dominic have never been a secret," I said firmly.

"I know, I just thought you'd realize that life with a demon will only lead you straight to hell."

His words were like a slap to the face. I stiffened, hurt by his callousness, but at the same time, enraged with blinding fury.

"If I was lingering in a gray area before, you just helped me cross over," I barked.

"Yeah," he murmured, his eyes sweeping across Dominic with a look of pure disgust. "To the *dark* side."

Dominic snarled, the skin over his hands tightening across his knuckles.

"I can't be too upset," Cayden continued. "I mean,

he's just doing his duty, right? Helping the innocent seal their sin?"

Something haunting flickered behind Dominic's eyes. Like spilled ink, drops of red swirled into the sea of black water. I squeezed his hand, trying to pull him back from a dangerous brink. His eyes darted to mine fleetingly, and then shot back at Cayden.

"You're wavering, angel boy. All this time on earth is making you think like a mortal."

Cayden glared at him, his chest heaving with budding rage.

Dominic sneered at him. "Jealousy is a child of pride," Dominic muttered. "That could get you cast out of Heaven."

"Dominic," I objected, pulling on his arm.

"Then who will be my annoyingly righteous partner?" Dominic added offhandedly, a sinister smile spreading across his face.

"I'm not going anywhere. As long as you're harping on people's weakness, I'll be right there, to lead them down the right path."

"Dude." Dominic held up a protesting hand. "Are you going tell me that with great power, comes great responsibility? Because if so, I think I might gag."

"Don't make me take off my gloves," Cayden threatened through gritted teeth.

Take off my gloves? Are those fighting words? Like when girls say, "Don't make me take my earrings out"?

"Go ahead, fly boy, let's see what you got." Dominic narrowed his eyes and arched one brow warningly.

I stepped away from Dominic, positioning myself between the two. *In the gray area again,* I thought crossly. "That's enough," I said, staring at each of them, one at a time.

"Come on, Kara," Cayden coaxed. "Don't you want to know what an angel's touch does to a demon?"

I studied his eyes. They were like blue flames, dancing wildly over gasoline. He removed one glove and wiggled his fingers intently at Dominic.

"You'll have to catch me first," Dominic said, crouching slightly as though he was ready to pounce.

"I said that's enough." I glowered at them, my hands outstretched, as though I could really keep the two apart.

The tension in the air slowly began to ratchet down. Dominic strolled confidently to my side, snaking his arms around my waist and pulling me into him.

"I'm going to talk to my father about my mother. He hardly speaks of her. I need to learn the history of their relationship. Maybe it can help us. Maybe there's a way I can rescind my role as a Damamah." He crushed his lips against mine. "I love you." Then before my eyes could follow, he was gone.

Cayden turned to face the wall, slamming a balled fist against it angrily. "There is a way."

I peered at him, trying to read his expression. He looked deeply saddened and almost reluctant to continue.

"What?"

"Damn these virtues," he said.

"Cayden? If you know something, please tell me," I begged, bounding across the room. I laid a hand on his back, feeling it flex at my touch. "Please."

"Ascension," he said simply.

I shook my head. "Okay, ascension. What does that

mean?"

"Demons can ascend out of the Underworld and become mortal."

I felt my lips curve into a smile and my heavy heart felt fifty pounds lighter. "This is fantastic! I've got to go tell Dominic!" I turned to leave, when Cayden grabbed me by the wrist. I snatched my head back and stared at him in confusion.

"There's more," he said quietly. I faced him. The pit of my stomach started churning anxiously. *More?* I waited, as he attempted to frame his next few words. His features looked conflicted, and I knew he was struggling internally.

"What is it, Cayden?" I pressed. He turned around and flopped back against the wall, leaning into it for support.

"In order for a demon to ascend to mortal status, an angel must…"

"What?" I urged, my stomach breaking into thousands of irritated butterflies.

"Die." Whispered so faintly, the word hit me like a lightning bolt. I scrambled to wrap my head around what he was telling me. Still, this revelation held a shred of promise that I could still be with Dominic, and I was going to sink my nails into it and hold on for dear life.

"Angels don't die of old age, do they, Cayden?" I asked.

"No," he whispered.

"Can they be murdered?" Not that I was thinking about knocking off an angel or anything. It just seemed like the next logical question.

"Yes." His eyes were now steady on mine. "But

not by the hands of a mortal."

My cheeks flushed with spiking embarrassment. "Cayden, I…"

"I know." He took a long intake of air and regarded me with weary eyes. "Angels can also descend willingly or fall," he added, unhitching himself from the wall.

"That doesn't sound like a pleasant process."

"If a demon wants to ascend into the mortal world, an angel must be removed from Heaven. And vice versa, if an angel chooses to vacate their place with God, then an evil spirit must be eradicated."

"I don't understand," I admitted, rubbing my neck fretfully.

"It's all part of the Natural Law. To balance nature, good and evil must be equal. One must never outweigh the other."

"But I thought…" My head ached as I floundered with this newfound knowledge. "You know…good versus evil. God versus the Devil. I thought the goal was to have peace and harmony on earth?"

"That's what they want you to believe. But there's already a place where good reigns." He looked down at me and gave me wry smile.

I mulled that over for a minute or so. *Heaven, of course.*

"Okay, so descending? How does that happen?" I had heard of fallen angels. Lucifer was one. He was an angel who got too big for his britches and got himself cast right out of Heaven by God himself.

"Angels can only willingly descend out of love."

"Love? Angels can fall in love with demons?" I asked, my voice lined with disgust. Although, wasn't I, in fact, in love with a demon? *Partial demon,* I sternly reminded myself.

"Absolutely not," he snorted. "We are natural enemies. I meant the angel must be in love with a mortal to descend from their place in the Heavens. They must be willing to give up their Godly abilities to live as a human."

"But this is a different situation. I mean, it would require an angel to trade their status, for a demon. What angel in their right mind would do that?"

"None."

I flinched at the word. "Oh," I mouthed. My stomach melted into my knees. I suddenly grew light-headed from the ebb and flow of hope and disparity and sank heavily to the floor. "Then that's it. It's over," I said despairingly. Tears sprung up along my eyelids.

"But one might do it for *you.*"

My eyes flew to his face and clung to the brilliant blue eyes looking back at me.

"No, Cayden. I won't let you do that." My voice trembled. I felt nauseous, and my head felt too heavy for my neck. All I wanted to do was crawl into a dark hole and hide.

"I want you to be happy," he hedged. "I just wish you could be happy with me."

My mind lingered on that for a moment, but suddenly flipped through the pages of my memory. Creeping like an ominous shadow, a gloomy idea unfurled in my brain. *An angel can descend out of love. An angel is created either by birth or by being murdered by a demon.*

Without giving it a second thought, for fear that I'd change my mind; I flung myself out the door and down the hall. Slamming through the double doors of the building, I ran toward the forest.

The sun was beginning to set, but its waning glow filtered through the trees, casting golden bars of light across the grass. Then I heard the whisper of movement behind me.

"Cayden," I said in surprise. "What are you doing here?"

His wings were out and spread wide behind him. Like the gleam of a pearl, the moonlight cast a glistening sheen across them.

"My part, as a Vocem. Keeping you from doing something stupid." He stepped toward me, drawing his wings tight to his back. I noticed his t-shirt was shredded where his magnificent wings must have sprang open, ripping the fabric easily as they shot out of the twin scars that sat between his shoulder blades.

"Kara, I won't let you do it," he continued. His voice was gentle, as he took slow and deliberate steps toward me. He approached with caution, as though he'd cornered a wild animal.

"Your influence won't sway me, Cayden."

"Kara, it doesn't work that way. In fact, it will only make things worse."

"I'll call out Vasuth. He'll be more than happy to kill me, and then I'll become an angel." My chest constricted with fear as I said the words—*kill me*—out loud. "And then I'll choose to descend for Dominic," I said with a shaky voice. I admit it wasn't a good plan, but it was all I had.

"But he'll still be a whisperer, a Damamah. He'll still be what he is…a demon."

"I have to try." I kept moving with determination,

my temples pounding in desperation with each of my hurried steps.

"But isn't this just another variation of suicide?"

His words drew me up short. *Suicide?*

"You may not be the one ultimately drawing the knife, but if you ask me, running head first into hell's arms is suicide in itself."

My chest tightened at the thought. The words *I am loved. My mother loves me. She needs me. I care enough about her to stay alive for her* danced around my head until I grew dizzy. I held my temples, grief-stricken as I considered that. *Was this suicide? No,* I thought. I was giving my all to the man I loved. I was going to fight, until my last intake of air for him, defying any and all to be with him. To live another day to love him.

The ground began to quake beneath Cayden's feet. Like a startled butterfly, he leapt gracefully in the air, his wings beating silently behind him. The dirt shifted and lurched violently, moaning in agony as the steel elevator penetrated the soil.

Darkness seemed to cascade out of it, sending a shockwave of prickling fear along my neck. I flinched at the sound of grinding metal. A sick feeling unfurled deep in my stomach as the heavy door lifted.

Cayden fluttered quietly to the ground, landing in a defensive stance. He looked stiff, but ready to tackle anything that moved. His eyes briefly touched mine before he steeled himself again, tightening his hands into fists before him.

Two shadowed figures poured out of the elevator. I swallowed back a lump of panic as I watched Dominic and his father emerge into view. Dominic's face was

pinched with seething frustration. Vasuth paraded
around on a cloud of bleak arrogance, his mock smile,
chilling and dangerous. He outstretched his arms
theatrically, as he pranced a slow, wide arc around
Cayden.

"Ah, I thought I felt the presence of one of God's
warriors on my hallowed ground," Vasuth said,
grinning, showing off his serrated teeth. I shivered at
the sight of them.

"Hell is no hallowed ground," Cayden said.

"Maybe to you it isn't," he snapped, his lips pulling
into a tight sneer. "Now, what brings an Angel of
Vocem, a mortal girl, and a Damamah to me, on this
fine evening?"

Dominic's gaze swung in my direction. For the
first time ever, he looked…*frightened.* Frightened for
me. I glanced at Vasuth and became frightened for
myself.

"I was requesting insight, Father, until we got
rudely interrupted by this…this…" He motioned to
Cayden with indifference. "Moth on steroids."

"I didn't interrupt anything, hell monger. I'm only
here because of Kara." Cayden's blue eyes shot to me
briefly before flicking back to Dominic.

"Come now, son," Vasuth said. "I had to
investigate why there was a do-gooder on my portal."

Cayden's lip curled over his tightly clenched teeth.
"I should kill you where you stand."

The only indication that Vasuth was unnerved, was
the slight twitch at the corner of his mouth. That was
until Cayden was suddenly whipped into a shroud of
swirling gray clouds.

He resisted, trying to tug himself free, but the dark

fog carried him away smoothly. Like a damp rag, Cayden was flung into the ancient contraption, the metal gate slamming shut with a definitive thud. He banged against the gate, rattling the metal like a crazed convict.

"Let me out of here!" he shouted, hurling himself against the walls. I cringed each time his body connected with the solid steel.

"It's crafted from demon metal and bounded with hell fire. There is no escaping, Child of Vocem," Vasuth hissed, his face breaking into a sinister grin.

"Dominic! Help him!" I cried.

"I don't give a flying fuck *about* that flying fuck!" he snarled, his eyes positioned pointedly on his father. "I'm here for only one reason."

"Since this dreadful girl is yet again within my sight, I can only assume it has something to do with her," Vasuth said, his tone almost bored.

"I wish to rescind my role as Damamah," he said. "I want to live as a human."

Vasuth's eyes were unreadable. He regarded his son with interest, but remained silent.

"You loved a mortal once," Dominic continued. "How—"

"*Loved* a mortal?" Vasuth's cold eyes rounded in surprised.

"Did you not love my mother?" Dominic questioned, his voice faltering. In that moment, he looked like a lost child, so vulnerable and frightened. I longed to embrace to him, to take the pain from him and bear it myself.

"Your mother was beautiful. I was drawn to her the moment I saw her, but my loins merely lusted for her."

His eyes hooded and his lips pulled into a demented grin. "I never *loved* her. It's a pity you have believed that for so long." His tone was biting, slicing Dominic to the quick.

"Then you seduced her."

"Easily," he said. "Just as you could, with this pathetic lamb." He jerked his chin toward me. My blood ran cold at the thought.

Dominic snarled, the sound, vicious and threatening. His eyes were set deadly upon his father. "I wish to rescind my role," he declared.

"You can't," he snapped. "You are a demon. You have *no* free will."

"My mother was human. Her blood runs through me."

"Just as mine does," Vasuth said vehemently. "Rise above this insignificant girl. If you're attracted to her, very well, love her flesh until you've had your fill."

Something guttural tore from Dominic's lips as he surged toward his father. Vasuth caught him by the throat, digging his claw-like hands deep into Dominic's flesh. Dominic sputtered and scratched frantically at Vasuth's bony fingers.

"Don't waste your existence on a human," he hissed as he straightened his arm. Blue veins bulged like highways on a roadmap, beneath his parchment-thin skin. Grunting through deadly teeth, he lifted Dominic high into the air.

I covered my mouth, holding in a scream as I watched him dangle in the air. *Oh God, Dominic!* He gasped for breath, then his eyes flashed a deadly shade of blood-red.

He threw an upper cut to Vasuth's chin, snapping

his head back. His grip faltered, and Dominic seized the opportunity to wretch himself free from his father's lethal grip.

With a roar, Vasuth leapt into the air and sprang forward like a wildcat. He landed softly in a crouch in front of Dominic. With a sadistic laugh, he rose up to his full height.

His razor sharp teeth shined in the moonlight as he snarled like a rabid dog, then with otherworldly strength, he shoved his hands into Dominic's chest, sending him soaring through the air like a limp noodle. With a sickening thud, Dominic's back smashed against an oak tree, crumbling to the dirt.

"Dominic!" I cried.

He rolled nimbly to feet, and crouched like a cat readying himself. At his feet lay exposed, gnarly roots. His eyes shifted down at them, and he reached forward, solidly grasping onto a set of thick roots. Flicking a toxic glare at Vasuth, he launched himself once again at his father.

This time, they locked arms, engaging in a bitter battle of upper strength. Dominic seemed to be getting the upper hand, when Vasuth jammed the heel of hand under Dominic's chin.

"I possess my mother's qualities," Dominic panted. "Her propensity for love. Her right to free will…"

"Foolish boy!" Vasuth growled, thrusting harder, nearly bending Dominic backward. *He'll kill him!* Terrified, I let out a high-pitched scream, rattling my vocal cords. Fearing Dominic's head would snap off from the pressure, I flung myself at Vasuth, ripping ruthlessly at his face with my fingernails.

"Let him go!"

Pus-like blood pearled and ran down his cheek. My stomach heaved at the sight of it, still I tore at him, feeling his skin embed deeper beneath my nails.

He bellowed, disentangling me from him and hurling me through the air. I crashed into the elevator, connecting with the solid steel.

A throbbing pain spread like heat across my forehead, as blood ran into my eyes, blurring my vision. I licked my busted lip; the coppery taste stung my tongue. *Fuck!* I spat on the ground, shivering when I noticed it was mostly blood. Everything around me dimmed, but I fought against the impending unconsciousness.

No! I squinted and forced myself to focus until I could make out Dominic's lean physique through the haze. *Oh God, what's happening to him?* His body thrashed wildly, but his feet remained planted firmly in the ground. Vasuth was smirking at him through eyes so narrowed they were merely slits.

"You're no match for a real demon, boy." He laughed menacingly. Vasuth's eyes then rolled across me. The emptiness of them seemed harsh and sent a shiver down my spine. The way he looked at me, chilled me straight to my marrow. *What's going through that madman's—?*

Suddenly darkness blanketed my vision. *Oh!* Flailing my arms outward, I groped at the elevator to remain steady, panic flaring with my chest. *What the hell?* I searched the black space, desperate to see something, *anything.*

Vasuth's ominous laugh erupted nearby. It was close. Too close. Every survival instinct within me screamed *danger!* I grew frantic, hot tears welling as I felt blindly around me. On the verge of insanity, I cried out for Dominic.

"No!" I heard him holler, but it sounded as though I was underwater. Drowning in darkness, my limbs felt as though they had filled with cement. Unable to hold my weight any longer, I fell to the ground. *What's happening?* A scorching fire flooded my limbs. I wanted to yell for help, but couldn't. Dirt caked my motionless lips, and my voice was rendered useless. *Help me please! Someone put out the fire!* My thoughts jumbled with fits of madness. *Dear God, please! Put out the fire!*

"*Tsk tsk, are we taking the Lord's name in vain?*"

I shrank back at the words in my head.

"*There's nowhere to run, child,*" Vasuth whispered. He laughed sadistically, and my body jerked upright. The movement was mine, but I was not at the helm of its control. My lids pried themselves open. Dominic stood several feet away. I wanted to run to him, but my body refused to move. I stared at him, wising I could claw my way out of my own skin, and leave it in a heap, just so I could go to him. He was trembling, his face even paler than normal.

"Leave her alone," he commanded. The severe angles in his face were shadowed, like a deeply etched tombstone.

"Or what?" a low voice rumbled from my throat. I yelped silently, locked within my own body. *He's in me! Vasuth has invaded my body!* "Or what, you'll *kill* me? I think not," the voice continued eerily. "You'd only be destroying your dearest in the process."

"Get out of her!" Dominic screeched, his fists clenching and his stare pulsating with pure hatred.

"You're going to kill her!"

"That's the point," he spat acidly. "Once I've depleted her of all life, you can have her body back." I began to move forward, with Vasuth directing my feet like a mad puppeteer yanking the strings. *Dominic!* I screamed his name, but it fell into silence, as though the word had never been uttered. Panic lanced through me, and a hopelessness surfaced and settled within my heart. It was suffocating. I considered retreating into the dark crevices of myself just to escape it. *No!* I thought. *I am loved. My mother loves me. Dominic loves me. I care enough about them to stay alive.*

An eerie stillness enveloped the forest, and though my eyes were no longer my own, I felt them squint against a blinding light. A surge of fear spiked my core, but it wasn't my fear. *It was Vasuth's.* A spark of hope unfurled within me as I felt my body shrink back. I could hear Cayden calling to me from a distance. He pounded angrily against the bars, slamming his weight against the door.

"Vasuth, I command you to exit that body," a hushed voice beckoned. Like a whisper carried on a breeze, it caressed my ears tenderly. A beautiful woman hovered in a misty vapor before me. Her transparent wings flapped gently, and like sparkling sand in an hourglass, her image materialized.

"Mia." Vasuth's words choked out raggedly from my lips. "Mortality hindered your beauty. You're even more radiant as a winged messenger." My feet back-pedaled, trying to put space between me and glittering creature.

Her raven hair swirled prettily around her, contrasting against her pale skin. Her gown of white was flowing, the delicate fabric hugging her curves like honey. She was barefoot, but her slender feet twinkled brightly as if they had been dipped in crushed gems. The angles of her face were stern, but it only enhanced her loveliness.

"Empty your wickedness from this vessel. Feeding upon her innocence will only mark you for a slow and painful demise." She glided toward me, her eyes charged with abhorrence for the loathsome Vasuth. A willowy arm reached out, and with a feathery touch, she traced a slight finger down my face.

It was like a hatchet carving its deathly route into my bones. A thread of raw blisters erupted in its wake. The taste of charred smoke flowed through my veins and bit at the back of my throat. My mouth hung open as a haunting scream tore at my vocal cords.

My body twisted and jerked uncontrollably, my muscles tearing painfully. My eyes rolled back into my head as the sound of shredding and gurgling pulsated through me. Just when I thought my body would split in two, I folded in half, falling limply to the ground. I heard a faded scream, but wasn't able to decipher who it came from. Through heavy lids, I tried to focus on the fuzzy figures around me, but I was too weak.

"Kara!" a voice called. My eyes fluttered closed and all went black.

Chapter 30

"Kara! Please, Kara. Wake up! Don't leave me!" Dominic laid his head on my chest; I could feel his hot tears against my skin. With a feeble hand, I reached up and stroked his mussed hair. He snatched his head up to peer into my face, searching my eyes with unrelenting pursuit. I was exhausted, mentally and physically.

"Kara," he breathed. His body sank against mine with relief. He covered my mouth with his, igniting my vitality with his. Sounds of trouble disrupted us, and I looked past Dominic and noticed the angel. She was slowly stalking Vasuth who was now back in his own body. His face was sliced open, the raw skin charred and oozing with murky blood. My hand flew to my cheek, it was unharmed. Her touch only reached Vasuth.

So that's what an angel's touch does to a demon, I thought. I looked back at Vasuth. One hand clung to his abdomen, his entrails visible as yellow fluid trickled down the fabric of his pants.

One arm dangled unnaturally. A bone, slick with the sheen of fresh blood protruded from his ashen skin. "Who is that?" I asked, bewildered.

"My mother," he said calmly.

"What?" My eyes grew wide, and I sat up with interest. "You're half angel? How's that even possible?"

"It's not. She wasn't an angel when she conceived me." His eyes washed with heartbreaking sadness. "She didn't die during childbirth. My father killed her, to raise me as a demon."

My heart felt as though it had been pricked with a thousand needles as I watched Dominic process his own words. He learned that his mother was an angel, and his father was more of a monster than he could ever imagine. *Poor Dominic.*

"She was converted to angel status upon her death," he said coldly. "And I never knew. The bastard killed my mother, so I could be raised with no free will!" he snarled, turning toward his parents. Dominic's features echoed his mother's, from their smooth pale skin to their beautiful dark hair. But in that instant, he looked just as menacing as his father did. The sharp angles in his face were severe, the dark rings around his eyes bold against his pallid skin. "I want to kill him myself!" he screamed as he vaulted his lean body toward the badly battered Vasuth.

His mother startled at the blur of motion zipping toward her. In the blink of an eye, Vasuth seized the moment and backhanded her. His organs slipped out of the cavernous hole in his stomach. They hung by bloody ribbons, causing my stomach to heave viciously. He was on her, slashing at her wings ruthlessly. Glistening pink blood seeped through the delicate membranes.

His clawed fingers circled her slim throat, but his skin began deteriorating like flaking ashes in the wind, until soon, he held her with a skeletal hand.

"No!" Dominic hollered, folding his arms around Vasuth's head, threatening to snap his neck.

"Don't do it, son," whispered Mia. Dominic looked at his mother, as she lay in a pool of her own glimmering blood. "Let him go," she said gently.

"Mother, even as an angel, you must see what a worthless being he is. Why grant him mercy?"

"So *you* can live."

Dominic's brow wrinkled and his full lips quivered with confusion. He clamped harder on his father's windpipe. "I don't understand," he admitted.

"Let me die, so you can live. If I leave my place in Heaven, you are free to ascend out of hell."

Dominic looked at his father, then back at his dying mother. His expression pained me, and I yearned to hold him. Finally he had a mother, and now she was telling him to let her go. His conflicted features tore at my heart.

"I know you love her deeply. Please, let me do this for you."

"I don't want to lose you," he whispered.

"It's the only way. You deserve a life of happiness. And she..." Mia took a ragged breath, her eyes fluttered and closed for one scary second. "She makes you happy. You love her, Dominic. And she obviously feels the same."

"I just can't let you sacrifice yourself for me," he said, his eyes welling with emotion.

"I never got to hold you. Your father ripped you from my womb before slaughtering me like a lamb," she said weakly. "After my heart stopped, I was bestowed the role of angel. With it, I acquired the angel's touch, forever forbidding me the joy of touching my son. It pained me to watch you grow; knowing that one moment of weakness could kill you. I couldn't risk revealing myself until I knew your heart was breaking out of the stone cast your father set." Like a mist rolling through a storm, her dark eyes began to glaze. "Allow me to do this for you."

Dominic looked back at me, his obsidian eyes flooded with crimson. I chanced a hesitant smile. His full lips trembled, and his eyes were rimmed with deep gray bruises. His fingers released slowly, allowing Vasuth to slip out his grip and bound stealthy toward the elevator, holding his innards in place he ran.

My stomach retched, as his slimy organs, coated in a sickly yellow excretion, sloshed, and squished around his hand. Stopping at the elevator door, Vasuth held his ugly, skeletal hand before the metal gate. It lifted with great effort, creaking loudly against the archaic device.

Cayden surged out, just as Vasuth darted in. They collided. Vasuth howled in pain as he scrambled backward. His skin bubbled with fresh welts. The gate slammed shut with a definite thud. Cayden surveyed the pitiful scene around him, his wings draped behind him like a flag waving in the wind.

He flanked my side after several long strides. The elevator rasped, like a grief-stricken widow, plunging into the earth with an unsettling wail.

"Will he die?" I shuddered, wrapping my arms around myself.

"He will heal, but it will take a very long time," Cayden answered solemnly.

I cast my eyes back to Dominic and Mia.

"I am so proud of you," she murmured. "You overcame evil in the name of love. Go to her."

Dominic moved hesitantly, as if considering something, then he threw himself across his mother.

I wanted to run to him, afraid of what her touch would do to him. Cayden laid a strong hand on my shoulder. It comforted me only slightly. *Please, don't hurt him.* I held my breath as I watched them.

Dominic's face flinched, as he gritted his teeth in agony. They embraced tenderly as he wept.

"I can think of no better way to part from this beautiful existence. I love you, my son."

Mia's eyes wavered, her thick lashes grazing her cheekbones. Her face slackened, and her hand slid limply off her chest. Dominic sat hunched over her body, his shoulders wracked with excruciating moans. I waited, giving him the space he needed. Finally, he rose and turned to face me. His singed shirt revealed raw skin, blossoming with painful blisters.

Unable to take our distance a moment longer, I loped toward him. He met me halfway, melting into me as I hugged his neck. He sought my lips hungrily, and I lost myself in the heated frenzy of our clashing mouths. My limbs spiked with the familiar fervor that only he could ignite.

When we pulled away, we reluctantly cast our eyes back to Mia. Her body was gone. I looked past Dominic and noticed Cayden; his features resigned, but peaceful as he wandered closer.

He jammed his hands into his pockets and said, "Her spirit has evaporated. It's part of the cosmos now.

Dominic whirled around, tucking me behind him slightly, studying him with uncertainty. Cayden showed no hint of animosity, offering a kind smile as he stepped closer.

"The exchange is complete. Now you just have to officially renounce your loyalty to Lucifer," he explained.

"It's time to complete the transformation," I whispered into Dominic's ear, my heart full of uncontainable happiness. *Soon, he'll be mine. All mine.*

Facing me again, Dominic slid his palms over my cheeks and I leaned into their warmth. Suddenly, I had a thought. "What if you're different, after this? What if your feelings change?" I asked, frightened by the possibility.

"Kara, nothing could change my feelings for you." He planted a tiny kiss on the corner of my mouth. "Not time." He brushed his lips to the other corner. "Nor distance." He kissed me fully on the mouth, and then dropped his hands.

He winked, and offered me a sweet smile as he backed away. His eyes held firmly to mine as he said with power, "I, Dominic Benenati, am no longer loyal to Lucifer. Unravel the thread of evil and lift Satan's creed from my fibers."

He lifted his chiseled face defiantly, raising his palms to the sky. Gray clouds churned and a soft rain trickled over us. It was as though the water freed him from invisible manacles.

He circled around himself once, wrapping his arms over his chest, as if checking himself for a physical change. He laughed once, and then his eyes settled on me. With a lopsided grin, he scooped me into his arms, swinging me joyfully in the air. Laughing, our lips merged, and I knew he had transformed. The shackles of evil had dissolved, allowing Dominic to love me wholly and without reservations. Finally, he was all mine.

****

A month later, everything was as it should be. School was back in session, Dominic and I were solid, and Cayden had accepted that. He even showed newfound interest in Cassie, which tickled her beyond delight.

"So what's going on between you and Cassie, fly boy?" Dominic asked one day.

"To be honest, I was so stuck on this one..." Cayden grinned shyly, and nudged me gently. "She barely registered on my radar. But over the last few weeks, I've seen Cassie in a different light." His eyes brightened, illuminating his entire face. "I swear she must be hiding a halo somewhere in that mop of curls."

"Aw, Cayden! That's great," I said smiling, swatting at him playfully. My eyes drifted past him, landing on Cassie as she flounced her way toward us. "Oh, here she comes now." I waved enthusiastically at my friend.

"Hey, Karonic." Cassie greeted us with the special term she often used for us. I pretended to hate the way she merged our names into one, but secretly I adored it. It described us perfectly. One being. One soul.

She winked at Cayden. "Hi, handsome. You ready to show off those putt-putt skills you've been bragging about?" She smiled up at him.

I nearly snickered. Cayden's eyes shifted to mine. He pursed his lips tightly, suppressing a grin as he scrubbed his chin.

Cassie took my hand, pulling me away to whisper in my ear, "I'm on cloud nine with this guy." I patted her, brimming with happiness that my friends had finally found each other. She giggled and skipped back to Cayden's side. They linked fingers and walked away happily.

Dominic swung his arm over my shoulder and kissed my temple. We crossed Belman's lawn to the parking lot, where he lifted, and sat me gently on the hood of his mean machine. Stepping between my legs, he leaned into my face. His hands grazed across my calves and slid seductively over my knees.

My body reacted, just as it always did to his touch. My insides hummed with desire, and my heart felt full of overwhelming love for this beautiful creature.

He gazed into my eyes with the intensity only he possessed. The kind that made me shiver and feel as though he had a direct connection to my soul.

His hands moved from my thighs to my face. He tunneled his fingers through my hair as he said, "Kara Maven, my *anima bella*, promise me that you will love me, each and every day, for the rest of our time on this crazy niche of the world, we call earth."

"Earth? Is that what you call it?" I asked.

"Well, what do you call it?" he asked, his handsome face lit up in amusement.

"Heaven," I said blissfully.

He glanced down at my wrist, and smiled. "Those charms. I love the way they look on you." Automatically, I touched them. Their meaning far more significant now than when he first gave them to me. "You *freed* me Kara," he continued. "Only to capture me again within your heart and it's a place I'll gladly stay forever."

Our lips melted into one, sparking my inner core like a lightning storm. *This is where I belong,* I thought. *In his arms. In his heart.*

The moment I cast my eyes upon him that day on

the school lawn, Dominic irrevocably claimed me. Though my own heart was battered and bruised, love softly crept in and struck me with a blow so mighty, I knew I would never recover. I didn't want to. I offered myself freely to Dominic, allowing him to possess me wholly, and without reservations. Love is undoubtedly selfish, but to feel even a shred of true love in a lifetime is rare and precious. One must seize it, and be willing to sacrifice for it. I know I was.

Dominic and I continued to love the hell out of one another, relishing each day in this piece of Heaven we found within each other's arms.

A word from the author...

I work full-time as a zoo curator, so when I'm not running a zoo, I'm trying to tame the one I live in! I have two kids, and a husband who sometimes acts their age.

I can usually be found jamming to Elvis Presley tunes, or diligently chipping away at my never-ending "to be read" pile.

I tend to gravitate toward anything paranormal. I love creatures who fly and characters who sprout fur or fangs. Sprinkle some romance and magic into the mix, and I'm a happy girl!

www.ingramcontent.com/pod-product-compliance
Lightning Source LLC
Chambersburg PA
CBHW051521260626
47170CB00003B/720